BAD MONKEYS

BAD MONKEYS

MATT RUFF

BLOOMSBURY
LONDON · OXFORD · NEW YORK · NEW DELHI · SYDNEY

For Phil

First published in Great Britain 2007

Copyright © 2007 by Matt Ruff

The moral right of the author has been asserted

Bloomsbury Publishing Plc
50 Bedford Square
London WC1B 3DP

Bloomsbury Publishing, London, New Delhi, New York and Berlin

A CIP catalogue record for this book is available from the British Library

ISBN 978 0 7475 9323 2
16

Printed and bound in Great Britain by CPI (UK) Ltd, Croydon CR0 4YY

Cain said to his brother Abel, "Let us go out to the field ..."

—Genesis 4:8

Conscience: the inner voice that warns us someone may be looking.

—H. L. Mencken

BAD MONKEYS

white room (i)

IT'S A ROOM AN UNINSPIRED PLAY-
wright might conjure while staring at a blank page:
White walls. White ceiling. White floor. Not featureless,
but close enough to raise suspicion that its few contents
are all crucial to the upcoming drama.

A woman sits in one of two chairs drawn up to a rect-
angular white table. Her hands are cuffed in front of
her; she is dressed in an orange prison jumpsuit whose
bright hue seems dull in the whiteness. A photograph of
a smiling politician hangs on the wall above the table.
Occasionally the woman glances up at the photo, or
at the door that is the room's only exit, but mostly she
stares at her hands, and waits.

The door opens. A man in a white coat steps in,
bringing more props: a file folder and a handheld tape
recorder.

"Hello," he says. "Jane Charlotte?"

"Present," she says.

"I'm Dr. Vale." He shuts the door and comes over to
the table. "I'm here to interview you, if that's all right."
When she shrugs, he asks: "Do you know where you
are?"

"Unless they moved the room ..." Then: "Las Vegas,
Clark County Detention Center. The nut wing."

"And do you know why you're here?"

"I'm in jail because I killed someone I wasn't supposed to," she says, matter-of-factly. "As for why I'm in this room, with you, I guess that has something to do with what I told the detectives who arrested me."

"Yes." He gestures at the empty chair. "May I sit down?"

Another shrug. He sits. Holding the tape recorder to his lips, he recites: "June 5th, 2002, approximately nine forty-five a.m. This is Dr. Richard Vale, speaking with subject Jane Charlotte, of ... What's your current home address?"

"I'm kind of between homes right now."

"... of no fixed address." He sets the tape recorder, still running, on the table, and opens the folder. "So ... You told the arresting detectives that you work for a secret crime-fighting organization called Bad Monkeys."

"No," she says.

"No?"

"We don't fight crime, we fight evil. There's a difference. And Bad Monkeys is the name of my division. The organization as a whole doesn't have a name, at least not that I ever heard. It's just 'the organization.'"

"And what does 'Bad Monkeys' mean?"

"It's a nickname," she says. "All the divisions have them. The official names are too long and complicated to use on anything but letterhead, so people come up with shorthand versions. Like the administrative branch, officially they're 'The Department for Optimal Utilization of Resources and Personnel,' but everyone just calls them Cost-Benefits. And the intel-gathering group, that's 'The Department of Ubiquitous Intermittent Surveillance,' but in conversation they're just Panopticon. And then there's my division, 'The Department for the Final Disposition of Irredeemable Persons ...'"

"Irredeemable persons." The doctor smiles. "Bad monkeys."

"Right."

"Shouldn't it be Bad Apes, though?" When she doesn't respond, he starts to explain: "Human beings are more closely related to great apes than—"

"You're channeling Phil," she says.

"Who?"

"My little brother. Philip. He's a nitpicker, too." She shrugs. "Yeah, I suppose technically, it should be apes instead of monkeys. And technically"—she lifts her arms and gives her bracelets a shake—"these should be called *wrist*cuffs. But they're not."

"So in your job with Bad Monkeys," the doctor asks, "what is it you do? Punish evil people?"

"No. Usually we just kill them."

"Killing's not a punishment?"

"It is if you do it to pay someone back. But the organization's not about that. We're just trying to make the world a better place."

"By killing evil men."

"Not *all* of them. Just the ones Cost-Benefits decides will do a lot more harm than good if they go on breathing."

"Does it bother you to kill people?"

"Not usually. It's not like being a police officer. I mean cops, they have to deal with all kinds of people, and sometimes, upholding the law, they've got to come down on folks who really aren't all that bad. I can see where that would give you a crisis of conscience. But the guys we go after in Bad Monkeys aren't the sort you have mixed feelings about."

"And the man you were arrested for killing, Mr.—"

"Dixon," she says. "He wasn't a bad monkey."

"No?"

"He was a prick. I didn't like him. But he wasn't evil."

"Then why did you kill him?"

She shakes her head. "I can't just tell you that. Even if I thought you'd believe me, it wouldn't make sense unless I told you everything else first. But that's too long a story."

"I don't have anywhere else I have to be this morning."

"No, I mean it's a *long* story. This morning I could maybe give you the prologue; to get through the whole thing would take days."

"You do understand you're going to be in here for a while."

"Of course," she says. "I'm a murderer. But that's no reason why you should have to waste your time."

"Do you want to tell the story?"

"I suppose there's a part of me that does. I mean, I didn't have to mention Bad Monkeys to the cops."

"Well if you're willing to talk, I'm willing to listen."

"You're just going to think I'm crazy. You probably already do."

"I'll try to keep an open mind."

"That won't help."

"Why don't we just start, and see how it goes?" the doctor suggests. "Tell me how you first got involved with the organization. How long have you worked for them?"

"About eight months. I was recruited last year after the World Trade towers went down. But that's not really the beginning. The first time I crossed paths with them was back when I was a teenager."

"What happened?"

"I stumbled into a Bad Monkeys op. That's how a lot of people get recruited: they're in the wrong place at the wrong time, they get caught up in an operation, and even though they don't really understand what's happening, they show enough potential that the organization takes notice. Then later—maybe days, maybe decades—there's a job opening, and New Blood pays them a visit."

"So tell me about this operation you stumbled into."

"Well, it all started when I figured out that the janitor at my high school was the Angel of Death …"

Nancy Drew, Reconsidered as a Bad Seed

IT WAS THE FALL OF 1979. I WAS fourteen years old, and I'd been sent away from home to live with my aunt and uncle.

Where was home?

San Francisco. The Haight-Ashbury. Charlie Manson's old stomping grounds.

Why were you sent away?

Mostly to keep my mom from killing me. We'd been fighting pretty much nonstop all that year, but towards the end of the summer things got especially bad. You know, physical.

What did you fight about?

The usual. Boys. Drugs. Me staying out all night with my friends. Plus there was my brother. My dad had taken off a few years before, and to support us my mom was working twelve-hour days, which she hated, and so I was supposed to watch Phil, which I hated.

How old was Phil?

Ten. Smart ten, I mean he knew enough not to drink Clorox or set fire to the apartment. Plus he was a really internal kid, the kind where if he had a book to read, he'd sit quiet for hours. Which is one reason I resented having to watch him: there was nothing to watch. It was like babysitting a pet rock. So what I'd do instead, a lot of the time, I'd take Phil out and park him somewhere, go off and do my own thing, and come back later and pick him up. And if my mom got home before us, or if it turned out she'd tried to call in from work to check on us, I'd just make up some story about how I took Phil to the zoo—and Phil, he'd back me up, because I'd threatened to sell him to the gypsies if he didn't.

That worked out OK for a while, but eventually my mother got wise. One time I didn't bring Phil home until nine o'clock at night, and she knew the zoo wasn't open that late. Then this other time, I got caught shoplifting at a record store, and by the time I talked my way out of it, the library where I'd left Phil was closing. One of the librarians found him in the stacks and reported him abandoned.

It was after that that my mother and I really went to war with each other. She started calling me her bad seed, saying I must have gotten all my genes from my no-good father. Looking back on it now, I don't blame her—in her shoes, I'd have done some name-calling too—but at the time, my position was "Hey, I didn't ask for a little brother, I didn't volunteer to be deputy mom, and if you think I'm a bad seed now, just wait until I get busy trying to earn the title."

You say the fights turned physical.

Yeah. Slaps and hair-pulling, mostly. I gave as good as I got—we were about the same size—so it wasn't like abuse. More like scuffling. She had more anger than me, though, and every so often she'd escalate to weapons: belts, dishes, whatever was handy. And like I say, I gave as good as I got, but long-term, that wasn't a healthy trend.

What about your brother? What was your mother's relationship with him like?

Oh, she loved Phil. Of course. He was the low-maintenance kid.

Did she display affection towards him?

She didn't throw plates at him. Beyond that, I don't know, maybe she kissed him on the forehead once in a while. I wasn't jealous, if that's what you're asking. The only thing that bugged me about their relationship was having to hang around for it. She expected me to help mind Phil even when she was home, which struck me as totally unreasonable. We had a bunch of fights about that.

Was it one of these fights that led to you being sent away?

No. That was a different incident. Phil was involved, but it wasn't really about him.

What happened?

It was kind of funny, actually. There was this big vacant lot across from our apartment building that some hippies had turned into a community garden. You could sign up for a plot of ground and raise vegetables or whatever. My friend Moon had some marijuana seeds, so we decided to try growing our own pot there.

In a public garden?

Not the brightest scheme ever, I know. But you have to understand, we'd only ever seen pot in baggies before, so we had no idea how big the plants got. We figured, it's a *weed*, and weeds are small. We thought we could grow bigger plants around it as cover, and then harvest it before anybody noticed what it was.

So I signed us up for a plot, but under Phil's name. The garden was one of the places I used to leave him; he didn't care about plants, but he liked animals, and there were these stray cats there that he could play with. That's what he was doing, herding cats, the day our marijuana patch got raided.

You'd think the hippies would have been the first to spot it, but it was a beat cop. The guy's name, I swear to God, was Buster Friendly. Officer Friendly's vice detector went off as he was walking past the garden one afternoon, and the next thing you know he had every adult in the place up against the fence, and he was waving the sign-up sheet in their faces, wanting to know which one of them was Phil. Then Phil came up and tugged him on the sleeve, and the officer asked him, "Are those your marijuana plants, son?" and Phil said yes, but without me right there whispering "gypsies" in his ear, he wasn't a very convincing liar, so it only took about ten minutes for Officer Friendly to get the real story out of him. Ten minutes after that, I came back from Moon's house to pick up Phil and got nabbed.

Did the officer arrest you?

He took us back to the police station, but he didn't book us. He ran us through the Scared Straight routine: showed us the holding cell, introduced us to some of the losers they had locked up in there, told us some horror stories about how much worse the actual jail was. Once I realized he wasn't actually going to do anything to us, I wasn't impressed, but I pretended like I was, because I figured I might need this guy in my corner once my mom showed up. So I called him "sir" a lot, and tried to come off like a little rascal instead of a little bitch.

Eventually my mom got there, and she went right for me, no preliminaries. By this point I had Officer Friendly halfway liking me, but he still needed me to learn a lesson, so if my mother had just smacked me around a little he would have let it go. But she was in full fury, screaming about the bad seed, and she started, like, *throttling* me, and then I lost my cool and started fighting back, and it turned into this big drama scene, with cops running in from other rooms to help pull us off each other. After they got us separated they called in a social worker, and we had this three-hour encounter session, during which my mom made it clear that if they sent me home with her, she wasn't just going to send me to bed with no supper, she was going to drown me in the tub. So they had to come up with a Plan B.

What finally happened, my mom agreed to see a shrink for anger management, and in exchange she got to take Phil home. I stayed at the police station while Officer Friendly went with them to pick up a couple bags of my clothes, and then he drove me out to my aunt and uncle's place in the San Joaquin Valley. It was the middle of the night by now, and it was at least a hundred-mile drive, but he insisted on taking me himself. So at first I was thinking, wow, he really bought my little-rascal act. And so I kept it up, kept playing him, until at one point I was in the middle of this completely bogus story about my mother, and he gave me this look, and I realized: he sees through me. He *knows* I'm bullshitting him, but he's cutting me this huge break anyway, not because he's stupid but because he's a decent guy. So that shut me up for a while.

Were you grateful, or just embarrassed?

Both. Look, I know what you're thinking: absent father, and now here's this male authority figure going out of his way for me, blah blah blah, and there is something to that. But also, him being smarter than I figured, that was a change in plan.

I mean, I had no intention of staying with my aunt and uncle. The way I'd already worked it out in my head, I'd let Officer Friendly drop me off, I'd spend the night, get some breakfast, maybe steal some cash, and take off. Hitchhike back to S.F. and see if Moon's parents would let me crash at their place. But now it turned out Officer Friendly had a brain, so of course he knew I was planning to do that.

We were almost there when he said to me: "Do me a favor, Jane?" And I said, "What?", and he said, "Give it two weeks." And I didn't have to ask, give *what* two weeks—he definitely had my frequency. So instead I said: "Why two weeks?" And he said, "That should be enough time for you to cool down. Then you can decide whether you really want to do something stupid." That pissed me off a little, but not as much as I would have expected, and I said, "What are you, my foster dad now?"

and he said, "Is that what it's going to take?", which shut me up again for a few seconds. Finally I said, "Twenty bucks," and he said, "Twenty bucks?" and I said, "Yeah. That's what it's going to take." But he shook his head and said, "For twenty bucks you've got to give it at least a month."

We spent the rest of the ride haggling. A part of me was thinking, this is ridiculous, but in spite of myself I was warming up to the guy, so it was a *serious* haggle. In the end we settled on twenty-five dollars, plus I promised that if I did decide to run away when the month was up, I'd call him first to give him a chance to talk me out of it. Getting me to agree to that last part, that was a sharp move.

How so?

Well, he'd gotten me to like him, right? As much as I liked any adult at that age. But at the same time, I wasn't stupid either, I knew in his job he must deal with hundreds of kids, most of them a lot more screwed up than me, so who knew if he'd even remember me in a month. And if I did call him up, and he said "Jane *who*?", I knew I wasn't going to enjoy that. But a deal's a deal, so the only way for me to *not* call him was to either not run away, or wait until things got bad enough that I'd feel OK about breaking my word.

So that's how I ended up at my aunt and uncle's place. How I ended up *staying* there.

They lived in Siesta Corta, which is Spanish for "wake me if anything happens." It was a wide spot on the road between Modesto and Fresno, with everything a truck driver or a migrant fruit-picker could ask for: a gas station, a general store, a diner, a bar, a fleabag motel, and a Holy Roller church. My aunt and uncle ran the general store.

What sort of people were they?

Old. They were my aunt and uncle on my father's side. My father had been fifteen years older than my mother, and my aunt was his older sister, so to look at her you'd think she was my grandmother. My uncle was even older.

Was it awkward for you, staying with your father's sister?

Not really. My father was completely out of the picture at this point; he'd cut ties with the rest of his family the same time he walked out on us. And my aunt wasn't anything like him. She'd been married to my uncle and living in the same house since the end of World War II.

How did they feel about you coming to live with them?

If there'd been some other option, I don't think they'd have volunteered to let me stay with them as long as I did, but they never complained about it.

So you got along with them?

I didn't really have a choice. They were the most nonconfrontational people I'd ever met: you couldn't pick a fight with them if you tried. And it's not that they didn't have rules, but their way of getting you to behave was to make it impossible for you not to.

Like my uncle, right, he was the kind of guy who liked to have a glass of whiskey before he went to bed. I thought that was a pretty good idea, so the second night I was there, I snuck into his study after he went to sleep and helped myself. And I didn't take much, but the thing about guys who drink every day, they know exactly what's left in the bottle they're working on, and if the level is off by even a quarter inch, they notice.

Now, if my mom had caught me drinking, especially her stuff? She'd have been in my face about it in two seconds flat. My uncle never said a word—but the next day, I passed by the study and heard drilling inside, and that evening when I went to fix myself another nightcap I found a brand-new lock on the liquor cabinet. A *big* lock, fist-sized, the kind you can't pick.

They were like that with every bad thing I did. They never lectured me; they assumed I knew right from wrong, but if I insisted on doing wrong, they found some way to lock out that choice.

One morning my aunt asked me if I'd like to come help out at the store. Normally there'd have been no chance, but I was already so bored that I said OK. At the end of the day she gave me fifty cents, which seemed pretty cheap for eight hours, even if I did spend most of that time flipping through magazines. Next day, same deal. The day after that, I bailed out around noon, and instead of waiting to get paid I swiped a couple dollars from the till. Then that night before bed, I went to put the two bucks into the drawer where I kept my other wages and my Officer Friendly money, and instead of the twenty-six dollars that should have been there, I only found twenty-four. It was obvious what had happened, but I pulled the drawer out anyway and shook it upside-down, just in case the rest of the money had gotten stuck somehow. A single quarter fell out.

Your pay for the half-day you'd just worked?

Right.

Did you say anything to your aunt?

What would I have said? No fair stealing back what I stole from you? Anyway I had to hand it to her, keeping a step ahead of me that way. And no energy wasted on yelling. It seemed, I don't know, *efficient.*

But it was also frustrating. If I haven't made it clear already, there wasn't a lot for me to do in Siesta Corta, and once you took away the stuff I *shouldn't* be doing, life got really dull really fast.

The low point came about ten days in. My aunt and uncle didn't own a TV—of *course* they didn't—but they did have a lot of books in the house, and one day in desperation I started rooting through their library. Now I don't want to give you the wrong impression. I wasn't illiterate, and I wasn't allergic to books the way some people are, but still, on my list of preferred leisure activities, reading anything more demanding than *Tiger Beat* ranked somewhere down around badminton and pulling taffy. But there I was, on a perfectly good Friday afternoon, curled up in an easy chair with a Nancy Drew mystery in my lap.

I wouldn't have guessed you'd be a Nancy Drew fan.

I wasn't, really. I was a Pamela Sue Martin fan. She was the actress who played Nancy Drew on television— *had* played her, until she got kicked off the show for being a troublemaker. She was one of my role models. On TV she was squeaky-clean, but in real life she had a reputation for being a bad girl who wouldn't take shit from people. She'd been in *Playboy*, and done R-rated movies—just that year she'd starred as John Dillinger's girlfriend in *The Lady in Red*. So because of Pamela Sue Martin, I had this image of Nancy Drew as a sort of closet bad seed, cooler than she had any right to be.

The book turned out to be strictly G-rated, but I got sucked into the story anyway, and by the time I came up for air, most of the afternoon had gone by. Which freaked me out when I realized, because, you know, sitting in the same spot for hours, barely moving, that's the kind of thing Phil would do.

You were worried about turning into your brother?

Yeah. I know it sounds comical now, but at the time? That really was a panic-inducing thought for me. So I got up right then, went and got my money, and made a beeline for the highway.

What about your promise to Officer Friendly?

Well, I wasn't *really* going to run away. It was more like a test run—kind of a hitchhiking feasibility study. Turned out to be good timing, too, because while I was standing there by the roadside, I spotted something really interesting.

It was a girl, about my age. Mexican, but with a cigarette in her mouth, which marked her as a member of my tribe. She was sitting out next to the diner, along the wall where they kept the dumpsters. She'd gotten a bunch of empty produce crates and built them into a sort of hunter's blind, and she was hunkered down in there with a pile of green rocks. Then I got closer and saw that the rocks were actually oranges. The girl had a homemade slingshot, and she was using it to fire these unripened oranges out across the road.

At cars?

That would have been cool, but no, *across* the road, at the gas station on the other side. There was a guy over there, Hispanic like the girl but older, eighteen or nineteen. He was supposed to be minding the pumps, but what he was actually doing was taking a late-afternoon nap. Or trying to; every time he started to nod off, the girl would cut loose with another orange.

She didn't try to hit him directly; that would have given the game away. Instead she aimed for the gas-station roof, which was made out of tin. Each orange would make this big thunderboom when it hit, and the guy would jolt awake and come running out from under the roof overhang just in time to get beaned by the orange rolling down. Then he'd stand there rubbing his head and shouting up at the roof, daring the orange-thrower to come face him like a man.

I watched this happen like five times, and each time, I fell a little more in love with the girl. I kept moving closer to her hiding place, too, until I was right on top of her. "Jeez," she finally said, "crouch down or something if you're gonna be there. He's not *that* dumb."

I joined her in the hunter's blind. She gave this big sigh, like she didn't really want company, but then she offered me her cigarette pack. I went to take one and realized they were candy cigarettes—so, maybe not a member of my tribe after all. But I took one anyway, just to be friendly.

"So is that guy your brother?" I asked.

"My *stupid* brother," she said. "Felipe."

Her brother was Phil, too?

Yeah. Weird coincidence. And not the only one: *her* name was Carlotta. Carlotta Juanita Diaz. "I'm Jane Charlotte," I told her, and she nodded like she already knew that, and said, "You're staying with the Fosters."

"For now," I said. "What about you?"

"I've always lived here. My parents came up from Tijuana when Felipe was a baby."

"Your family owns the gas station?"

"And this place." She jerked her thumb at the diner. "And my dad's a deacon in the church."

"Wow," I said. "Important people."

"Yeah, we're the kings and queens of nowhere, all right."

Across the way, Felipe had settled back into the lawn chair he was using for a cot. Carlotta handed me the slingshot. "Remember," she said, "aim high." I did, and I did manage to hit the roof, although instead of rolling back the orange popped up over the peak and fell down the other side. No matter: Felipe jumped up just the same, and this time, instead of going back to his siesta, he ran inside the gas-station office. When he reappeared a moment later, he was dragging an extension ladder.

"So Carlotta," I asked, "how long have you been out here doing this?"

"You mean like today, or just in general?"

"This is a regular thing for you?"

She shrugged. "There's no movie theater in town, so I gotta make my own fun ... Here we go."

Felipe had gotten the ladder set up and started climbing. Carlotta waited until he was on the roof, then used one last orange to knock the ladder away. Game over.

"So," she said, "you want to get ice cream?"

Carlotta's parents both worked in the diner. Her mother ran the cash register and waited tables. Her father managed the kitchen—although Señor Diaz's management consisted mainly of sitting around, reading the

Bible and the sports pages, and occasionally yelling at the cooks for not moving fast enough.

"Hey you!" he called, as Carlotta led me in the back door. "Where have you been?"

"Walking to and fro on the earth," said Carlotta, with a nod to the Good Book in her father's lap. The crack earned her a scowl that could have come from the Old Testament God Himself.

"That's not funny, Carlotta. Your mother has been looking for you. She needs help out front."

"Yeah sure, in a minute," Carlotta said. She ducked into the walk-in freezer, leaving me alone with Jehovah.

"Hi," I said. "I'm Jane."

Señor Diaz cleared his throat like he was going to spit. He started to return to his Bible study, then looked up again and gave me this long, thoughtful stare.

"You're the new girl," he finally said. "At the Fosters'."

"Yeah, that's me. The new girl."

"You'll be staying with them a while?"

"Looks like."

"So you'll be going to school here, then."

I hadn't given it any thought, but of course he was right. The prospect didn't thrill me. "I guess so."

He nodded. "And how are you planning to get to school?"

"I don't know. I guess … Is there a bus?"

"Ah! A bus!" He waved the idea away. "Why would you want to take a bus to school?"

"Well …"

"I'll tell you something—Jane, is it?—the school bus here, it's not very good."

"No?"

"No. I would never let my daughter take the bus. We drive her to school. You could ride along with her, if you'd like."

"I could?"

"Yes. In fact, I think that would be an excellent idea."

It sounded like an OK idea to me, too, but there was obviously a catch. "Well," I hedged, "of course I'd have to ask my aunt and uncle first ..."

"Oh, I'm sure they won't object. You just let me talk to them. Here!" He stood up, and dusted off the stool he'd been sitting on. "Here, sit down, relax! Would you like some ice cream?"

Later, Carlotta told me what was up. The previous spring, she'd been kicked off the school bus twice for fighting, and after the second time, the driver refused to let her back on without a written apology. But Señor Diaz wouldn't hear of it: "He wanted the bus driver fired, you know, for violating my civil rights? But the superintendent wouldn't do that, so now my father wants to send me to a private school, only he wants the superintendent to pay for it. So we've got this lawsuit, but until we win, I've still got to go to the public school." But not by bus. Instead, Carlotta's mother would drive her to school in the morning, and her brother would pick her up at the end of the day. "Which is OK, except it means a lot of waiting, especially in the afternoon. Felipe can't leave the gas station before somebody else takes over for him, and some days that's not until five or six."

"So you've just got to hang out at the school until then?"

"Well, I don't *have* to—I could walk back, it's only like two miles—but my father gets real mad if I do that. He says it's too dangerous, especially now, with the death angel."

"The who?"

Most newspapers referred to him as the Route 99 Killer—an anonymous somebody who'd been traveling up and down the highway for the last year, grabbing kids out of rest stops while their parents were distracted—but a couple of tabloids, noticing that he only took boys, had given him a new name.

"The Angel of Death," Carlotta said. "Like the one in Egypt, who killed the firstborn sons? And I told my father, 'Hey, *I'm* not a boy, what do I have to worry about?' but he said, 'What if the guy makes a mistake? You think once he gets you in his car and sees you're a girl, he's just going to let you go?'"

Which explained why Señor Diaz wanted me riding along with his daughter: he figured with someone to keep her company, she'd be less likely to get bored and go for a stroll along the roadside. Plus, of the two of us, I was definitely the more butch-looking, so if the worst happened, chances were the Angel would take me.

Señor Diaz sounds like a great humanitarian.

Eh, you know. Parents. I couldn't really bring myself to be offended. Anyway, this is going to sound twisted, but it was kind of exciting, thinking about the danger. I mean that's one reason people believe in the bogeyman, right? It makes the dark more entertaining.

And it's not like I thought we were ever actually going to run into the guy. If I had any doubts on that score, they disappeared the minute my aunt and uncle said OK to Señor Diaz's offer. I had to figure if there was any real risk, they'd have made me take the bus.

Instead, first day of school, my aunt got me up extra early so I'd be ready when Carlotta's mom came by. That was the only time I had second thoughts, when my bedroom door banged open at five a.m. Half an hour later I was in the car, and by quarter to six Carlotta and I were in front of the school, eating candy cigarettes with a handful of other early birds.

Around six-fifteen the school librarian showed up. She let us into the building and had us come upstairs to the library until classes started. Then after final bell, we went back up there and killed time until Felipe came with his pickup.

Did the school library have Nancy Drew?

A full set. The Hardy Boys and the Bobbsey Twins, too. Carlotta was nuts about the Bobbsey Twins, which I never got—she really was a strange girl in a lot of ways.

What about your classes? What were those like?

Boring.

Did you make any other friends?

Not really. I tried to find a bad crowd to fall in with, but Carlotta with her sugar Pall Malls was the closest thing to a real j.d. that the place had to offer. Most of the other kids, I don't want to say they were dumb hicks, but they *were* dumb hicks. So I stuck with Carlotta, and we made our own fun.

And did this fun include amateur detective work?

Not deliberately. You're talking about the janitor, right? Me getting wise to him, that was mostly an accident.

What happened?

The school was only running at about sixty percent capacity, so to save money, an entire wing of the building had been closed down. The closed wing was officially off-limits, but of course that was just an invitation for students to try and break in; Carlotta and I had already talked about getting a crowbar from the gas station so we could go exploring.

Then one afternoon I was on my way to the bathroom when I saw the janitor open up one of the connecting doors that led into the closed wing. He went inside and pulled the door shut behind him, but I didn't hear him relock it. It seemed like a golden opportunity; I almost ran back to the library to get Carlotta, but then I thought about it a little more and realized that it was maybe more than one kind of opportunity.

See, one thing I was definitely missing in Siesta Corta was dope. And it was making me crazy, because I was in the middle of goddamned farm country, and I *knew* people had to be growing it. But nobody would tell me

who. Carlotta was no help; the only controlled substance
that ever passed her lips was communion wine, and not
much of that. I had higher hopes for Felipe, but when it
came to drugs he turned out to be even more straitlaced
than his sister. The one time I tried to raise the subject
with him he just gave me the evil eye.

You thought you might have better luck with the janitor?

Sure. I mean, four o'clock in the afternoon, the guy
goes into an abandoned part of the building. What for?
Not to mop floors. And he wasn't carrying any tools, so
he couldn't be doing repairs. So what's that leave?

*Any number of things, I'd imagine. But I take it you were
hoping for vice?*

You bet I was. And we're talking about a young guy
with long hair and a Jesus beard. So what kind of vice
was he likely to be into?

But it wasn't what you thought.

No, actually, it was what I thought. It's just, it was
also *more* than what I thought.

Past the connecting door was a long hallway lined
with empty classrooms. The janitor was in the last room
on the left, but halfway down the hall I could already
smell the pot. Good stuff, too—he obviously knew the
right people. So I tiptoed down there, trying to work
out how to play this. I figured I could either go in casual and friendly—"Hey, can I get a hit off that?"—or
I could be a hard-ass and threaten to turn him in if he
didn't give me his whole stash.

Which approach did you decide on?

I couldn't make up my mind. I didn't know the guy
at all, right, so I had no idea how easily he'd scare, or
share. And meanwhile—I was standing right outside the
room, now—I started hearing these monkey noises.

Monkey noises?

Yeah. *Literal* monkey noises, I thought at first, like
maybe he had a pet chimp in there with him. Farfetched,
I know, but who can tell with pot-smokers? So I took a

peep around the doorframe to see what kind of side-show I was about to burst in on.

The janitor was over by the windows. He had a tele-scope set up, and his face was mashed down over the eyepiece like it had been glued there. His left arm was curved above his head, like this, holding a joint in the air, and his right arm was curved down towards his waist, like this, holding ... Well, I couldn't see exactly what he was holding, for which thank God, but from the way his elbow was pumping it wasn't hard to guess.

As for the monkey noises, that was actually two sounds in one. He was grunting, of course, but also, to sort of brace himself, he'd pulled a pupil's chair up sideways be-hind him and planted his butt on the armrest, and the feet of the chair were going *squeak-squeak-squeak* in time with the grunts: voilà, instant chimp sounds. Which, all things considered, wasn't too far off the mark.

So I'm watching this, and I'm like, *yuck*, but at the same time, I still really wanted some dope. I definitely had the goods to blackmail this guy now, but the idea of confronting him in the act was too gross to contem-plate, so I decided to wait him out and see if he'd leave the roach behind when he was done with his business. That was something Moon and I used to do at her par-ents' parties, go around collecting leftovers out of the ashtrays and recycling them into bong hits. It was a great way to get high without actually having to talk to any freaks.

I hid in another classroom across the hall and prayed for a quick finish. The monkey noises got louder—they were more gorilla than chimp towards the end—and then there was a bang as the desk fell over, then silence, and then, very faint, the zip of a zipper. And then foot-steps, going out and down the hall, not running but hurrying, like he'd suddenly remembered an appoint-ment he had to get to.

When I was sure the coast was clear I came out of

hiding. I was out of luck on the dope: he'd left some-thing behind, all right, but it wasn't marijuana.

I took a look through the telescope to see what he'd been spying on. I was expecting the girls' locker room, something like that, but the guy's tastes turned out to be weirder than I'd thought. The telescope was aimed at this little picnic area about a quarter mile south of the school. It was nothing fancy, just a turnaround by the side of Route 99 with some wooden tables and a tire swing. The place doubled as a make-out spot, and on a Friday or a Saturday night I suppose there'd have been plenty to keep a Peeping Tom interested, but at the moment the only people there were this tourist fam-ily: Mom, Dad, two boys, a golden retriever, and an RV plastered with Disneyland stickers.

I didn't see the attraction. I mean, there's no account-ing for perverts, but this family just didn't strike me as, you know, masturbation material. So I was trying to puzzle it out—was it the mom that turned him on? Was it the *dog*?—when I heard a door slam. And I'm like, oh crap, he's coming back, but it wasn't the door in the hall, it was the school's front door. I looked out the window and saw the janitor down in the parking lot. He walked over to this brown van, got in, started up the engine ... and just sat there, idling.

Then after another minute I noticed smoke wafting out of the driver's-side window: the son of a bitch had fired up another joint. That got me mad, because I was already thinking of it as my dope, so I started sending out mental vibes to any of Officer Friendly's country cousins who happened to be in the area, begging them to drive by and bust this guy.

Well, of course that didn't happen. But who did drive by, a few minutes later, was the family in the RV. And no sooner had they passed the school than the van's taillights finally winked out; the janitor pulled onto the highway right behind the RV and started following it.

Was that when you began to suspect that the janitor was the Angel of Death?

No. The guy was a creep, obviously, but at that point I was still thinking voyeur, not psycho killer. I figured he was tailing them because he wanted to whack off some more—or maybe he was hoping to steal some panties, or a chew toy.

Then the next morning, I went out to catch my ride and Señor Diaz was driving the car, which had never happened before.

"What's going on?" I said. "Is it the Rapture?"

"The death angel," said Carlotta. "He grabbed another kid yesterday, right outside Modesto."

Modesto was north, the same direction the RV had been headed. That should have been enough to start me thinking, but the lightbulb didn't go on until Carlotta said: "Get this. He didn't just take the kid this time. He killed the kid's *dog*, too."

"Dog?" I said. "What kind of dog?"

"I don't know, a big one I guess. They think the dog tried to protect the kid, so the angel, like, gutted it."

"What about the boy? Did they find his body yet?"

"Yeah."

"Where?"

Carlotta looked excited. "You'll see."

A half mile out from school, we hit a traffic jam. This was something else that had never happened before—the road was usually empty at this hour—but when I saw the flashing lights up ahead, I immediately understood.

"The state police found him around two in the morning," Carlotta said. "Mrs. Zapatero from the motel was coming back late from visiting her sister and saw them roping off the crime scene. She said the kid was laid out on one of the picnic tables, like a human sacrifice."

As we got closer to the turnaround, Carlotta and I

rolled our windows down and leaned out, hoping to
catch a glimpse of the corpse. Señor Diaz yanked us back
into the car and gave us each a swat on the head. "Show
some respect!" he demanded, adding, to Carlotta: "You
see why I don't want you walking?"

Did you tell Señor Diaz about the janitor?

No. I know I should have, but I was pissed at him for
hitting me. Besides, telling what I'd seen meant explaining how I'd happened to see it, and I didn't think he'd
appreciate the part about me looking to get stoned. I
needed time to come up with a sanitized version of the
story—one that would stand up to questioning.

Meanwhile, I decided to ask some questions of my
own. When we finally got to school that morning, I
quizzed the librarian about the janitor. She didn't know
much. His name was Whitmer, Marvin or maybe Martin, and like me he was new; she'd heard he'd worked
at another school before this one, but she couldn't say
where.

"So you wouldn't know whether this other school was
also by the highway?"

"No, dear."

I thanked her and sat down. Then Carlotta started
interrogating me: "What are you so interested in the
janitor for?"

"It's nothing," I told her.

"Like hell it's nothing. Hey, I'm not stupid like Felipe."

"OK, it's not nothing. But I'm not ready to talk about
it." I didn't think Carlotta would care about the dope—
at least, not enough to give me shit for it—but she *would*
care that I'd gone into the closed wing without her.

Of course, now she was mad at me anyway: "What do
you mean you're not ready to talk about it? Since when
do we keep secrets?"

"Carlotta … It's not a secret, exactly, it—"

"You asked about the highway," she said. "You think

the janitor had something to do with that kid who got killed?"

Good guess; maybe there was something to the Bobbsey Twins after all. "Yeah, I do."

"But why would you think that? What happened? Did you see something?"

"I told you, I'm not ready to talk about it … Look, Carlotta, I promise I'll tell you later, OK? But first … I need your help with something. I want to search the janitor's van after school today, and I need you to be my lookout."

Now, I came up with this purely as a way of stalling, but when I thought about it, I realized it wasn't a bad plan. If I did find incriminating evidence in the van, I could turn the janitor in for that, and forget about the other thing.

Wouldn't you still have to explain your decision to search the van?

Well, that was the beauty of it: if I found proof that the janitor was a serial killer, people would be so excited they'd accept pretty much *any* explanation. At that point I could just say I had a hunch, and even Carlotta would probably buy it.

So after final bell that day, instead of going back to the library, we went to the lobby and waited for the other students to leave. Not long after the last of them had cleared out, the janitor passed through, pushing a cartload of garbage bags towards the rear of the building.

"What do you think?" I asked Carlotta, once he was out of earshot.

"I think this might not be such a smart idea, Jane. What if he really is the death angel? If he catches you—"

"He won't. You just stay here, and if you see him coming back, stick your head out the front door and yell something."

"What should I yell?"

"Anything but my real name."

The teachers had all taken off too by now, so aside from the librarian's Volkswagen, the janitor's van was the only vehicle left in the lot. It was a utility-style van, with no windows in the rear side panels; the windows in the back doors were small, and tinted so you couldn't see in. Add a little soundproofing, I thought, and it'd be perfect for kidnappings.

Its doors were all locked, but like Nancy Drew I'd come prepared: during lunch period, I'd stolen a coat hanger from the closet in the teachers' lounge. I slipped it in at the base of the driver's-side window and fished around until the lock button came up.

The inside of the van smelled like cleaning products. I was struck right away by how tidy it was. I mean I guess it's no surprise that a janitor would be a neat freak, but still: the dashboard was completely clear, with none of the crap that usually collects there, and there wasn't a scrap of trash on the floor or under the seats. Even the ashtrays were empty. There was nothing in the glove compartment but the van's registration papers.

The back of the van was a similar story. The floor was covered with a blanket that looked like it had just come out of a washing machine, and there was a gray metal toolbox stowed away neatly in one of the back corners. Other than that, I couldn't see so much as a stray gum wrapper.

Did you look inside the toolbox?

Yeah. I almost let it be—it seemed obvious now that the janitor wasn't the kind of guy to leave body parts lying around—but I decided I'd better be thorough.

The blanket crackled when I stepped on it. I crouched down and lifted up a corner; underneath it was a double layer of plastic sheeting. Then I lifted *that* up, and found a set of luggage straps, pre-positioned for easy bundling.

I smoothed the blanket back in place and turned to

the toolbox. It was padlocked; my coat hanger was no help here, but I had a couple different-sized paper clips, too, and one of them did the trick. I slipped off the padlock and lifted the lid.

And? What was inside?

Tools. A pair of handcuffs, for starters; a fat roll of electrician's tape; gloves. Also four sets of pliers, three ice picks, and a loop of piano wire.

Oh yeah, and one more thing: a hunting knife. It was a foot long, with a jagged-edged blade. Like the pliers and the ice picks it was shiny clean and smelled like it had been soaking in detergent, but when I took a closer look at it I saw that there was a hair stuck to the handle. A golden hair. I couldn't tell whether the hair was from a person or a dog, but I was pretty sure the police would be able to.

"Got you," I said, and that's when I heard footsteps outside the van.

For a moment I hoped it might only be Carlotta, bored with sentry duty and come to help me search, but then I heard keys jangling and knew I was in trouble. Dumping the garbage must have been the janitor's last chore for the day; instead of coming back through the building afterwards like I'd expected him to, he'd walked around the outside, bypassing my lookout.

As he fumbled with his keys, I packed the knife away in the toolbox and got ready to make a run for it. But when I reached for the back-door handle to let myself out, the handle wasn't there.

The janitor opened the driver's door. I froze. I was totally exposed; there was no way he wouldn't see me.

Then Carlotta called out from the front steps of the school: "Guadalupe!"

The janitor paused with one foot in the van and looked to see who she was yelling at. That bought me an extra few seconds. I did the only thing I could: moved up into the blind spot directly behind the driver's seat and made myself as small as possible.

The janitor slid behind the wheel. I crossed my fingers that he'd hang out for a while, maybe give Carlotta a chance to start lobbing oranges onto the van's roof, but not today: quicker than you can say "Guadalupe!" we were on the road. The janitor drove north again, away from Siesta Corta.

I couldn't see out, so I passed the time by staring at the toolbox. Although I'd closed the lid, I'd forgotten to latch it, and every time we hit a bump it threatened to fly open and dump its contents. Also, I'd left the padlock lying in plain view on the blanket; I kept waiting for the janitor to notice it in the rearview mirror and pull over to investigate.

After we'd gone about fifteen miles, he *did* pull over. I raised my head up as high as I dared, trying to get a sense of whether we were coming into a gas station or some other place where people would hear me if I screamed. It didn't look like it. It looked like we were in another roadside turnaround.

The janitor set the parking brake and killed the engine. He didn't get out. He rolled his window down, dug around in his pockets for a moment, and lit a joint.

Today I didn't begrudge him. Let him smoke all the dope he wanted; as long as he didn't come in back and kill me, I'd be totally cool with it.

I listened to the cars buzzing past on Route 99. *Come on, Officer Friendly*, I thought. *Get your vice detector working* ... There was a lull in the traffic, and I heard a new sound: voices.

Voices approaching the van?

Voices off in the distance. Boys' voices, shouting, excited, like in a playground. Then I heard a wooden *crack!*, and I thought, ball field, and I thought, oh shit.

I really didn't want to die, you know? But I didn't

think I could just sit quiet if the janitor started with the monkey noises again. If it came down to that, I thought I was probably going to have to bash him over the head with the toolbox.

But he kept his fly zipped. Maybe he was worried this spot was too public, or maybe he was storing up images for later. Whichever, he just sat and watched, and smoked—first the joint, then half a dozen cigarettes.

Finally he'd had enough, and got moving again. He drove another three or four miles up the highway before turning off on a side road. The road was in bad shape, and the toolbox lid started jumping again—and just to make things more exciting, we were going uphill, so the blanket kept sliding underneath me. I had to hook my hands under the bottom of the driver's seat and hang on.

We made a last turn, onto gravel, and pulled into a garage. The janitor parked and got out. My adrenaline level spiked as he walked to the back of the van, but he continued around to the passenger's side without stopping, jangling his keys. There was a hum of an electric motor as the garage door rattled shut, followed by more key jangling, and the squeak of another door opening and closing. And then, incredibly, I was alone. He hadn't even come close to discovering me.

I crawled back to the toolbox and got the knife. I thought about taking everything, but I didn't want to overload myself without knowing how far I might have to run. I figured the knife was the most important piece of evidence, not to mention the most useful if I happened to get cornered.

I got out of the van on the passenger's side and looked for the button that activated the garage-door opener. I couldn't find it, but on the wall right where you'd expect the button to be, I saw a small metal panel with a key-hole in it. I whipped out one of my paper clips and with a couple deft moves managed to break off the tip in the keyhole.

Shit. A quick check of the garage door confirmed that I'd need superstrength to open it by hand. I thought seriously about trying to crash the van through it, but it looked sturdy enough to withstand a collision, and anyway, my j.d. skill set didn't extend to hot-wiring.

I was going to have to sneak out through the house. Worse, now that I'd jammed the garage-door opener, I was going to have to do it soon, before the janitor decided to go out to dinner or another Little League game.

I went and pressed my ear to the house door, and when I didn't hear heavy breathing on the other side, I tried the knob. I expected it to be locked, which was going to create additional problems, but I guess the janitor wasn't a total security fanatic after all. The knob turned, and I opened the door a sliver.

Water was running somewhere in the house. I opened the door wider, and the running-water noise resolved itself into the sound of a shower.

I couldn't believe my luck. I *didn't* believe it: as I slipped through the door, I held the knife at the ready.

I found myself in a little alcove equipped with a washer and dryer. The alcove opened into a kitchen. To my left as I came out of the alcove was another doorway; it led into a bedroom, which led, in turn, to the bathroom with the shower. I hovered at the bedroom doorway, listening.

The janitor was definitely in the shower stall; I'll let you guess how I knew that. My nose wrinkled in disgust, but at the same time I relaxed, sure that I was safe now for at least the next few minutes.

Relief made me stupid. Instead of beating it for the front door, I started snooping around, opening drawers and cabinets. I was over by the pantry, trading glances with the Trix rabbit, when the phone on the kitchen table rang.

I reacted as if a burglar alarm had gone off. I dropped the knife in a panic, and snatched at the phone before it could ring a second time.

The shower kept on running. I raised the phone to my ear.

"Hello?" I said.

There was a pause, and a series of sharp clicks, and then a man's voice said: "Jane Charlotte."

It was the janitor, of course; he'd tricked me. All this time he'd been stringing me along, letting me think he hadn't noticed me. The sounds in the shower stall must have been some sort of recording, meant to lull me into a false sense of security. The game was over now, though, and in a moment he'd tell me to turn around, and he'd be standing right behind me, and then I would die.

But what the voice on the phone said next was: "You don't want to be messing around in there, Jane. He's a bad monkey."

Then the voice broke up in a screech of static—or maybe it was me who screeched—and the next clear thought I had I was outside, running screaming for the road.

Two state police cars were pulling up in front of the janitor's house. Felipe's pickup truck was right behind them, with Felipe, Carlotta, Señor Diaz, and the school librarian all jammed into the cab together.

A cop got out of the lead car, and I ran straight into his arms, shouting: "He's the Angel of Death! He's the Angel of Death! The janitor is the Angel of Death!" The cop grabbed me by the shoulders and tried to get me to tell him what had happened, but I just kept on shouting: "He's the Angel of Death!"

The other cops drew their guns and advanced on the house. They were almost at the front door when the janitor came out, still damp from the shower, wearing a T-shirt and a pair of boxer shorts. I'd started to calm down a little, but when I saw him I lost it again, screaming "Bad monkey!" and scrambling around to the far side of the police cars.

The cops pointed their guns at the janitor and told him to put his hands up, and he did. He was smooth. Instead of looking scared he acted bewildered, like he was this totally innocent guy who couldn't imagine what the police were doing on his property.

They handcuffed him. "Come on now," the lead cop coaxed me. "It's all right, we've got him. Talk to me." So I started babbling about the hunting knife, and eventually he nodded and said, "OK, just stay here," and went inside the house.

The Diazes formed a protective huddle around me. "Are you OK, Jane?" Carlotta said. "Did he hurt you?"

I shook my head. "Just scared me out of my wits is all … But it's fine now."

Only, it wasn't fine. I started figuring that out as soon as the cop came back with the wrong knife.

"Is this it?" he asked, holding out a scrawny little steak knife with a five-inch blade.

"No," I said. "I told you, it was a *hunting* knife. It was *big*."

"Show me." He took me back inside with him. The hunting knife had disappeared; when I pointed to the spot on the floor where I'd dropped it, the cop said, "That's where I found this," and held up the steak knife again. "Are you sure this isn't it?"

"Of course I'm sure," I said, annoyed. "The janitor must have hidden the real knife before he came outside." Then I remembered the toolbox: "Wait a minute … This way!"

I led him into the garage and around to the back of the van. "In there," I said. "You'll probably need his keys …" But the van's back doors were unlocked now. The cop pulled them open.

"So," he said, "what am I supposed to be looking at?"

The back of the van was empty. No blanket, no plastic sheeting, no luggage straps, no toolbox.

"Damn it!" I said. "He must have hidden this stuff, too."

"What stuff?"

"His kidnapping equipment."

"Equipment, huh?" The cop's expression changed, in a way I didn't like. "And you think he gathered up this … equipment … and hid it away just as we were arriving?"

"The stuff was here before, and now it's gone. So yeah. What's your problem?"

"No problem. It's just, he must have been moving awfully fast, don't you think?"

"Look, I'm not making this up."

"I didn't say you were making it up. Why would I think you were making it up?"

I should have just shut my mouth then. The thing was, he was right—the janitor would have had to move quickly, which meant he couldn't have hidden the stuff very well. I'm sure I could have found it.

But the cop was giving me the same I-see-through-your-bullshit look that Officer Friendly had—only not, you know, so friendly—so not only did I keep on running my mouth, but I immediately brought up the one subject you never mention when you're trying to get somebody to believe you.

"Take a whiff," I said.

"A whiff?"

"Inside the van. Smell it."

He leaned in and sniffed. "Air freshener?"

"Pot."

His eyebrows went up. "Marijuana?"

"The janitor smokes it."

"Really. You'd never guess that, looking at him."

"Not to get high," I said. "I mean, that too, but he smokes it to excite himself. Before ..."

"Oh! Before he uses his kidnapping equipment, you mean ... And you're familiar with the smell of marijuana, are you?"

It was a fast trip downhill from there. The more skeptical he became, the more I talked—when he asked me what had put me on to the janitor in the first place, I actually told the truth, or at least enough of it to make myself sound like a complete idiot. "Monkey noises, eh? Well, I can see why you'd be suspicious of a man who made noises like a monkey ..."

To complete my humiliation, he brought me back outside and asked Carlotta whether she knew anything about these monkey noises. "Monkey *what*?" said Carlotta.

"That's what I thought," said the cop, and told his buddies to turn the janitor loose.

My mouth wouldn't stop running: "You're letting him *go*?"

"You should be worried about whether I'm going to let *you* go," the cop said. "If this gentleman wants to press charges against you for trespassing, I'll be only too happy to run you in."

But the janitor, still playing the innocent, said he didn't want to press charges—he just wanted to know what was going on.

"Just a big misunderstanding, sir," the cop told him. He shot me a look: "One that had better not happen again."

The Diazes took me home. Señor Diaz made me ride in the back of the pickup, which I didn't particularly mind, since he and Carlotta spent the entire trip arguing in high-decibel Spanish; when we stopped at the school to drop off the librarian, she stumbled out of the cab looking pale and half-deaf. Then when we got to my stop, Señor Diaz had a quieter conversation with my aunt and uncle. I didn't need to listen in to know that I'd be taking the bus to school from now on.

After the Diazes left, my uncle told me that it "might be best" if I didn't go by the diner or the gas station anymore, and my aunt added that they wouldn't need my help at the store "for a while," which I understood was her way of saying I was grounded. I got really mad, and started going on about how stupid it was that no one believed me, and how it wasn't going to be my fault if the janitor killed another kid; but my aunt and uncle just shook their heads and left me alone to rant and rave.

It was Friday, so I had the whole weekend to feel sorry for myself. Monday was a little better; I got to sleep an extra hour and a half, which almost made up for having to take the school bus. I didn't see Carlotta until second-period English. She ignored me during class, and afterwards I had to run out into the hall to catch up with her.

"I'm not supposed to talk to you, Jane," she said. "My dad thinks you're a bad influence."

"I am a bad influence. It's one of the reasons you like me."

The joke fell flat, but at least she didn't walk away. After a moment, she asked: "Did you hear about the janitor?"

"What about him?"

"He quit his job over the weekend. The librarian told me he called up the school superintendent on Saturday and said he was leaving."

"Leaving as in moving away?"

"I guess so."

"Well don't you see what that means? He's guilty! Even though the cops let him go, he's afraid they'll remember him next time a kid disappears."

"Maybe," said Carlotta. "Or maybe he's afraid people will jump to conclusions when they hear the cops were at his place."

"Carlotta, I swear, I didn't make any of that stuff up."

"Well, it doesn't really matter now, does it? I mean, if he's really gone for good." She looked at me. "You should probably be careful until we know that for sure, huh?"

The thought had already occurred to me. Friday afternoon, as we were about to leave the janitor's house, I'd caught the janitor eyeballing me. The cops were already in their cars, and Felipe was revving the pickup, and I looked over and saw the janitor standing in his front doorway, still in his underwear, staring at me. He'd dropped the bewildered routine and put a whole new face on.

A hostile face?

No. He didn't show any emotion at all. He was just ... *intent*. Like he wanted to make really sure he'd recognize me next time we met up.

It was good for a few weeks' nightmares. In my dreams, he'd drive up to my aunt and uncle's place after midnight with his headlights off, and sit smoking dope and looking up at my bedroom window. Sometimes he'd just sit there, thinking about how he was going to get even with me, and other times he'd get out and walk around the outside of the house, looking for a way in. One night I woke up in a sweat, sure I'd just heard a van driving away, and when I opened my window to look out, I smelled pot smoke.

I also dreamed about that voice I'd heard on the phone in the janitor's kitchen. When I was awake I didn't think about it so much—I mean, it's not like I forgot about it, but it was just so *weird*, I sort of pretended I forgot about it. But it got into my dreams, and in my dreams, it wasn't scary. I'd be like clutching this phone in the dark, petrified because the janitor was coming for me, and then the voice would say my name, "Jane Charlotte," and there'd be this wave of relief, because somehow, dream logic, I'd know the voice was *good*, and it was on my side, on the side of *all* good people. And it was more powerful than the Angel of Death.

So I dreamed about this stuff for a few weeks, and then the dreams started to taper off. The janitor hadn't come calling on me, nobody at school or in town had seen him, no more kids had gone missing, and while I still knew the guy was guilty, more and more it seemed like that was somebody else's problem.

Then one evening my aunt and uncle drove down to Fresno to visit some friends of theirs. Originally I was supposed to go with them and catch a movie while they played bridge or whatever, but the day before, I'd gotten busted for cheating on a test, and after the school superintendent called home to narc on me, my aunt went from talking about "when we go out tomorrow night" to "when your uncle and I go out tomorrow night."

They left around six. Storm clouds were blowing in from the west, and I was pissy enough to hope they'd get caught in a downpour. By seven the sky was overcast and lightning was flickering on the horizon, but there was still no rain.

I read a few chapters of Nancy Drew—I'd worked my way through most of the series by now, so I'd had to start rationing the books that were left—then ate the cold meatloaf my aunt had left me in the fridge. After I cleared my plate I sat back down at the kitchen table to work a crossword puzzle from the Fresno *Bee*. This was another Phil-type activity that you couldn't have paid me to do back in S.F. But with no TV, a looming Nancy Drew shortage, and Señor Diaz hanging up the phone every time I tried to call Carlotta, my entertainment standards just kept getting lower and lower.

It was a hidden-message crossword, which they did sometimes: certain of the clues were highlighted, and if you solved them and strung the answers together, they'd form a saying or a quotation, like RED SKY AT MORNING, SAILOR TAKE WARNING, or THAT WHICH DOES NOT KILL US MAKES US STRONGER. Usually the special clues were hard enough that you had to finish the whole crossword to get them, but sometimes, like tonight, you could solve them directly.

The first highlighted clue, 1 across, four letters, was "Defunct *Life* magazine rival," and I knew that was LOOK. The second clue, 9 across, five letters, was "Opposite of over," or UNDER. The third clue—and this one was *so* easy I almost laughed—was a fill-in-the-blank, 13 across, three letters, "Winnie ____ Pooh."

There was a rumble of thunder and the rain finally started. It was the downpour I'd wished for and then some, but instead of making me happy it set me on edge. I went down the hall to the front door, flicked on the front-porch lights, and spent a long time looking out, making sure that the hiss of the rain was just rain, and not tires creeping up the drive.

The next clue was the only one I didn't get right off the bat: 20 across, four letters, "Where the NC gun is hidden."

NC gun?

Capital N, capital C. I thought it might be a typo, so I moved on to the next clue, 24 across, four letters, "Tarzan's girlfriend." My scalp prickled a little when I saw that, but what really made my hair stand up was the last clue, 31 across, nine letters, "The loneliest Brontë."

Now, ordinarily I wouldn't have gotten that one either, but it just so happened that we'd been reading *Jane Eyre* in class that week, and the teacher had given us the rundown on the whole sorry Brontë family, so I knew that the loneliest Brontë was CHARLOTTE. After Branwell and Emily and Anne all died, Charlotte was the one left over, the one left alone in the house, kind of

like I was right now. And so if you added it all together,
tonight's hidden message was—

LOOK UNDER THE blank, JANE CHARLOTTE.

Yeah. And maybe it was because it shared a couple of
letters with "blank," or maybe it was because I was sitting with my back to it, but all at once I knew that the
missing word was SINK.

My aunt and uncle's kitchen had this huge sink—"Big
enough to slaughter a pig in," my uncle said one time,
and he made it sound like that was more than a figure
of speech. It had a big cabinet space underneath it too,
and once when we were visiting a few years earlier, Phil
crawled under there during a game of hide-and-seek
and split his head open on the drainpipe. So between
thoughts of pig slaughter and the memory of Phil with
blood streaming down his face, I wasn't exactly eager to
stick my nose down there.

Of course I had to look. I told myself that it was just
a coincidence anyway, there was no way that message in
the crossword could really be intended for me personally. Maybe "Look under the sink, Jane Charlotte" was a
line from Shakespeare.

So I opened up the cabinet, and there was nothing
there but the usual assortment of under-the-sink junk,
and I'm like, see, just a coincidence. But then I'm like,
not so fast, if there *is* a gun, it's not just going to be lying out next to the silver polish. So I felt up in the space
between the wall and the back of the sink basin. And at
first I was just touching air, but then I moved my hand a
little and my fingers brushed something rough. A pack-
age.

It was rolled up in a piece of potato sack and tied
up with twine. I brought it out into the light and unwrapped it. And there it was.

It looked like a toy zap gun. It was bright orange,
with a puffy barrel, and it seemed to be made of plastic.
It was heavy, though, and from the weight and the fact

that it was slightly cold, I thought it might be a water pistol. But when I checked the base of the handle there was no rubber plug, just a flat plate embossed with the letters NC.

There were more markings on the side of the gun. Near the back of the barrel, right above the trigger, was a dial with four settings. One setting was labeled SAFE in small green letters; the next setting was labeled NS, in blue; the last two settings, both labeled in dark red, were CI and MI. The dial was currently set to MI.

I did the thing that you traditionally do when you're a teenager and you find a gun, which was point it at my own face. The dark hole of the NC gun's muzzle seemed more real than the rest of it, though, so I decided not to pull the trigger. Instead I looked around to see if one of my aunt's cats was in the room. But the cats had made themselves scarce, and before I could choose something else for target practice, all the lights in the house went out.

For the first few seconds I was amazingly calm. Then lightning flashed outside and I turned towards the window above the sink, drawn by an afterimage of something that didn't belong. When the next flash came I saw it clearly: out beyond the backyard, in the orange groves that ran behind the house, a van was parked with its headlights off.

Something big walked across the back porch, passing right in front of the window—I say *something*, but of course I knew who it was, and what he was here for. He went straight for the porch door, which was locked but flimsy, and banged on it hard, real hammer blows. I could feel it shaking in its frame. There was a pause, and then he started attacking the doorknob, rattling it like he meant to pull it off.

By this point I was practically shitting myself with fear. I still had the gun, but I'd gone back to thinking of it as a toy, and in another moment I would have dropped it in the sink and started running blind through the house.

Then the phone rang, a beautiful sound. The janitor immediately stopped rattling the doorknob. The phone rang again, and again, and I moved towards it, terrified that if the ringing stopped before I reached it the attack on the door would begin again. I racked my knee on a chair, and banged my side against the corner of the kitchen table, but I held on to the gun.

I answered the phone on the seventh ring: *"Hello . . . ?"*

"Jane Charlotte."

"I don't know who this is," I whispered, "but I need help. Your bad monkey is right outside my back door."

"No," the voice on the phone said. "He's in the house."

Down the hall in my uncle's study, a board creaked.

"Now don't panic," the voice advised. "He won't expect you to be armed. Just hold the gun steady in both hands . . ."

I hung up. From the phone to the porch door was about a dozen steps, but my feet didn't touch the floor more than twice.

The door wouldn't open, even after I remembered to unlock it. Something—one of the porch chairs, probably—had been jammed under the knob on the other side.

Behind me, another board creaked: he was coming down the hall. I whirled around and raised the gun, even as his silhouette filled the kitchen doorway.

The NC gun doesn't make any noise when you fire it. I didn't realize that at the time, though, because just as I pulled the trigger, the lightning came again, striking so close behind the house that there was no pause before the thunder. The kitchen filled up with sound and light, so bright that the janitor himself seemed to glow like a real angel, an angel with a flaming dagger in one hand and a sparkling wire halo in the other. I screamed, and he screamed too, and by the time the brightness failed he was already falling.

In the dark I heard his body hit the floor. I lowered my aim and pulled the trigger again, but this time there was nothing, not even a click.

The rain stopped. The thunder and lightning moved off, and after a while the power came back on. I could see him, then, sprawled on his back in the kitchen doorway, not moving. He was just a man now; his eyes were glassy, and he had a new expression on his face.

He looked surprised.

Now, this next part may be a little hard to believe.

Really.

You know normally, if you shoot an intruder in your house, especially a serial killer, the first thing you do afterwards is call the police.

Right.

Or just run like hell to the neighbors'.

Right.

Right. But I didn't do either of those things.

What did you do?

I got sleepy. I mean, the guy was dead—I kicked him a couple times to make sure—so it's not like notifying the cops was *urgent* anymore. And now that I knew I was safe, I just really felt like lying down for a while. I thought, my aunt and uncle will be home in a few hours, and we can deal with the aftermath then.

So I went upstairs to my room. I barricaded the door with my dresser—just in case—and lay down. I slipped the NC gun under my pillow. I closed my eyes.

When I opened them again, it was morning. My bedroom door was wide open, and I could hear my aunt making breakfast in the kitchen. I got up and went downstairs, and stood in the empty doorway where the janitor's body had been.

"Good morning, sleepyhead," my aunt said. "Would you like bacon with your eggs?"

The porch door was open too, and I could see my uncle out back, walking around the remains of a lightning-blasted tree.

"Hold off on the bacon," I said. "I'll be right back."

I ran upstairs and looked under my pillow.

The gun was gone too, wasn't it?

Yeah. But there was something else in its place. A coin. A gift from the pistol fairy, maybe.

It was the size of a quarter, but thicker and heavier. It looked like gold. It had the same image on both sides, a hollow pyramid with a glowing eye inside of it, you know, kind of like the capstone from the pyramid on the dollar bill. Running around the rim of the coin was a three-word slogan: OMNES MUNDUM FACIMUS.

My Latin is rusty. Mundum *means "world"?*

Yeah. I got a Latin dictionary from the school library and worked it out. *Omnes* is "all of us," and *facimus*, that's "create" or "make," so *omnes mundum facimus* is like, "We all make the world." That's how it translates; as for what it *meant*, though, that was trickier. It was a puzzle, see? A sort of aptitude test, like the hidden message in the crossword, only much harder, so it took me a lot longer to get it.

How much longer?

Twenty-two years.

white room (ii)

THE NEXT TIME THE DOCTOR ENTERS the room, he's carrying a second file folder, thick with evidence.

"Checking up on my story?" she guesses, as he deals the folder's contents into three neat piles on the table.

He nods. "I don't like to confront patients, but in prison psychiatry I find that taking an aggressive tack early on can be very useful."

"For separating the con artists from the genuine head cases?" She looks amused. "So what's the verdict on me?"

He offers her the first of his evidence piles. "This is a report filed by the Madera County sheriff's office in October 1979. A man named Martin Whitmer was found dead in his van in a roadside ditch outside Fresno. Whitmer had worked as a janitor at a rural high school, but quit his job after an unidentified student accused him of being the Route 99 Killer."

"Well there you go. It's just like I said."

"Not quite." He flips to a page near the bottom of the pile. "There's no mention of a bullet wound in the autopsy. Mr. Whitmer died of a coronary."

"Yeah, I know. I told you, I shot him with an NC gun."

The doctor thinks a moment. "NC stands for Natural Causes?"

"Right. Sorry, I thought that was obvious."

"The gun shoots heart attacks."

"Myocardial infarctions," she says, tapping a finger on the cause-of-death line in the autopsy report. "MIs. And the CI setting, that's for *cerebral* infarctions. Heart attack and stroke, the two leading killers of bad monkeys ..." She smiles. "So what else have you got?"

He pushes forward the second pile, which consists of just two sheets, printouts from a newspaper microfilm reader. It's a story from the San Francisco *Examiner*, with the questioning headline ANGEL OF DEATH HANGS UP WINGS?

"'Sixteen months after the Route 99 serial killer claimed his last victim,'" she reads aloud, "'state police are beginning to hope that the so-called Angel of Death—whose identity remains a mystery—may have gone into retirement ...' Yeah, see, I told you the cops didn't believe me about the janitor. So even after he turned up dead, they thought the Angel was still out there."

The doctor points to a circled paragraph farther down the page. "Keep reading."

"'Thirteen-year-old David Konovic, the boy believed to have been the Angel of Death's eighth and final victim, disappeared from a Bakersfield gas station on December 12th, 1979 ...'"

"December," the doctor says. "Two months after Whitmer was found dead."

"Are you sure the newspaper didn't screw up the date?"

He slides the last evidence pile across the table. "The sheriff's report on David Konovic's abduction. The date matches. And when the boy's body was recovered, he was found to have been tortured and strangled in the

same manner as all the other Angel of Death victims. So
what does that tell us?"

"I don't know."

"Come on, Jane."

"You want me to say that Whitmer couldn't have
been the Angel of Death, is that it?"

"Doesn't that seem like a reasonable conclusion?"

"No."

"Why not?"

"Because he *was* the Angel of Death."

"Well if that's the case, how do you explain this last
victim?"

"I don't."

"You mean you can't."

"It's a Nod problem," she says.

"An odd problem?"

"A *Nod* problem. You know, the land of Nod, east of
Eden? In the Bible?"

"I know the reference, but . . ."

"Cain kills his brother Abel," she says, "and God
sets him wandering in the wilderness as a punishment.
Cain ends up in Nod, where he settles and gets married.
Which is a problem, logically, because Adam and Eve
are supposed to be the first people on earth, and as far
as we know, Cain and Abel are their only children. So
where did this wife come from?

"Now, people who don't believe in the Bible tend to
think the Nod problem is a big deal. Like for example,
there was this guy my mother dated one time for a
couple months, Roger, who was this totally rabid atheist, and he used to pick on Phil—"

"Your brother was religious?" the doctor asks.

"In a little-boy kind of way. My mother was raised
Lutheran, and even though she didn't really believe, she
took us to church because she thought it would be good
for us. I stopped going as soon as I was old enough to

say no, but Phil really got into it. Said his prayers every day, the whole bit. So along comes Roger, and he's constantly razzing Phil about inconsistencies in Scripture. 'Hey Phil, it says here in the Gospels that Judas hanged himself because he was sorry for betraying Christ. But it says in Acts that Judas wasn't sorry, and he died when his stomach exploded. How come there are two different versions of the story?' Or, 'Hey Phil, if all the disciples fell asleep in the Garden of Gethsemane, how did Matthew know what Jesus said in his prayer?' The Nod problem, though, that was his favorite: 'Hey Phil, it says that God put a mark on Cain to warn other people not to harm him. What other people, Phil? His parents? The same ones who didn't listen when God told them not to eat the fruit?'"

"And how did Phil respond?"

"Well like I said before, Phil was a big-time nitpicker himself, so at first he kind of got into it. He tried to play along, only Roger wasn't playing. Roger would shoot down every explanation Phil came up with, until finally Phil had to admit he didn't have an answer, and then Roger would say, 'So does that mean you're going to give up this Bible nonsense?' and Phil would say, 'No,' and Roger would say, 'That's because religion makes people stupid.'"

"What did you think of that?"

"Oh, I definitely think religion makes people stupid," she says. "But Roger was still a hypocrite."

"Why a hypocrite?"

"Because the Nod problem didn't have anything to do with him being an atheist. If the Bible had been perfectly consistent, he still wouldn't have believed a word of it. His mind was made up, and pointing out contradictions was just a way of being smug—and meanwhile, he completely missed where Phil was coming from.

"Phil *did* believe in the Bible. Part of believing that the Bible is true is believing that any problems in the text have solutions. Actually knowing what those solutions are isn't important. It's like, just because I can't tell you what killed the dinosaurs doesn't mean they aren't extinct. And so to Phil, looking at it from that perspective, it was Roger who was being unreasonable. So Phil didn't know where Cain's wife came from. So what?

"And it's the same with this." She waves a hand at the papers in front of her. "Don't pretend this is some kind of objective inquiry for you. You've already decided what you believe. All you're doing now is looking for a club to beat me with until I agree to see things your way."

"Jane ..."

"But that's not going to happen. I know my story is true. If something about it doesn't add up for you, we can discuss it, but don't try to blow a little discrepancy out of proportion. It's just a Nod problem."

"Well, you're putting me in a difficult position," the doctor says. "If I can't question inconsistencies in your account—"

"You can question them. I just said we can discuss it."

"But you're unwilling to entertain any real doubt."

"Which makes us even," she says. "Just like Phil and Roger."

The doctor frowns.

"Sorry to spoil your game plan. Does this mean you don't want to hear any more?"

"No, I still want to hear the whole story."

"Good. Because it would make you a liar if you didn't. I mean, you're already a liar for saying you'd keep an open mind, but if you bailed on me now you'd be a double liar."

"Well I wouldn't want to be that," says the doctor. "So after you killed the Angel of Death, what happened next?"

We All Make the World

I GREW UP.

I lived in Siesta Corta until I turned eighteen. It wasn't supposed to be for that long, but my mother refused to take me back, and not even my aunt and uncle could come up with a way to make her.

Were you upset about not going home?

No. Before the incident with the janitor, I would have been, but after … My perspective on pretty much everything was different.

I can understand that.

I'm not sure you can. I mean yeah, I'd been through a life-and-death experience, I'd *killed* someone, but in hindsight, it wasn't the shooting that most affected me. It was hearing that voice say my name on the phone. It's like, imagine if God called you up one day, not to give you a message but just to let you know He existed. Imagine how you'd feel right after you hung up.

You thought the voice on the phone was God?

No! But it was *like* that: like I'd been in contact with something big and mysterious, and the fact that it was out there made the whole world more interesting.

So it was like a conversion experience.

I suppose. Only not bullshit—it really happened, and I had the coin to prove it. And that was another thing:

the fact that they'd left me even that tiny bit of evidence told me it wasn't over. I'd be hearing from them again.

You saw that as something positive.

Sure. Why not?

I think many people, having been through the experience you describe, wouldn't be eager to repeat it.

Well yeah, but *those* people wouldn't have even gotten the first phone call. Not everyone is cut out for Bad Monkeys, and that's OK. But for me, once the initial shock wore off, of course I wanted to go again. I mean, Nancy Drew with a fucking lightning gun, what's not to love?

So with that to look forward to, living in Siesta Corta wasn't such a drag anymore. You can wait for a bright future pretty much anywhere, right? And while I was waiting, just in case it mattered, I cleaned up my act. I never became a model citizen, but I did cut out most of the bad-seed crap. I gave up trying to outsmart my aunt and uncle, and at school, I actually applied myself— enough so that when I finally graduated, I was able to get a scholarship to Berkeley.

So you ultimately did go back to San Francisco.

Yeah. I almost didn't, I mean I thought about not taking the scholarship, but Phil convinced me I'd be an idiot not to.

You were in contact with your brother?

By then, yeah. The first couple years in Siesta Corta I didn't hear from him, but on his thirteenth birthday he came out to see me. He stole a page from my old playbook: told Mom he was staying at a friend's place for the weekend, then hitchhiked out to the Valley. I came home from working at the store one afternoon and found him playing with the cats on the front porch.

At first I was pissed about the hitchhiking: "Do you have any idea what kind of psychos are out on the road, Phil?" But he just laughed and said I was the pot calling the kettle black, and anyway he was big enough to take care of himself. And the truth is, he was; he'd gone through this major growth spurt, so even though he was barely a teenager, he had the height and weight to make a bad monkey think twice.

It ended up being a good visit. The same time he'd become more like me, I'd become more like him, so we were able to sort of meet each other halfway. Turned out we actually liked each other. So from then on we kept in touch, and when he could he came out to see me. He had a knack for showing up when I needed advice, like about the scholarship.

What about your mother? Did you and she ever reconcile?

No. I thought about going to visit her once I was back in S.F. I talked to Phil about it—I figured he'd be all in favor—but he thought it was a lousy idea. "You know you'll just end up fighting with her, Jane. Why would you want to do that?" So I put it off. When she died in '87, I still hadn't seen her.

I'm sorry.

No, Phil was right. There was no love lost there, and no sense pretending, either.

Tell me about Berkeley. What was your major?

Christ, *that* question … Which one do you want to hear about first? I had like five.

You had trouble deciding?

I didn't think I needed to decide. Look, there are basically two reasons people go to college. Some people actually go there to learn something, something specific I mean, a trade or a vocation. Other people—like me—just go for the experience. I was like one of those starving-artist types, people who convince themselves back in grade school that they have a destiny to become actors or musicians or writers. For them, college is a place to mark time until their destiny kicks in.

And you believed that you had a destiny … to become Nancy Drew with a lightning gun?

See, when you say it that way it sounds crazy. It was

never that explicit. I didn't even know what the organization was at that point, so it's not like I ever thought to myself, "One day I'm going to join the fight against evil, and here's how." It was a lot more subtle than that, just this general sense that I was covered—I didn't need to make a plan for my life, because the plan already existed, and eventually it would come clear to me.

But the wait got long. When I left Berkeley after five years, my destiny still hadn't kicked in yet, and suddenly it didn't seem so smart that I hadn't studied anything useful. To survive, I ended up doing what the starving artists did, taking jobs that even a high-school dropout could get: waitress, pizza-delivery girl, liquor-store clerk … Name an occupation with no entry qualifications and no future, and I probably tried it at least once.

So I was poor, and living in one shitty apartment after another, but I was young, and having fun—too *much* fun, sometimes—and I still felt like I was covered. And then one day I turned around and I was thirty years old. And like I say, my destiny, I never thought about it that explicitly, but on milestone birthdays, you *do* think about things, and the day I turned thirty it occurred to me that it had been a really long time since I'd seen the coin. I decided I needed to see it, to hold it in my hand and remind myself, you know, *omnes mundum facimus*, we all make the world, whatever the hell that meant.

But I couldn't find it. I trashed my apartment looking for it. And it was no surprise—I'd moved so many times, it was a wonder I hadn't lost more stuff—but I was still very upset. So I went out and got really fucked up, and to make a long story short, my birthday ended with cops and an ambulance ride.

Afterwards, Phil came to see me, and we had a long heart-to-heart about what I was going to do with my life. I'd never told him about the coin, or the voice on the phone, or any of the rest of it, but he talked like he knew: "You don't need an engraved invitation to do good works in the world, Jane," he said. "You want to do them, you just go out and do them." Which, once I got done gagging, actually made a lot of sense to me. So that kind of became the theme of my early thirties.

Good works?

Well, *attempted* good works. Turns out it's not as easy as it sounds.

The first couple years, I did a bunch of gigs with groups like the Salvation Army and Goodwill, but I found out I don't really have the temperament for charity work, especially religious charity work. I decided to try more white-collar stuff—March of Dimes, CARE—but that was just boring, plus I'm even worse at office politics than I am at charity. So then I thought, getting back to basics, maybe what I needed was something with a more disciplinarian bent to it.

Law enforcement?

Yeah. But there I had a different problem: to become a cop, or a prison guard, or even a parole officer, you need to pass a background check, and there were things in my history—like that meltdown on my thirtieth birthday—that made that a deal-breaker. About the best I could do was a job as a security guard, and protecting the inventory at some department store didn't really count as good works in my book.

So as time wore on, my thirties started looking more and more like my twenties: lots of pointless, dead-end jobs. And then I was thirty-five, and thirty-*six*, and forty was just up ahead, and Phil didn't have any more suggestions for me.

And then one day I bumped into my old pal Moon. I hadn't seen her in twenty years, but this one day I was feeling nostalgic and decided to go back to the Haight, to the street where we grew up. I was standing in front of the lot where the community garden used to be—it had been paved and turned into a skateboard rink—when Moon came along, dragging a pair of kids with her.

She looked great. Young and skinny, not like someone who'd been through two pregnancies. Meanwhile I was definitely the worse for wear, so it took her a minute to recognize me, but when she finally did she gave me this big hug and introduced me to the brood. Then—like this wasn't depressing enough already—she told me that she and her husband had started their own consulting firm and were pulling down six figures a year working from home. So I came back with this story about how I'd been in the Peace Corps, and if I seemed a little run down it was because I'd spent the last decade fighting AIDS in Africa. Then she had to go, so I gave her a fake e-mail address and told her to keep in touch.

And I was on my way home when I passed by this pay phone, and just on impulse I picked up the receiver. There was no dial tone, but the phone wasn't dead—it was an open line. "Hello?" I said. There was no answer, but still it felt like someone was listening at the other end, so I said, "If you're ever planning to call me back, do it soon."

The next day, I got a jury-duty summons in the mail. I'd gotten calls to jury duty before, and I was about due for another, so it could have been a coincidence. But maybe not ... and either way, I figured this was an opportunity to do some good in the world, exactly what I'd been looking for.

It was an arson-murder trial. This guy Julius Deeds, reputed gangster, found out his girlfriend was cheating on him and threw a gasoline bomb into her living room in the middle of the night. She escaped through the back door of the house, but she left three kids upstairs and none of them made it out.

So I was in the jury pool for this, and I was pretty psyched, until it dawned on me that I'd met the defendant before. He'd been at my dealer's place the last time I went to make a buy.

That's your drug dealer?

Yeah. Guy named Ganesh.

May I ask what kind of drugs?

The usual kind. Pot of course, speed, Valium, coke on special occasions, acid when I needed a cheap vacation. I know that probably sounds like a lot, but at that point in my life I had it under control.

Anyhow, the last time I'd gone to see Ganesh, about a month before the jury call, he'd come to the door looking scared. Now Ganesh was always a little shaky. He'd studied to be an oncologist before flunking out of med school, and I'm guessing he had a failure mantra playing 24/7 in his head: "I was supposed to be curing cancer, instead I'm one bad day away from doing twenty years in Leavenworth." This time, though, he wasn't just nervous, he was sick with fear, *ashen* with it, like he'd just come from watching his twin get autopsied.

"I can't see you right now, Jane," he said, and started to shut the door on me. Then the door jerked open again, and this giant ape of a guy stepped up behind Ganesh and belly-bumped him so hard he nearly fell on his face.

"Hi there, Jane," the ape said, grabbing Ganesh by the back of the neck to steady him. "What brings you here?"

I kept my voice casual: "Just dropping by to say hi."

"Oh yeah?" He looked down at Ganesh, turning him like a can whose label he wanted to read. "You sure about that? Because Ganesh here, he likes to sell things to people—he's not so good about paying bills, but he likes to sell. You sure you didn't come to do some shopping, Jane?"

"No, really ... I'm just here to say hi. But if you guys are busy ..."

"Yeah, we kind of are ..." He started dragging Ganesh back inside. "So come back later. Much."

I hadn't seen or heard from Ganesh since, and I naturally assumed the worst.

I hadn't seen Julius Deeds since, either. His lawyer had him cleaned up for the trial, but King Kong with a haircut is still King Kong, so I should have recognized him right off the bat. But I was so gung-ho to get on the jury, I spent my first half hour in the courtroom focused on the juror questionnaire. It wasn't until I got done bullshitting my way through that and handed it in that I noticed Deeds staring at me, trying to work out where he knew me from.

We both got it at the same time. Then he smiled, like Christmas just came early, and all my good intentions went straight out the window. I started hoping three things in quick succession: one, that I didn't get picked for the jury after all, two, that Deeds hadn't made bail, and three, that if he *had* made bail, Ganesh was either dead or out of the country, because Ganesh knew where I lived.

I'm going to guess that none of your hopes were realized.

Of course they weren't. I'd done such a great job on the questionnaire that I was the first juror seated—Deeds looked *really* happy about that—and then later, after we were dismissed for the day and I'd snuck out of the courthouse, I saw him on the sidewalk shaking hands with his lawyer.

So I tried calling Ganesh, but his phone had been disconnected. I didn't know whether that was good or bad. I thought it might be a smart idea for me to skip town regardless, but first I made a stop at the house of this other dealer I knew, to re-up my Valium stash. And it gets hazy after that, but I guess between the Valium and the bottle of vodka I kept in my freezer, I decided *not* to skip town.

Now there's one other important thing I haven't told you, and that's the date that all this happened. I got summoned to jury duty on Monday, September 10th, 2001. And so the next morning I came to in my living room at around six a.m., and the TV was on, and at first I thought it must be tuned to the Sci-Fi Channel because there was this image of the World Trade Center, and one of the buildings was on fire. Then I saw the CNN logo in the corner of the screen, and I'm like, hang on a minute. And it had just registered that this wasn't a bad movie, this was *real*, when the second plane flew in.

I turned up the sound and sat there for about an hour with my jaw hanging open. Then my phone rang.

It was King Kong: "Hi there, Jane."

Instead of being freaked out like I should have been, like I was *supposed* to be, I actually felt sorry for the guy, because the world had just turned upside-down and he obviously hadn't gotten the memo yet. So I said: "Are you near a TV set?"

That wasn't the reaction he was looking for. "Listen, you stupid bitch," he said, "do you know who this is?" And I said, "Yeah, I know who it is, and I know you think you're a badass, but the thing is, you've just been trumped." And he went off, all threats and swearing, but I didn't really hear it, because it was right then that the first tower went down. A hundred-ten-story building, and it turned to rubble right in front of my eyes, and I realized in this weirdly detached way that I was witnessing a mass murder.

On the phone, Deeds was raging: "Are you listening to me? Are you listening to me?" And I said, "Get fucked, killer," and hung up on him. There was a moment right after I set the phone down when I thought, *That probably wasn't too smart*, but then I looked back at the debris cloud on TV, and by the time the second tower collapsed, I'd put Julius Deeds completely out of my mind.

I took some more Valium and went for a long walk. Around noon I ended up at Coit Tower on Telegraph Hill. By then all the planes had been grounded, and the city was quieter than I'd ever heard it—the only sounds were the wind and a few people crying. I was looking for a place to light up a joint when I saw Phil. We didn't say anything, just wandered off together and sat down to watch the day go by.

It was after dark when I finally went home. The drugs had worn off enough for me to start worrying about Deeds again, but by then I couldn't remember whether that early-morning phone call had really happened or was just something I'd imagined. I was wary going into my building, but when I found my apartment door closed and locked, not kicked off its hinges, I figured I was safe.

I let myself in. My TV was on, and that seemed wrong, but I told myself not to be paranoid. I started hunting around the living room for the remote, and then the television shut off on its own, and Deeds said, "Hello, Jane."

He was sitting in the darkest corner of the room, with a baseball bat across his knees. I looked at him, and the bat, and then at the door I'd just come in by, and he said: "You won't make it."

"OK," I said, standing very still. And he said: "You were right about me being trumped. This morning when we talked, I had no idea. You know they say the body count could be as high as five thousand?"

"Five thousand ..."

"Yeah. Kind of puts things in perspective, doesn't it? Still, it's not all bad news. My trial, for example: it's been postponed."

"Postponed?"

"Yeah. The courthouse was closed today, and the way things are, my lawyer says it could be months before I get a new trial date."

"I'm happy for you," I said.

"Oh, it's not just good luck for me. It's lucky for you, too."

"Oh yeah?"

"Yeah." He stood up. "You'll have time to recover."

That's my last clear memory from that night. I know I did try for the door, and I eventually made it—I was bleeding out on the landing when the neighbors found me—but not before he worked me over. He broke my collarbone, and my right arm in two places, and cracked or broke half my ribs. He also got in one really good shot to my skull—the doctors told me later it was a miracle I didn't end up dead or a vegetable from that.

I was in a coma for ten days. I woke up in a darkened hospital room with a television playing somewhere nearby. Tom Cruise was talking about a priest who'd died giving last rites to a fireman at Ground Zero. Then Mariah Carey started singing that we all have a hero inside us, and I thought maybe *I'd* died, and this was hell. But the show went on, with more celebrities coming out to sing and tell stories, and there were calls for donations, and eventually I realized I wasn't in hell, I was just in America.

The cops came around. I told them I didn't know who'd attacked me. Then Phil came to see me, and I told him the same thing, but he knew I was lying. I told him to mind his own business.

I had another visitor, too. I first noticed him about a week after I woke up, and for a long while I wasn't sure he was real. I was in a lot of pain, but because of the coma the doctors were nervous about drugging me. But I kept after them, and eventually they put me on a morphine drip. And I was floating on that when this guy showed up.

He was black, with a round face. He sat in a chair over by the window, watching me.

What made you think he wasn't real?

The way he was dressed. He had on this cheerleader's uniform: pink checked skirt, pink sweater with OMF across the chest, pink pom-poms, plus this wig—a *yarn* wig, like a pink mop head with pigtails.

That does sound a little strange. On the other hand, San Francisco ...

Yeah, I thought of that too, but the other thing about this guy, nobody else seemed to be able to see him. The woman I shared the room with had end-stage brain cancer, so she was out of it, but there were nurses and doctors coming through all the time, and they never so much as glanced at him. I tried to draw attention to him without, you know, actually saying anything—if it turned out he wasn't real, I didn't want my morphine drip pulled—but no dice.

So finally I gave in, and tried talking to him: "What do you want?"

"What's the magic phrase?" he said.

"What?"

"What's the magic phrase?" He lowered his pom-poms and puffed his chest out.

"Omnes mundum facimus," I said.

"That's it ... Now look under your pillow."

It took some major maneuvering, but eventually I slipped my good arm under the pillow. My hand closed around a coin. *The* coin.

I was more relieved than I could say, but I was also pissed off: "*Now* you show up? Where the hell were you when that asshole was beating the shit out of me?"

"That was an oversight," he said, frowning. "Not my department, you understand, but I am sorry—it was a busy day, and details got missed." He brightened again, and laughed. "'Get fucked, killer ...' I like that. That showed spirit. Not a lotta brains, but spirit."

"So why now?"

"Well I know you got hit in the head, but you are aware of recent events, right? The organization I represent—that that coin represents—is holding a recruitment drive."

"You want me to help fight terrorism?"

"No! There's people all over the country lining up to do *that*."

"Well what, then?"

"Well the thing about one big evil taking center stage, it tends to draw attention away from all the other evils. So now somebody's got to swim against the tide, to make sure those other evils don't flourish from neglect. You could be a part of that, if you're interested."

"But why now?" I persisted. "Those other evils, they were always there, so why didn't you come for me sooner?"

"*Omnes mundum facimus*," he said. "You looked up the translation for that, right? You know it doesn't mean 'Wait for further instructions' or 'Stand around with your thumb up your ass.'"

"No, but …"

"Let me lay another saying on you: 'Many are called, but few are chosen.' Now the implication is that the few are special—brave enough to answer the call, or worthy enough to be chosen. But there's another way of looking at it. If many are called, and few are chosen, maybe that's because most of the many have better things to do." He shook a pom-pom at me accusingly. "You had a life. It was *hoped* you'd do something with it."

"Great," I said. "So you're telling me you're the booby prize?"

He laughed again. "I do like that spirit. I—we—can use that spirit. So the question becomes, are you willing to let it be used? Are you ready to be one of the few?"

"You know I am."

"All right, then … Tomorrow night, between seven and seven-fifteen, you're to go to the top floor of this building. Turn left out the elevator, and look for a door marked Examination One. If you come early, or show up late, it'll be just an empty room. But if you come on time, you'll meet a man named Robert True, who'll tell you what the next step is."

That was all he had to say to me, but still he sat there, watching me and smiling. "Go ahead," he finally said. "Ask it."

"OK. Why are you dressed like a cheerleader?"

"You know what a nondisclosure agreement is, Jane? This outfit serves the same purpose. What do you suppose would happen if you told the hospital staff about our conversation?"

"They'd cut off my drugs."

"You got it," he said, and winked. A few moments later a nurse came in and gave me a shot; I fell asleep, and when I woke up again, my visitor was gone. But the coin was still there, safe under my pillow.

The next evening, I made sure I was awake. At quarter to seven I hauled myself out of bed, and wheeled my IV stand to the elevator. I went up to the fourteenth floor and found Examination One, and at 7:01, I knocked.

"Come in," a voice said.

Inside, the room was a lot like this one. Spare, I mean, with just a table and a couple of chairs. Robert True was standing when I came in. He was wearing a gray flannel suit that might have been stylish back when *Ozzie and Harriet* was a hit TV show; he was short, and heavy, and didn't have much hair.

"Welcome, Jane," he greeted me. "I'm Bob True."

"Hi," I said. *"Omnes mundum facimus."*

"That's all right. I don't need the magic phrase. But as long as we're on the subject, have you worked it out yet?"

I had, finally. "It's a comeback," I told him. "To that thing people say when they don't want to be blamed for a bad situation: 'I didn't make the world, I only live in it.'"

"Very good."

"So that's what you're about, your organization? Making the world a better place?"

"By fighting evil in all its forms," True said, nodding.

"Are you the government?"

He seemed surprised by the question. "Does the government fight evil?"

I thought about it. For some reason, the first thing that came to mind wasn't the FBI or the justice system, but my last trip to the DMV. "Well," I said, "it *can*."

"Lots of things *can* fight evil," True replied. "Cinderblocks, for example—if a cinderblock had fallen in Josef Stalin's crib, the twentieth century might have been a bit more pleasant. Even if one had, though, I doubt most people would say that the *purpose* of cinderblocks is to fight evil."

"So you're not the government. What are you, then? Vigilantes? You hunt bad guys, right?"

"The organization pursues its goal through diverse means, most of them constructive. We employ Good Samaritans, Random Acts of Kindness, Second and Third Chances ..." He went on, ticking off more than a dozen of what I eventually understood were division names, actual organization departments that fought evil in positive, life-affirming ways. My eyes must have glazed over, because suddenly he stopped and said, "Am I boring you?"

"A little," I admitted. "So which are you, a Good Samaritan or a Random Actor?"

"I work for what's known as the Cost-Benefits division."

"You handle the money."

"I help allocate the organization's resources. Which are substantial, but still finite."

"'Resources' includes people?"

"Of course."

"Well then, if you know anything about people, you know I'm *not* a good Samaritan."

"No," True said, "I don't suppose you are ..." He placed a green NC gun in the center of the table. "You'll recognize this."

"The one I had last time was orange."

"The one you had in Siesta Corta was standard issue. This is a special model."

"What's special about it?"

"We'll get to that. First I have a hypothetical question for you. A test question."

"OK."

"There are two men, both evil. One is a former concentration-camp commandant, responsible for the murder of half a million people; he's ninety years old, living in hiding in the South American jungle. The other man is much younger—barely twenty-five, in excellent health—and living openly in the middle of San Francisco. He's only killed once so far, but he's discovered he has a talent and a taste for it, and it's likely he'll kill again many times … though of course, the total number of his victims will never be more than a fraction of the commandant's.

"The death of either of these men would leave the world a better place. You have the power to kill one of them—but only one. Whom do you choose?"

"That's easy," I said. "The young guy."

"Why?"

"Because killing the Nazi is the obvious choice, and this is a trick question."

"Clever," True said, in a tone that suggested it was anything but. "Now how about a less glib answer."

"In this hypothetical situation, I'm supposed to be you?"

"Someone with my job description, let's say."

"Then the answer's the same. Kill the young guy."

"Why?"

"His worst days are still ahead of him. With the Nazi, the Holocaust is already out of the barn—killing him might be more satisfying, but the net benefit is smaller."

"What about deterrence?" True said. "Wouldn't kill-

ing the Nazi discourage other people from following in
his footsteps?"

"It might, if it were a public execution. If I were the
government, I could put him on trial for genocide and
then hang him on pay-per-view. That might turn some
heads. Trouble is, I'm not the government, I'm a member of a secret organization that dresses its agents like
cheerleaders so people can't talk about them. An execution that no one knows about won't deter squat."

"What about justice?"

"Is this a hypothetical *real* situation, or a hypothetical
comic book?"

"And what about vengeance?"

"It's fun. But it doesn't have anything to do with
fighting evil."

"No," True agreed, "it doesn't."

"Does that mean I pass the test?"

"The first half. The second half is less theoretical ..."
He laid a couple booklets on the table. They looked
like those question booklets you get when you take the
SATs. A name was written on the cover of each one in
felt-tip pen. The one on the first booklet was BENJAMIN
LOOMIS; the one on the second was JULIUS DEEDS.

"Two men," True said. "Both evil. One you've already
met—"

"Yeah, I have," I said. "And he's not ninety years old,
if that's where you're going with this."

"Julius Deeds has been indicted for murder. The case
against him is strong, and despite his efforts at jury tam-
pering he'll probably be convicted. Even if he avoids
prison, his actions have made him enemies on both sides
of the law. A ninety-year-old might well outlive him."

"And Loomis? Let me guess: he's barely twenty-five,
in excellent health ..."

"Twenty-seven, actually. And he's killed four times,
not just once. Other than that, yes, he's just like the
younger man in the hypothetical. A predator. He's been

operating on a three-month cycle, so unless someone stops him, we expect he'll take his next victim in early December."

"The police don't have a clue who he is?"

"The police aren't even aware of his crimes yet. He hunts male prostitutes, men who've been abandoned by their families and have no one to report them missing. He kills discreetly and buries the bodies. In time he'll be found out, of course—they almost always are—but it could be years from now."

I stared at the tabletop. "The gun's a one-shot, isn't it? That's the special modification. And the test is I have to choose."

"We need to know what your real priorities are," True said. "In a moment you'll select one of these booklets; inside, you'll find all the information you need to complete your first assignment. The other booklet will go back into our files, with a notation that its subject is never to be harmed or otherwise acted against by any agent of the organization."

"So if I pick Deeds, Loomis gets a free pass? You'd really do that?"

"It wouldn't be much of a test, otherwise." He looked at his wristwatch. "You have one minute to decide."

"Screw that. I don't need a minute." I reached for a booklet. True took the other one. "Don't lose the gun," he said. "You'll see me again when the job is completed."

I was in the hospital for a few more weeks. Towards the end of my stay, even though I hadn't said a word about the organization, the doctors downgraded me from morphine to Vicodin. This made me cranky.

They released me right before Thanksgiving. I had a quiet holiday at home—just Phil, a couple microwave turkey dinners, and some nonprescription painkillers—and then, on the last day of November, I killed Julius Deeds.

It happened like this: Deeds' favorite hangout was a nightclub in the Mission District. He'd show up most nights around ten, driving a red Mustang convertible that he'd park asshole-fashion in front of a hydrant, or just facing the wrong direction—like to say, you know, I'm the king of the jungle, the normal rules don't apply to me. If it wasn't raining, he'd leave the top down, too. I figured the deal with that was he wanted to show what a tough guy he was, so tough that nobody would dare steal his car. Or maybe he hoped someone *would* steal it, so he'd have an excuse to get in some batting practice.

That night, I was hiding in an alley across the street from the club when he drove up. I watched him go inside, and gave him half an hour to get comfortable. Then I set his Mustang on fire.

Gasoline would have been poetic, but besides being really conspicuous, a gas can is tough to sling one-handed, and my right arm was still in a cast. I used charcoal starter instead—a twenty-ounce container, small enough to slip inside my jacket. I strolled up to the car during a lull in the street traffic and stood there casually, peeing lighter fluid over the front-seat upholstery. When the container was empty, I took out a strike-anywhere match and lit it off my cast.

The Mustang's interior was burning nicely by the time the nightclub's bouncer raised the alarm. People started coming out of the club. Most of them hung back, but one particular Cro-Magnon went charging at the car. For a second it looked like Deeds was going to do my job for me by diving headfirst into the fire.

Where were you at this point?

A couple blocks up the street, by the entrance to this park. It was on a rise, so I had a clear line of sight to the nightclub, and vice versa. I was standing under a streetlamp, spotlit.

You wanted Deeds to see you?

That was the plan. It took a while, though. You know

that expression, "a blind rage"? I know what that means now. Deeds was still trying to decide whether to throw himself on the flames when the bouncer came up with a fire extinguisher. The guy was trying to help, right, but as soon as he started spraying foam onto the Mustang, Deeds went berserk and swung on him. The guy went down, and then Deeds grabbed the fire extinguisher himself, and spent about a minute trying to figure out how to work it. Then he went berserk again, and tossed the extinguisher through a shop window.

In the middle of this tantrum he suddenly stiffened up, and I knew he'd finally sensed me watching him. "Over here, killer," I whispered. He turned slowly in place until he was looking straight at me; I raised my good arm and gave a little wave. Then I ran like hell into the park.

About a hundred yards in, I stopped to look back. Deeds had already reached the park entrance, and was ripping a two-by-four off a sign on the park gate. I ran on, my cast banging against my ribs; when I looked back again, Deeds had closed about half the distance between us and was swinging the two-by-four in big warm-up circles.

I made a last dash downhill past a swing set and out the far side of the park, onto a street lined with houses. I went to a house near the end of the block, pulling out a key as I ran up the front steps. Deeds was right on my heels now—I'd barely got the door shut behind me when the pounding started. The lock splintered on the third blow, and gave way on the fourth; the door chain snapped and then Deeds was inside.

This time I was the one sitting in a dark corner of the living room. Instead of a baseball bat I was holding a double-barreled shotgun. I had it up and ready with both hammers cocked, the barrels balanced on my right wrist, my left hand on the triggers.

"You're a dead woman," Deeds announced. Then he

blinked, noticing the gun, and added: "You're kidding me, right?"

"No," I said, "I'm not kidding. Now here's what's going to happen: you're going to drop that piece of wood you're holding, and we're going to go downstairs to the basement ..."

"No," Deeds snarled. "What's going to *happen* is, you're going to give me that fucking gun. You can either hand it over easy, or I can take it from you—but if you make me take it, I'm *really* going to be angry."

I pulled the left-side trigger. The shot struck Deeds in the arm, knocking him back and tearing a big chunk out of his bicep. He grunted and dropped the two-by-four.

"I'll tell you what," I said. "You want to start worrying about *my* feelings."

Deeds cupped a hand to his ruined bicep. "You *shot* me!" he complained. "You're crazy ..." He glanced over his shoulder at the broken front door.

"You won't make it," I said. I stood up, and gestured towards the back of the house. "Basement door's that way. Start walking."

He moved slowly, hoping I'd come up too close behind and give him a chance to grab at the gun. When we reached the basement stairs, he slowed down even more and tried goading me: "I don't know how you think you're going to come out on top here, Jane. I mean, I know you're not going to kill me."

"Keep moving."

"I *know* you're not going to kill me. Maybe you've got the guts to pull the trigger, I'll grant you that much, but you don't want to go to prison, do you?"

"Keep moving."

"Or are you stupid enough to think you can claim self-defense on this? Is that the plan? Tell the cops you had to do it, because of that beating I gave you? You think they'll care about that?"

I wasn't going to argue with him, but I couldn't help myself: "I think they'll care about those three kids you burned to death."

"Those kids ... So that's what this is about?" He laughed. "Let me tell you something about those kids, Jane. I didn't even know they were in the house that night. But their mother—my so-called girlfriend?—she knew. And I'll bet the selfish bitch didn't look back once when she was running to save herself ... You want to pass judgment on someone, Jane? What about a mom who leaves her own kids to fry?"

"Shut up and keep moving. I'm not going to say it again."

"All right, all right ... But I'm telling you, Jane, I really don't see this ending well for you. I don't ..."

He trailed off in mid-threat. We'd finally reached the bottom of the stairs.

The basement was lit by strings of hanging bulbs. Its floor had originally been wood, but the planks had been pried up and set aside, exposing bare dirt beneath. Here and there—four places in all—long, narrow holes had been dug in the dirt, filled in again, and sprinkled with lime. In between the water heater and the furnace a fifth hole had been started, but it was only half-finished. The handle of a shovel jutted out of it at an angle; lying facedown in front of it, one hand still reaching for the shovel, was the figure of a man.

"What the hell is this?" Deeds said.

"The greater of two evils," I told him. "His name was Benjamin Loomis. He was a serial killer. Earlier tonight he had a heart attack. Died in the act—at least, that's what the cops will think."

"Died in the act of what?"

"Burying his last victim."

Deeds turned and lunged for the gun then, but my finger was already tightening on the trigger.

"Bad monkey," I said.

After, I went back into the park, and found True sitting on a bench near the swings. He wasn't happy.

"I told you to choose *one*," he said.

"One booklet," I reminded him. "But I didn't need your help to track Deeds down. He was in the damned phone book. And then when I went to take care of Loomis and found that shotgun in his closet ... Well, I figured it was part of the test, to see if I had the initiative to take out both of them."

"Did you really think that? Or did you kill Deeds because you wanted to?"

I shrugged. "Does it even matter? You said it yourself, they were both evil. The world's better off."

"Yes, but now there are discrepancies for the police to wonder about. Such as the fact that Loomis died several hours before Deeds."

"They won't be able to tell that, I bet. I mean yeah, if they came right now, while Deeds is still warm ... But I don't hear any sirens, do you? And once his body hits room temperature, it'll be a lot harder to fix a time of death. That basement was cold as a meat locker."

"And when they discover that Loomis's other victims were poisoned, not shot?"

"So? Maybe Deeds wasn't a normal victim. Maybe he found out what Loomis was doing, and tried to blackmail him, or just walked in on him somehow."

"Somehow."

"It's a Nod problem. The police will believe that Loomis killed Deeds because it's the simplest explanation. They'll *want* to believe it, especially when they find out who Deeds was. Tell me I'm wrong."

True shook his head. "This is not how we do things."

"Look, you said you wanted to know what my priorities were. You want to give me grief for bending the rules? You want to blackball me for it? Fine. But we all make the world, right? And if that's true, I'm not going to settle for just one bad guy when I can get two. I saw my chance and went for it, and I'm not sorry. I'd do it again." I stopped there, worried about overplaying it, but after a minute had gone by and True hadn't given me the chop, I went on, in a softer voice: "So do I pass the test? Am I in?"

Another minute. True sighed.

"You're in."

white room (iii)

"WHAT'S THE PROBLEM THIS TIME?" she asks. "Did I screw up the body count?"

"No, your description of the scene in Benjamin Loomis's basement was accurate," the doctor says. "And there are details in your account, such as the fact that Deeds was shot in the arm, that were never released to the press. So it's plausible you were there, or at least spoke to someone who was."

"But ...?"

"But, there's no evidence to support the rest of your story. If Julius Deeds was a vicious gangster, you seem to be the only person who knew about it. There's no record he was ever indicted for murder; no record of *anyone* committing an arson-homicide of the kind you say he was charged with; no record, either, of the beating you claim you received at his hands."

"Back up a second. You're telling me Deeds didn't have a rap sheet?"

"He was a criminal, all right, just not a violent one. He had a long history of petty drug offenses, including one early charge for theft of a doctor's prescription pad. The prescription pad theft happened while he was an intern at Saint Francis Memorial Hospital, studying to be an oncologist."

"No, you're mixed up. The oncology student, that was—"

"Your dealer friend Ganesh, yes. Of whom there's also no record. Or none that I could find: I wasn't sure if Ganesh was a first or last name, or an alias."

"I'm not sure either," she says, "but I didn't just imagine him. Hey, I bought dope from the guy for years."

"Well if Ganesh is a real person, Jane, can you explain how Julius Deeds ended up with his biography? Or is that another Nod problem?"

"No, it's not a Nod problem." She frowns. "It's Catering."

"Catering?"

"Organization counterintelligence. They must know I'm talking to you."

"The organization altered the police records?"

"Somebody did. And I know how this is going to sound, but if it is Catering? You can forget about fact-checking my story anymore."

"I see. That's a rather convenient development, isn't it?"

"Oh yeah, it's very convenient, having you think I'm full of shit ..."

"Why 'Catering'? That's a strange name for a counterintelligence division."

"They do a lot of logistics work," she explains. "One way the organization keeps itself off the radar is by not having a fixed headquarters. Cost-Benefits, the whole bureaucracy, it's constantly moving around, and Catering are like the movers. They scout new locations, pack and set up equipment, and provide transport for personnel. And as sort of a natural extension of that, they're also in charge of meetings and special events: scheduling, security, hors d'oeuvres, whatever."

"So if you needed to arrange a rendezvous with another operative, you'd contact Catering."

"Right."

"And how does that work? Is there a number you call?"

"No number. You just pick up a phone and start talking."

"Operators are standing by?"

"Unless the phone's in an insecure location. Then you just get a dial tone and look stupid."

"All right," says the doctor. "Let's get back to your story. Once you'd been accepted into the organization, I assume you underwent some sort of training regimen ..."

"They call it Probate. Training is part of it, but also they're still testing you, making sure it wasn't a mistake to offer you the job. They team you with a senior operative called a Probate officer, and you're given a Probate assignment, which is like a standard op but more complicated, with more ways to screw up."

"What was your Probate assignment?"

"A guy named Arlo Dexter."

"Another serial killer?"

"More like a serial maimer. His thing was explosive booby-traps: he'd take, like, a Scooby-Doo toothpaste dispenser, fill it with black powder, ball bearings, and a motion trigger, and leave it on a store shelf for someone to pick up. He hadn't actually killed anyone yet, but he was definitely working his way up to it—and then, right before the organization stepped in, he met some people who wanted to leapfrog him straight to mass murder."

"You stopped him?"

"No." She frowns again. "I was supposed to, but it went wrong."

"What happened?"

"He saw me coming."

Look Both Ways

THE VOICE ON THE PHONE SAID: "Jane Charlotte."

"Yeah, I'm supposed to make an appointment to meet my Probate officer ..."

"Southeast corner of Orchard and Masonic, tomorrow, eight-thirty a.m."

"Do you know what this guy looks like? Or will he know me?"

"Southeast corner of Orchard and Masonic," the voice repeated, "tomorrow, eight-thirty a.m."

Dial tone.

Oh well, at least I knew where I was going. That intersection was in the Haight, and assuming I had my compass directions straight, the southeast corner was just across Orchard Street from the elementary school that Phil and I had both attended.

Next morning I was there, standing under the awning of a candy store where I used to shoplift Mars bars, and playing "Who's the Probate officer?" with the other pedestrians. Despite the drizzle there were plenty of prospects: a guy waiting at the bus stop who didn't check the numbers of the buses pulling up; another guy who'd been out in the wet so long that the newspaper he was reading had soaked through; a bag lady who had her forehead pressed up against a utility pole like she was trying to mind-meld with it; a bored-looking school crossing guard.

My money was on the crossing guard. His uniform didn't fit him, and he held his stop sign the way a circus bear would, like this meaningless prop some midget had just handed to him. He also didn't seem to care whether any kids made it across the street in one piece. At the school, the second bell had already rung, but there were still a few members of the Jane Charlotte tribe racing to get in under the wire; if the guard happened to be facing the right direction when they darted out into the crosswalk, he'd make this token gesture to stop the traffic, but for the most part they were on their own.

So I decided this was probably my guy and tried to make contact with him, which wasn't easy, because he wasn't paying any attention to the adults around him, either.

"Hey," I said, waving a hand in his face. "Hello?"

Three more kids ran into the street behind the crossing guard's back, on an intercept course with a speeding delivery truck. Out of the corner of my eye I saw the bag lady come to life. She whipped her shopping bag up in a circle and let fly; the bag arced above the heads of the jaywalkers and burst on the truck's front hood, spraying cans everywhere. The truck screeched to a halt; so did the rest of the traffic, and every pedestrian within earshot.

The bag lady went charging at the kids, shrieking, "Look both ways! Look both ways!" Two of them bolted straight off; the third, definitely my tribe, stood his ground long enough to give the woman who'd saved his life a one-finger thank you.

She went after the crossing guard next: "Not ... paying ... attention!" She started smacking him on the chest and shoulders—"Pay attention! Pay attention!"— sloppy, overhand girly slaps that he was too stunned to defend himself against. Then her slaps turned into punches and he got mad; he stiff-armed her and raised his stop sign threateningly. The bag lady fell back into a cringe, chanting "Hit me? Hit me?" (Or maybe it was "Hit me! Hit me!"—when I thought about it later, that seemed more likely.)

"Get the hell out of my face!" the crossing guard said, and she did—but as she turned to go she stumbled and fell into me, hissing three words in Latin into my ear. Then she was gone, fast-walking east along Orchard.

"What do *you* want?" said the crossing guard, finally acknowledging me. I gave him the tribal salute and took off after my Probate officer.

By the time I caught up to her she was in full schizophrenic muttering mode. Most of it was impossible to make out, but here and there I'd catch a few words: "Pay attention!... Watch! Watch!... Not on the rocks, Billy!"

She led me to a delicatessen called Silverman's. A sign in the window said CLOSED FOR FAMILY EMERGENCY, but when she stepped up to the door, it opened for her.

Inside, Bob True was sitting at a table by the meat counter. The bag lady breezed right past him, going into a back corner of the room and putting her face to the wall. True gave her a moment, then called out gently: "Annie. We need you in the present day."

She straightened up and came out of her corner. The craziness in her eyes had gone back a bit but it hadn't disappeared, and when she offered her hand to shake I had to push myself to take it.

"Annie Charles," she introduced herself.

"Hi," I said. "I'm the last of the Brontë sisters."

"Let's begin," said True, gesturing. I joined him at the table. There was a third chair, but rather than sit, Annie stood behind it, wringing her hands and making little noises.

"Your Probate assignment," True said. He handed

me a school notebook, the kind with the black-and-white speckled covers; the name ARLO DEXTER had been scrawled in the "I belong to" box in red Crayola. I figured it was an official case file, like the Deeds and Loomis SAT booklets.

The notebook was full of crayon drawings. Page one showed a frowning stick-figure boy—ARLO, according to the caption—in a short-sleeve shirt and black short pants.

On page two, Arlo stood on a chair beside a work-bench, his tongue sticking out in concentration as he performed some kind of surgery on a teddy bear. On page three, Arlo was walking, holding the teddy bear out in front of him. On page four, he'd set the teddy bear on the ground and backed away; a second stick-figure boy—ROGER OLSEN—approached from the op-posite direction. On page five, Roger picked up the teddy bear, and Arlo covered his ears. On page six, the teddy bear vanished in a cartoon explosion. On page seven, Roger stood crying with his face covered in soot and smoke rising from his head; Arlo, watching from the sidelines, smiled.

On page eight, Arlo was alone again, and unhappy …

The same basic sequence was repeated over and over. Each explosion was a little more powerful than the last one. A boy named Gregg Faulkner who picked up a booby-trapped cereal box didn't just lose his hair, one of his eyes was X-ed out. A girl named Jody Conrad lost both her eyes, and a boy named Tariq Williams lost a hand. In the most gruesome scene of all, a boy named Harold Rodriguez jetted so much blood from the stumps of his arms that Arlo had to break out an umbrella.

I looked over at True. "You know, I know you guys are obsessed with secrecy, but this is like *beyond* tasteless …"

"What you're holding isn't an internal organization report," he told me. "It's a facsimile of a notebook dis-covered during a search of Arlo Dexter's apartment."

"He drew this himself? How old is he?"

"Thirty-two. That's chronological age, of course. His mental self-image—"

"Who cares?" I interrupted. "When do I kill him?"

"Soon. But there are some questions we'd like answered first, if possible. Turn to the next page."

On the page following the Harold Rodriguez bloodbath, Arlo was center stage again, but this time he'd been joined by three other stick figures. Not people. Monkeys. Two of them had him bookended and were whispering to him in stereo; the third monkey stood nearby, holding a black briefcase.

On the next page, the briefcase was lying open on the ground, and Arlo was on his knees beside it with his hands clasped and his mouth forming an O of perfect joy. The monkeys clustered behind him, looking pleased by his reaction. As for the briefcase, the drawing didn't show what was in it, but whatever it was was pumping out yellow and orange rays of light, and given Arlo's habits it wasn't hard to come up with possibilities.

"Do we know who these other guys are?" I asked.

"That's one of the questions we'd like answered."

"I suppose Al Qaeda would be too obvious, huh?"

"Not too obvious, just unlikely. Arlo Dexter is an apolitical psychopath, not an Islamic jihadist. Besides, look at the way he's drawn them. To depict Arabs as monkeys would almost certainly be an expression of contempt. But Mr. Dexter isn't contemptuous of his new associates. He admires them."

"How do you know that?"

"Turn the page."

On the next page—actually a two-page spread, and the last drawing in the notebook—Arlo was on the move again, carrying the black briefcase towards some sort of fenced-in area where a huge crowd of stick-figures was gathered. I could tell it was Arlo carrying the briefcase because he was still wearing his shirt and short pants.

But he had a new head on his shoulders: he'd become a monkey too, now.

"I take it you don't know what his target is, either."

"No," said True, "and that's the most important question of all. If Dexter's confederates aren't imaginary, then stopping him may not be enough; there could be other monkeys with briefcases."

"Have you thought about just asking him who his buddies are? I mean, you guys do do interrogations, right?"

"We do, and it may come to that. But the more effective methods of extracting information tend to be time-consuming, and we don't believe we have much time. So we've decided instead to keep a close watch on Dexter and see what he does. Your job will be to help with the surveillance and perform any other tasks that may come up; and if it looks as though Dexter is about to complete his mission, you'll see to it that he doesn't succeed."

"Cool," I said. "Where's my gun?"

"It'll be delivered to you shortly. For now, go with Annie and do as she says; she's been fully briefed on the details of the operation."

"With Annie, right … Listen, True, can I talk to you privately for a second?"

"Later," True said, getting up. "We're on a tight schedule, and I have other things to attend to."

Right. I knew a brush-off when I heard it—and Annie, for her part, knew a vote of no confidence when *she* heard it. When we got back outside, the first thing she said was: "You're frightened of me."

"'Frightened' is kind of strong," I lied. "You do freak me out a little, yeah, but—"

"You don't need to be frightened." She flashed me this brittle smile. "I know how I seem, but I'm really very dependable. God keeps me focused."

"Oh-kay, well that's good to hear … So what does God want us to do first?"

"How much money do you have?"

"Not a lot. Maybe twenty bucks and change."

"Give me the twenty."

Two doors down from the deli was a corner grocery that sold scratch lottery tickets. "Which kind do you like?" Annie asked me. There were fifteen varieties to choose from, most with some type of gambling theme: Lucky Poker, Scratch Roulette, Twenty-One, Three-Card Monte ... Then I noticed this one kind called Jungle Cash that had pictures of animals on it, including a baboon that was being stalked by a pair of tigers. "That one," I said, and Annie nodded approvingly.

Jungle Cash tickets were two bucks each. Annie bought ten, and when we scratched them all off, nine were winners. We left the store with over three hundred dollars.

"Does that always work?" I asked.

"'There will be water if God wills it,'" Annie replied, and flagged down a taxi.

The cab took us to an address in the Richmond, a Pentecostal church called the Chapel of the Redeemer. It reminded me of the Diazes' church in Siesta Corta, and, already keyed up by Annie's God-talk, I got worried that my training curriculum was going to include speaking in tongues. But then I noticed the chains on the front doors, and the sign that said PROPERTY FOR LEASE.

"What is this place?" I asked, thinking maybe Arlo Dexter was using it for a bomb factory.

"Home," said Annie.

"You live here? You and God?"

"Not inside," she said. "Around back."

Around back was a small cemetery. Like the church doors, the cemetery gate was chained and padlocked, but Annie had a key.

Her home was a refrigerator box covered with a waterproof tarp. The open end of the box faced a grave marked WILLIAM DANE. The grave plot had been neatly outlined with stones, and Annie was careful to step around it.

"I'll just be a minute," she said, and crawled into the box.

Some questions you don't ask, especially of a crazy person. So while I was waiting, I decided to treat this situation as one of the organization's test puzzles, which for all I knew it was. I hadn't seen a ring on Annie's fingers, so William Dane probably wasn't her husband. He could have been her lover, I thought, but then when I took another look at the plot, I noticed the stone outline was too small for an adult-sized coffin.

"All right ..." Annie reappeared, wearing a light blue knapsack that clashed with her bag-lady couture. She crouched beside the grave and patted the headstone in a way that dispelled any doubt Billy Dane was her son. Then she looked up at the sky. The rain had stopped but it was still overcast, and I could tell she didn't like the idea of leaving the kid alone in bad weather; I half expected her to pull the tarp off the refrigerator box and use it as a blanket. But she resisted the impulse, and got back up after giving the headstone one more pat.

"Where to now?" I asked.

"Just follow me. And pay attention."

We set off on foot in the general direction of downtown. We'd gone maybe a block when Annie started doing the muttering thing again. This time I couldn't make out a single word. I tried to just ignore it, but I couldn't do that either—the babble coming out of her mouth had this weird insistent edge to it, like fingernails on a blackboard.

"Annie?" I said. "Snap out of it, Annie," but all that did was up her volume a couple notches. People on the street were turning to stare at us, and so I started craning my head around, looking up at the clouds, at the buildings we passed, my body language sending out the message: "Just because I'm walking *next* to this person doesn't mean I'm *with* her."

Then suddenly the mutter cut off, and Annie's hand caught my wrist. I looked down; my right foot was in midair, about to step down onto the jagged base of a broken wine bottle.

"Pay attention," Annie said.

So after that I watched where I was walking, while Annie's mutter wormed its way into my ear and set up shop in my back brain. Next thing I knew we were back in the Haight, in front of a hotel called the Rose & Cross. The doorman nodded to Annie and slipped her a set of keys.

We went up to the second floor, to a room with a single twin-size bed. The bed was just made, the covers turned down invitingly; Annie pushed me towards it and said, "I'm going to take a shower. You sleep."

"Sleep?" I said. "It's like eleven o'clock in the morning ..." But the truth is I was exhausted; the miles of listening to her babble had worn me out. I kicked off my shoes and climbed under the covers. By the time my head hit the pillow I was elsewhere.

I was in a classroom, sitting at a pupil's desk, third row center. Up at the blackboard, a younger, saner-looking Annie was sketching out an organizational chart. The boxes in the chart formed a rough pyramid; the one at the very top was marked T.A.S.E. Directly below this, connected to it by a double line, was a box labeled COST-BENEFITS. More lines radiated downwards from there, linking to other divisions and subdivisions, some of which I already knew about (Catering, Random Acts of Kindness), but most of which I didn't (Scary Clowns?). I was kind of disappointed to see that despite having a direct link to Cost-Benefits, Bad Monkeys was at the bottom of the pyramid.

While Annie finished up the chart, I looked around for a distraction. There were no other students, so note-passing was out, and the classroom windows didn't offer a view, just this white glow, like the school was floating in a cloud. Then I lifted up my desktop and found a textbook inside, something called *Secrets of the Invisible College*. It sounded interesting.

It wasn't. The pages were full of that dense, tiny type that you know is going to be boring even before you try to read it. I started flipping through the book to see if there were any pictures (there weren't), and somebody kicked the back of my chair.

Phil had materialized in the seat behind me. Not the grown-up Phil, who I liked; the ten-year-old Phil, who'd bugged the shit out of me back before I was sent away. "Knock it off," I warned him. I turned back to the textbook, and Phil kicked my chair again.

"Knock it *off*!" I whirled around, brandishing the book with both hands. But Phil was gone.

A sharp rapping came from the front of the classroom. "Jane," Annie said. "We need you in the present day."

"Yes ma'am," I heard myself say.

"The subjects to be covered in today's lesson include the organization's command structure, the proper handling of the NC gun, and the use of the Daily Jumble as a covert communication channel. Please turn to page one thousand, four hundred and sixty-five ..."

Long dream. The worst part of it was, unlike a real classroom, I couldn't just drift off, because I already had.

When I finally woke up, it was nighttime. Annie was over by the window, looking out; she heard me fumbling for the bedside lamp and said, "Leave it off."

I joined her at the window. Across the street from the hotel was a model-railroad store; there were apartments above it, and in one unit on the second floor, I could see a thirtysomething guy walking around in his underwear. "That's him?"

"That's him." Annie gave a nudge to a shoebox on the windowsill. "This came for you."

My NC gun. I took it out, hefted it, and did a couple quick integrity checks that I'd learned about in dream class. Once I'd verified it was in working order, Annie said: "Now let's review ... Suppose I asked you to shoot him from here. Could you?"

On the MI setting, the NC gun's effective range is about fifty feet; on the CI setting, around half that. "I could probably nail him with a heart attack," I said. "But I'd need to open this window, and get him to open one of his."

"Why not just shoot him through the glass?"

"Doesn't work. The gun can penetrate ordinary clothing, but anything more substantial will either absorb the shot or bounce it in a random direction. Reflective surfaces are bad."

"And another important implication of that is ...?"

"Unless I'm so close that I can't miss, I never want to shoot at anybody standing in *front* of a reflective surface, either."

"Good," Annie said. "You were listening."

"Yeah, so now I've got a question: *are* you asking me to shoot him? Because I could just go over there and ring his buzzer."

"Not tonight." She handed me a wireless headset. "This will put you in touch with the rest of the surveillance team. If it looks like he's going to leave the apartment, let them know. Otherwise, just keep an eye on him." She went over to the bed. "Wake me at dawn, or sooner if something happens. And Jane—"

"Yeah, I know. Pay attention."

Annie didn't go to sleep right away. I heard her praying, and then, for a while, she talked to William. Maybe a half hour after she finally got quiet, the lights went out at Arlo's place. After that it was just me in the dark, with nothing to do but twiddle my thumbs.

I was tired. I know that probably sounds strange seeing as I'd slept the whole day away, but the thing about
dream school is, it's not restful. Also I hadn't eaten anything since breakfast, and my feet hurt from the walking. I decided to sit down for a while, only there weren't
any chairs in the room, so I ended up on the floor with
my back to the wall beneath the windowsill. At first I
was good about poking my head up every few minutes
to check on Arlo's apartment, but pretty soon I was nodding.

I started awake in gray dawn light. A fog had come
in off the bay while I'd slept; through the haze, I could
see that Arlo's windows were still dark, but whether that
meant he was still in bed or had already gone out was
anybody's guess.

What did you do?

Said "Oh, shit!" a few dozen times. Then, for variety,
I tried calling myself a stupid bitch. I had some other
choice phrases lined up, but before I could get to them,
someone came out the front door of Arlo's building. In
the fog, all I could make out was a figure, but this person, whoever he or she was, was carrying some kind of
case.

I tried calling it in to the surveillance team, but all I
got for an answer was static. The figure with the case
went into an alley beside the model-railroad store. I
gave the headset one more try, then grabbed my gun
and ran downstairs.

By the time I got to the alley, the figure was nowhere
to be seen. The headset went on hissing static. I was
going to look for a pay phone, but then something else
caught my eye, something that seemed out of place in
the dinginess of the alley: a china doll with a bright yellow bonnet. It was jammed into a dumpster, with its arm
jutting out over the lip like it wanted to shake hands.

Without thinking, I started to reach for it, only realizing at the last second how stupid that was. I backed

up, grabbed a rock, wound up to throw it, realized that that was pretty dumb too, and then just stood there indecisively.

"What are you doing?"

True had come up behind me, silent in the fog. I nearly brained him.

"What are you doing?" he repeated.

I looked at the rock in my hand like, *How did that get there?*, and tossed it aside as casually as I could. "I thought I saw Arlo come this way. I tried to call it in, but the headset's broken or something."

"It's not broken. The surveillance team got tired of your snoring and turned off the receiver."

Oops. "Why didn't they just wake me up?"

"They tried. The volume only goes up so high."

"Oh … Well look, I'm sorry about that, but Arlo—"

"Dexter is still in bed."

"How do you know?"

"How do you think?"

"You bugged his apartment?"

"Of course."

"Well if you've got him covered, what do you need *me* watching him for?"

"Are you sure this is a line of questioning you want to pursue?"

"When you put it that way, no."

"Good. Now get back upstairs, and try not to fall asleep until you're told to."

He started to turn away.

"True."

I thought I heard him sigh. "Yes?"

"Annie," I said. "What's her deal?"

"You've already worked out most of it, I'm sure. She had a young son, and a house on the bay. One day, she let her attention wander."

"The kid drowned."

"Yes."

"And now she's insane."

"Not clinically," True said. "She was a grammar school teacher, but she'd studied to be a psychologist. In the aftermath of her son's death, she used her knowledge of mental illness to construct a refuge for herself."

"She pretends to be crazy to keep from going crazy?"

"It's slightly more complicated than that, but essentially, yes. Spend enough time with her, and you'll notice she only acts out when it's safe or advantageous to do so. Where sanity is required, she's sane. She's very dependable."

"Yeah, I got that memo. 'God keeps me focused'?"

"You don't believe in God."

"No. Sorry."

"No need to apologize to *me*. But I'll tell you a secret about God: if you're careful not to ask too much of Him, it doesn't really matter whether He exists. Annie doesn't ask much."

"Just three squares a day and a cardboard roof over her head, right?"

"She wants to be useful. It would be very easy for someone in Annie's position to spend the rest of her life paralyzed by guilt, but she wants her remaining time to count for something. The organization gives her a purpose; God holds her to it."

"And you're not worried about the Almighty countermanding your orders during a mission?"

"If I feel a need to worry about disobedient operatives," True said, "Annie won't be the first one who comes to mind."

"Yeah, yeah, OK ... Point taken."

"I hope so."

"Seriously, True, I get it." I reached up and tapped my headset. "So can I order breakfast on this thing?"

It was actually a couple more hours before I got to eat. After I went back and woke Annie, she took forever in the bathroom—I guess when you live in a box, you can't get enough of indoor plumbing—and nearly as long choosing an ensemble from the collection of rags in her backpack. I was good, though: I only got a *little* impatient. Finally we made it out the door and went to Silverman's Deli, where I pigged out on bagels and lox.

From there, we fell into a routine: we went for a post-breakfast walk; Annie muttered; I listened. Then, back to the hotel, where I had dream class while Annie—the waking Annie—took another shower. Then, all-night sentry duty. Then, more Silverman's. Rinse and repeat, for seven days straight. By the time we were done, I knew everything a Bad Monkeys operative is supposed to know.

On the morning of the eighth day, Annie told me I'd completed the initial phase of my training. "Go home and relax," she said. "We meet back here in seventy-two hours."

"What about Arlo?"

"If we're very lucky, he'll have been taken care of by then. If not … you'll want to be sharp."

I went home, crashed, and slept for a day. I woke up starving, but the thought of more smoked salmon made me queasy, so I gave the deli a rest and went to this pub I knew instead. I was working on my second plate of cheese fries when Phil showed up.

"Those must be really good," he said. "You look happy."

"It's not the fries. I got a new job."

"Is it the one you've been looking for?"

"Yeah," I said, "I think it might be. If I don't fuck it up."

Did you tell him what the job was?

No. I could have, I mean, Phil's probably the only person I know who'd have *believed* me, but … no. I just called it a "public service" job, stayed vague on the details, and Phil, he knew enough not to push. He smiled like he was proud of me, though—like he *would* have been proud of me, if I'd told him everything.

I did tell him about Annie. I called her my supervisor and had her living in a homeless shelter instead of a cemetery, but other than that I stuck pretty close to the truth. "She's growing on me. At first I didn't want to be around her, but now that I know the crazy thing is mostly an act—well, not an *act*, exactly, more like a coping strategy—I'm starting to like her … The God thing still bugs me, though."

"Why?"

"Besides the fact that it's just stupid? I can't see giving the time of day to a God who let your kid drown."

"Well," said Phil, "it wasn't God's responsibility to watch the kid. It was hers."

"What, and God's too busy to pick up the slack the one time she takes her eyes off him?"

"Was it just the one time?"

"Shut up. Annie's not like that. She wasn't a bad mother."

"How do you know?"

"Because I know her, OK? She's a little weird, but she's not a bad person. This organization we work for, they've got standards. They wouldn't keep her on if she was bad."

"Maybe she's not a bad person now. But before …?"

"Oh yeah, I'm sure she used to be a real terror. Hey, here's a theory, maybe God killed her kid as a character-building exercise: 'Go on, Billy, jump in the bay, it'll help Mommy get her priorities straight …' How's that sound?"

"I don't know. Could be."

"*Could be?* Are you fucking serious?"

"Or maybe it's the job. You say you're doing important work. But would this woman even be a part of that, if her son hadn't—"

"Jesus, Phil, are you *trying* to piss me off?"

He swore he wasn't, but he kept doing it anyway, and pretty soon I told him to take a hike. Goddamned Phil … Nine times out of ten, you know, talking to him made me feel better, but that tenth time left me wondering why I even bothered. I spent the rest of my break alone at home, sacked out on the couch with a bottle and my post-Ganesh drug stash, watching spy shows on cable.

When I reported back to work, Arlo Dexter was still alive. Eleven a.m. on a weekday morning, Annie and I were watching from the Rose & Cross as he opened up the model-railroad store.

"So is that his shop?"

"He runs it," Annie said. "But his grandmother holds the lease and pays for the inventory. She covers the rent on his apartment, as well."

"Generous grandma. Did the organization check her out?"

"Yes. She's not evil, just lonely."

"What about employees?"

"He doesn't have any. Not many customers, either. He's not what you'd call a people person."

"So basically the store is just a private playroom for him."

"That's about the size of it."

"And what's our play? We just hang out while Arlo fools with his trains?"

"That depends," Annie said. "I spoke with True earlier this morning, and he told me that Cost-Benefits is divided on how to proceed. Some members feel that we should continue to watch and wait. Others, including True, think that this is taking too long. They'd like to provoke Dexter into making a move, if we can come up with some way of doing that."

"You mean if *I* can come up with some way of doing it, right? Is this my final exam?"

"Do you have any ideas?"

"Yeah, actually … Did your son like model trains?"

Her expression got all brittle again, but then she said: "Model planes. Billy wanted to be a pilot when he grew up."

"OK, planes, same difference. The point is, you've been to a hobby shop."

"We went every Saturday."

"And the geeks who ran the place, you remember how they reacted to having a woman in the store?"

She nodded, seeing where I was going. "Yes."

"Yeah—and those guys probably *liked* having customers."

Annie turned back to the window and looked down at Arlo's shop. "You want me to go in?"

"No," I said. "Let me mess with him. I've got a mood I feel like sharing."

A taxi sat just up the block from the model-railroad store, its driver working the Daily Jumble and picking at a carton of chicken vindaloo that had come from Catering's kitchens. If Arlo made a break for it, the taxi would help track him, or, if necessary, run him down. That was the plan, anyway, but there was a wrinkle. As I crossed the street, this black guy approached the cab and tried to hire it, and when the driver belatedly flipped on his off-duty lamp, the black guy took it personally. They were arguing as I slipped inside Arlo's shop.

The front of the store was packed with shelves and display cases, but the back was given over to a huge train layout, complete with model scenery and a scale-model town. Arlo stood in front of the layout reading a magazine, while toy passenger and freight trains made an endless circuit of the town.

I gave the door a good slam. Arlo jumped and dropped his magazine.

"Hi there!" I said, in a loud and cheery stupid-chick voice. "Do you sell *trains* here?"

Instead of answering, Arlo just stared, wide-eyed, as if he expected me to whip out a gun and shoot him on the spot. That should have been a hint, but I was way too pleased by his reaction to pick up on it.

"Sorry," I said. "Didn't mean to *scare* you ... But can you help me out? I need to get my brother a birthday present ... Oh, neat!" On a shelf to my right was a stack of boxed miniature evergreen trees. I grabbed one off the bottom and brought the entire stack tumbling to the floor. "Whoops!" Bending to pick up the trees, I slammed my butt into the opposing shelf, scattering more boxes.

This broke Arlo's paralysis. He came dashing up the aisle, but stopped short as I straightened up again.

"Sorry," I repeated, waving my hands at the mess. "Maybe I'd better leave this for you, huh?"

"What do you want?" Arlo said. He had a high voice, and sounded like he might break down crying at any moment.

"Well like I said, I need a birthday present for my brother. I mean, between you and me, he's been kind of a shit lately, so it's not like he actually *deserves* anything, but lucky for him I'm not the type to hold a grudge ... Anyway, this last year he's gotten into the whole toy-train thing, so I wanted to get him some stuff."

"What kind of trains?"

Reverting to stupid-chick mode: "Oh, you know, the kind with *wheels*?"

"What *scale*?"

"Scale?"

"HO? O? N? Z?"

"You see, this is why I had to come to a brick-and-mortar store instead of just buying off the Internet. I have no idea what you just said."

"The *scale* of the *trains*. HO is 1:87. O is—"

"One to eighty-seven what?"

"It's a *size ratio*. HO-scale model trains are one eighty-seventh the size of real trains."

"Oh ... Well, I'm not sure. I know the trains he's got

are *small*, but I'll be honest, I was never that good with fractions ... What scale are those?" I raised my arm to point; Arlo ducked sideways as if my finger were the tip of a spear, which gave me an opening to move past him. I walked up to the train layout. "Yeah, these look about right ..." One train was approaching a bridge near the edge of town; I plucked the locomotive from the track, sending half a dozen passenger cars plunging into a river gorge. "Is this HO size?"

Arlo's cheeks were billowing in and out, and he'd just about bitten his lower lip off. "Sorry," I said again. "This is the right size, though, I'm almost sure ... Do you have any like this?" Unable to speak, Arlo gestured to a nearby display case—and immediately regretted it.

The display case was locked, but by jiggling the glass doors I managed to knock over a couple of the train cars inside. I turned to Arlo: "Could you open this up for—"

"No."

"I just want to look at—"

"*No.*"

"OK." I shrugged, and jabbed a finger at a random locomotive. "What's that one called?"

"The Burlington-Northern."

"And that one?"

"The Union Pacific."

"And that one?"

"The Illinois Central ... Listen, I don't have time to name every—"

"Ooh! What about that one up there?"

"The Southwest Chief."

"That one's pretty slick. Does it come in other colors?"

"No, it doesn't ... Now I'm really kind of busy this morning, so if you aren't sure what you want—"

"What about monkeys?" I said.

"Wh-what?"

"Monkeys." I smiled at him. "It's freakish, I know, but when we were kids my brother was a big-time Curious George fan, and he never totally outgrew it. Do you have any trains with monkeys on them?"

"No. I don't have anything like that. I've never *heard* of anything like that."

"What about a case?"

Arlo bit his lip again.

"You know," I continued, "like a carrying case? Since my brother got into the hobby, he's made some … interesting new friends. So I thought he might like a case to carry his trains in, when he goes to visit them. You got anything like that, say about this big? In a nice black, maybe?"

A phone began to ring in the store's back room. Arlo turned his head towards the sound. "You want to get that?" I asked him. It was obvious he did—at least, he wanted to get the hell away from me—but it was just as obvious he was afraid of what might happen to his toys if he left me alone with them. "It's OK," I assured him. "I promise I won't touch anything while you're gone."

That *really* made him nervous—as he headed into the back, he took a last look at the train layout, like he was sure I was going to trash it the minute he was out of sight.

Which, come to think of it, wasn't a bad idea …

As I stepped back towards the layout, my foot kicked something. It was the magazine Arlo had been reading when I first entered the store: *Model Train Enthusiast's Monthly*, something like that. The cover photo showed a sleek locomotive chugging towards a railroad crossing, where—this was weird—a pewter figurine of a boy with a soccer ball had been placed on the tracks, his back to the oncoming train.

The locomotive had a monkey on its side. Not Curious George, or any other friendly cartoon simian—this was a badass nightmare monkey, with sharp fangs tipping a blue-and-red snout. THE MANDRILL, screamed the caption, ON SALE *TODAY*.

Inset in a box in the lower right-hand corner of the magazine cover was a second, smaller photo, of two women in train-conductor uniforms. The uniforms must have been digitally added, but the doctoring job was so skillful that I almost didn't notice that the women were me and Annie. The caption on this photo read: "They're coming for you—details, pg. 23."

The door to the store's back room was locked. I kicked it until it wasn't. The space beyond was lined with more shelves, but instead of trains they held teddy bears, cereal boxes, and toothpaste dispensers ... There was a workbench, too, covered with papers and tools, and a couple of empty soccer-ball cartons.

Arlo was gone, of course. I ducked out a side door into the alley. There was no sign of him there, either, but that china doll I'd first seen almost two weeks ago was still sitting in the dumpster, still holding out its hand to shake. Someone had dropped a paper bag over its head.

I broke out my headset: "Hello? Anybody?"

"This is True."

"Arlo's on the run," I told him, hoping this wasn't news.

"What happened?"

"The short version is, his monkey friends sent him a warning ... Please tell me you saw him leave."

"We've had some difficulties with the surveillance."

"Ah, man ..."

"I'm tasking additional resources to the search as we speak; Dexter shouldn't get far. How long ago did he—"

"Hold on."

A corkboard had been mounted on the wall above Arlo's workbench. Looking back at it from the alley door,

I noticed that the board didn't hang quite flush. When I grabbed it by the edge and pulled, it swung outwards. "Holy shit."

"What?"

"I found the briefcase."

"You did?"

"Arlo must've been in too much of a hurry to take it with him."

"Perhaps," True said warily. "But before you open it—"

"Too late."

There was a brief silence, and I had this clear mental picture of True pursing his lips. "Very well," he continued. "Describe the contents, *without touching them*."

"Right ... The case is foam-lined, with slots holding what look like digital stopwatches. Each watch has three small buttons on the left side and one big one on top—don't worry, I'm not going to push any of them. The brand name on the watch-casings is—"

"Mandrill."

"Yeah."

"This next question is very important, Jane. Are any of the stopwatches *running* right now?"

"Counting down, you mean? No—trust me, that's the first thing I'd have mentioned. But there is some bad news: Arlo may have left the briefcase behind, but it looks like he took a couple of the watches with him. Two of the slots are empty."

"All right, I'll notify the other teams. What I need you to do next is look around the area where you found the case. Can you see anything that might indicate where Dexter is headed?"

"Maybe ..." I moved aside a soccer-ball carton. "There's a map of SFO airport here."

"Are any of the terminals circled?"

"Yeah, all of them ... Listen, True, assuming these

watches are what I think they are, is Arlo going to be able to get them through airport security?"

"That's an irrelevant question."

"Why?"

"He wants to blow up a crowd, not an airplane. All a security checkpoint will do is save him a few steps."

Oh, right. "OK then, let's stop him before he gets there. You want me to go after him on foot, or—"

"No. Stay with the briefcase until Catering secures it."

"What? Wait a minute, I'm supposed to be hunting Arlo, not—"

"You've done your job," True said. "Stay with the case; another operative will get Dexter."

"Shit, True …"

He wasn't listening. I could still hear him on the headset, but he was talking to other people now, ordering a close watch on all bus stops, cab stands, BART stations, even the parking garage where Arlo's grandmother kept her car. Between that and the general surveillance blanket already covering the neighborhood, Arlo would almost certainly be picked up within a matter of minutes, and there was no way he was getting to the airport. I should have been happy about that, and content to have done my part without any foul-ups, but of course I wasn't.

I stuck my head out the alley door again, on the off chance that Arlo had doubled back to let me take care of him personally. No such luck. I locked the door, and carried the briefcase into the front of the shop to wait for Catering.

Arlo's train layout was still running. I watched the remaining passenger train wend its way through town, past the miniature city hall, the department store, the candy shop, the church, the police station, the school …

The school. It was wood, not brick, but just like the real elementary school at Orchard and Masonic, it had an attached playground: a fenced-in lot, packed with tiny figures.

I got back on the headset: "True, forget about the airport. I know where he's going ... True? ... True?"

I ran outside. The taxi had taken off, and when I looked up at the second floor of the hotel, Annie was gone from the window. I kept trying the headset, getting back mostly static; but in between the stretches of white noise I caught snippets of other transmissions, enough to figure out that I wasn't the only one having communication problems.

The school was only seven blocks away, and Arlo had enough of a head start that he might already be there. I had to hope that, knowing we were looking for him, he'd opt for a slow and stealthy approach.

I took off running. Four blocks later, as I rounded the corner onto Masonic, I saw an off-duty cab stopped for a red light just ahead. "Hey!" I shouted, and started towards it.

The world changed color. Like the firing of an NC gun, the explosion of the Mandrill bomb was silent: a bright noiseless flash of orange and yellow with a translucent cab-shape at its center. I felt something pass through me—the shockwave, I guess, though it was more like a jolt from a power outlet—and then I was flat on my back.

I sat up slowly. Steam was rising from my arms, and my face felt hot. I got to my feet—we're talking at least another minute, here—and went to check on the taxi.

The vehicle itself had suffered remarkably little damage. The windows and mirrors had all shattered and fallen out, but the chassis seemed untouched, not even lightly scorched. The driver was a different story. It was like he'd spontaneously combusted: all that was left of him was a pile of smoldering clothes. I leaned in for a closer look, caught a whiff of something awful,

and pulled back gagging. That's when I noticed the pedestrians: three separate pairs of shoes in the crosswalk
in front of the taxi, each with its own accompanying
clothes-pile.

I gagged again, and my knees buckled. It was OK: I
needed to check beneath the taxi anyway. Sure enough,
in the shadow of the undercarriage I saw the remains of
a burst soccer ball.

I got back on my feet. In the distance I could hear the
school bell ringing: recess. I tried to hurry, but the best
I could manage was a drunken stagger.

By the time I reached Orchard Street, the school
playground was already full of kids. Arlo Dexter stood
just outside the fence, slipping another soccer ball from
a canvas bag. I pulled my gun and tried to draw a bead
on him, but my arm wouldn't steady.

I needed to get closer, like point-blank range. I
stepped off the curb and immediately stepped back as a
car swerved to avoid me. Arlo heard the horn blare and
looked over his shoulder. We locked eyes. He smiled
and stuck his tongue out, then raised the ball above his
head and cocked his arms to throw.

A shopping bag full of soup cans caught him square
in the face. He went down hard, dropping the ball,
which only bounced once before Annie swooped in and
grabbed it. She did a neat half-pirouette and relayed the
ball down the block to another cab driver, who dropped
it into an open manhole at his feet.

"Are you all right, miss?" someone asked. It was just
some guy walking by; he'd missed the show across the
street, but noticed me. "You should be careful waving
that around," he said, pointing to my NC gun. "The
cops, especially these days, they might not realize it's a
toy until it's too late."

"You're right," I said. "Thanks for the tip."

I swayed a little on my feet, and he reached out to

steady me. "You sure you're OK? You're not on anything, are you?"

"Not yet," I told him, "but I hope to be, soon." I started laughing.

Then I looked across the street, and my laughter died. Arlo had gotten back up and had his hands around Annie's throat; she was smacking him in the head to try to get him to let go. As they grappled, they were edging towards the curb.

"Annie!" I shouted. I raised my gun again, but this was an even more impossible shot. All I could do was watch as their fight carried them out into traffic.

This time, the delivery truck didn't even try to stop. Arlo went down and got swept under the wheels, but Annie was knocked up and away. She flew diagonally across the intersection and crash-landed on the hood of a parked car.

She was still conscious when I got to her. I pushed my way through the crowd that was already gathering around her, and immediately launched into a line of bullshit about how she'd be OK if she could just hang on. She shut me up with a glance.

I'd like to tell you that she died at peace, relieved at the thought of being reunited with her son. But this was no Hallmark ending. She was in a lot of pain, and she was scared. Maybe just scared of dying, but maybe—I think this is it—scared that saving that playground full of kids hadn't been enough, and where she was going now, she *wouldn't* see Billy again, even looking both ways.

Right before she went out, she grabbed my wrist and said, "Pay attention," one more time. Then she muttered something, which, as usual, I couldn't quite make out. But I was in tune with her now, and so I knew it had to do with the truck that had hit her.

I looked up, and the crowd parted, and I saw it: a

black-paneled truck, idling in the distance. The driver was leaning out the cab window, watching Annie's death scene through a pair of binoculars. Watching me. When he saw that I saw him, he pulled his head back inside the truck cab. The truck's taillights flashed, drawing my attention to the mandrill painted on the back door.

"Hey!" The crowd had closed up again; I started pushing people aside, flailing my arms. "Hey! Stop that truck! Stop that truck!"

But no one would listen to me, and by the time I fought my way clear, it was already too late—the truck had turned a corner, and like a model train going into a tunnel, it vanished.

white room (iv)

ONE OF THE FLOOR TILES HAS TURNED black. She's prodding it with her foot as the doctor comes in.

"Maintenance had to replace it," he explains. "One of the other inmates was feeling claustrophobic. She tried to dig her way out."

"What did she use, a chair leg?"

"A ballpoint pen. My colleague Dr. Chiang got called away in the middle of a session, and he made the mistake of leaving his belongings on the table."

"Your colleague. So you weren't there when it happened."

"No, it was on one of my days off. You doubt the story?"

She shrugs. "Nice job of color-matching."

"If you'd like, I could call maintenance back in and have it pried up."

"Don't bother. Even if the organization put something under there, all you'd find is an ordinary patch of floor."

"What would they put there, though? Some sort of microphone?"

She shakes her head. "The spy gear won't be in the floor."

"Meaning it is here somewhere?"

She glances at the smiling politician on the wall. "Eyes Only," she says.

"You'll have to decode that for me, Jane."

"I told you about Panopticon, right?"

"'The Department of Ubiquitous Intermittent Surveillance?'"

"That's the one. Eyes Only is one of their intel-gathering programs. It uses these miniature sensor devices that are kind of like contact lenses, only smaller and thinner—so much so that they're undetectable without special equipment. Now in theory you could plant these things anywhere, but in practice Panopticon only puts them on eyes. *Representations* of eyes, that is: photographs, paintings, drawings, sculpture ... Any time you see an eyeball that's not in an actual person's head, there's a chance it's monitoring you."

"How much of a chance?"

"Nobody outside Panopticon knows for sure. If you ask, they tell you, 'Less than a hundred percent, but more than zero.' It's a joke, see? 'Ubiquitous intermittent surveillance' means they aren't always watching, but they always *might* be."

"Do you think they're watching now?"

"I think the odds are closer to a hundred percent than zero."

The doctor reaches to take down the photograph, but it's fixed firmly in place. "Well," he says, "I suppose I could get a towel or a washcloth to drape over it."

"Don't bother. I don't really care if they're watching. Besides, those aren't the only eyes in the room." She points to the identification badge clipped to the front of his lab coat. "And you've got more photo I.D. in your wallet, right? And maybe some snaps of the family?"

"They can see out of my wallet?"

"No, but they can hear."

"The Eyes have Ears?"

"It's an imperfect metaphor. Panopticon's run by geeks, not poets."

The doctor takes out his wallet and does a quick survey of its contents. Peering into the billfold, he asks: "Do they put these devices on currency, too?"

"Oh yeah. Smart money, they call that. They use it to track cash transactions."

"Interesting," says the doctor. "And disturbing."

"It's scary when it works. But that's the other half of the joke: the Eyes go blind a lot, and they miss stuff— whole *trucks*, sometimes."

"Who told you about Eyes Only? Annie?"

"We covered it in dream class. But I guess you could say it was Dixon who really schooled me on the subject."

"Did Mr. Dixon work for Panopticon?"

"A subdivision of Panopticon," she says. "One that you really *don't* want watching you . . ."

Malfeasance

I PASSED PROBATE.

I wasn't expecting to; you'd think letting your Probate officer get killed would pretty much guarantee an F. But the Loose Ends team that collected Annie's personal effects found a half-finished progress report that said I showed "real potential," which I guess was enough to bump me to a D-minus.

A month later I got my first assignment as a full-fledged Bad Monkeys operative, at an old folks' home in Russian Hill. A doctor in the critical-care ward was playing God with the senior citizens. He'd put stuff in their IVs to cause a cardiac arrest, then call an emergency code and bring them back to life. Sometimes he'd "save" the same patient two or three times before their systems couldn't take it anymore.

He'd been at this long enough that the nurses on the ward were starting to get suspicious, and he probably would have been busted eventually, but the organization got wind of him first. Panopticon did a background check and found out he'd worked at three other old folks' homes before this one. When Cost-Benefits heard that, they decided enough was enough.

I got a job sweeping floors on the night shift. My first

night on, I caught Dr. God alone in the break room and gave him a taste of his own medicine.

That was it for the Bad Monkeys op, but I decided to keep working at the home for a while. I needed the money. It turned out Annie's lottery stipend was a special deal just for her; whenever I bought scratch tickets, they were losers.

You didn't ask Bob True to provide you with a salary?

Nah. After squeaking through Probate, I figured I wasn't in a position to ask for anything. Besides, when I thought about it, it made sense: I was supposed to be doing this for the good of the world, not for a buck. And it's not like they had me killing bad guys every day. I had more than enough downtime to manage a second job.

So I stayed on at the home, and even took a shot at having a personal life. I made friends with some of the night nurses and started going to breakfast with them after our shifts ended. There was also this cute doctor, John Tyler, who came in to replace Dr. God. I tried to get something going with him.

Did you?

No. I'd hang around the break room with him, you know, dropping hints, but he wasn't interested. And not that I'm God's gift, but I figured that probably meant he was gay. Then one night when he was off-duty I was sweeping the floor outside his office and noticed the door was unlocked. I decided to snoop a little, see if I could confirm my suspicions—or if he wasn't a lost cause, find some clue to what might float his boat.

There was nothing out in the open. Nothing in his Rolodex, either. I started checking desk drawers, hit one that was locked, grabbed a paper clip ... and then, when I had the drawer open and saw what was inside, I reached for the phone.

True was waiting for me on the roof of the nursing home at dawn. Catering had set out chairs and a buffet table, and as I came out of the stairwell, I saw a guy puttering around the tea service. I might have taken him for a waiter, except he looked more like nearsighted Gestapo: blond crew cut, black leather trench coat, and these thick pebble glasses, you know the kind they stopped making once plastic lenses were invented?

And this was Dixon?

Yeah, although I didn't catch his name right away. He didn't introduce himself, and I was in too much of a hurry to tell True what I'd found to insist on the niceties.

"The drawer was full of pictures," I said. "Pictures of little boys. Not, like, hardcore stuff; they were cutouts from mainstream magazines, product ads mostly: little boys in blue jeans, little boys in bathing suits, little boys in underwear … I suppose there could be an innocent explanation, but what makes that hard to believe is how many of them there were. I mean, we're talking stockpile, *hundreds* of images …"

"Five hundred and forty-four, at last count," said True. "There's also a catalog of parochial-school uniforms hidden at the back of the X-ray drawer in his filing cabinet."

"You already knew about this?"

"Eyes Only," True said.

It took me a minute to get my head around the concept. "You *bug* children's underwear ads?"

"An obvious strategy for identifying pedophiles. Though perhaps not as cost-effective as initially hoped." He glanced at the guy in the pebble glasses, who was sitting down now, stirring his tea.

"So I was right. Dr. Tyler is a bad monkey."

"He has potential."

"What does that mean?"

"It means that so far as we know, he's never laid a hand on a real child, or even tried to. He just thinks about it."

"So what?"

"So, wicked thoughts alone aren't enough to classify someone as irredeemable."

I couldn't believe it. "You're not going to do anything?"

"We're evaluating him. If it's warranted, we'll arrange a Good Samaritan operation to get him some counseling."

"That's it? You *might* make him see a shrink?"

"I was referring to moral counseling, actually," True said. "If his own conscience isn't enough to keep his impulses in check, I doubt psychiatry will be much use … What is it you'd like us to do, Jane? Execute someone for keeping magazine clippings?"

"Well if you're not going to send me in, you could at least let people know about him."

"And beyond ruining the reputation of a man who's done nothing wrong, what would that accomplish?"

"Jesus, True, do you really need me to spell it out?"

"I do appreciate your feelings in this matter …"

"You *appreciate*—"

"You're a proactive personality," True said. "When you see a potential threat, you want to eradicate it. That's a useful instinct in a hunter, and it's one of the reasons you're in Bad Monkeys. My desires are a bit different, however. Like you, I want to fight evil, but I want to fight it effectively. In particular, I want to make sure that when the organization acts, it's out of a reasonable expectation of a positive result, and not just for the sake of doing something. That's why I'm in Cost-Benefits. And that's why you take your orders from me."

I didn't trust myself to respond to that, so instead I jerked a thumb at Pebble Glasses. "And what does *he* want?"

"This is Mr. Dixon. He's attached to Malfeasance."

Malfeasance is the Panopticon subdivision that investigates operatives; it's the organization equivalent of Internal Affairs. "Did I do something wrong?"

Dixon looked up from his tea. "In my experience," he said, "the proper question isn't 'Did I?', but 'How much do they know?' Then again, there's a first time for everything. I've always wanted to meet a truly innocent person; maybe you'll be her." He plucked a card from a hidden pocket in his coat sleeve. "This is the current location of my office. Come by this evening at eight o'clock. We'll chat."

"Uh, my shift here starts at nine-thirty. Will that be enough time?"

"Eight o'clock," Dixon repeated. He stood up. "Don't be late."

I waited until he'd left, then turned to True: "What the hell is this about?"

"I don't know. Dixon called me last night, right after you did, and said he wanted to meet you. I assume it has something to do with your background check."

"I thought I passed Probate. Why would Malfeasance still be running a background check?"

"They're always running it."

"And you have no idea what they might have turned up?"

"Dixon didn't say."

"Well, is there some way I could find out before I go see him?"

"Try asking yourself," True suggested.

"Asking myself what?"

"Whether you've ever done anything evil."

The address on the card was for a video arcade in the Mission District. I was surprised to find it open for business. I stood by the entrance, checking out the crowd—most of them were too young to be anything but civilians—and wondering if I had the right place, until this guy in a change apron came up and tapped me on the shoulder. He pointed to a sign on the wall that read, ALL TOY WEAPONS MUST BE SURRENDERED BEFORE PROCEEDING.

I looked at the guy. He tugged at his earlobe, which was pierced with a monogram earring that had the letters OMF in gold. I gave him my NC gun. He tucked it into his apron and brought out a yellow elastic band that he slipped around my wrist. The wristband was tight and had some sort of metal contacts on the inside, and right away it started my skin tingling. While I was still adjusting to that, the guy slapped an ice-cold can of Coke into my other hand. He pointed to another sign: FREE SODA WITH SURRENDER OF WEAPON. Then he nodded towards the rear of the arcade and said, "He's waiting for you."

I started back. The Coke can was freezing my hand, so to warm it up I popped the tab and took a big gulp. It was like drinking liquid nitrogen; my whole mouth went numb, and when the Coke hit the back of my throat I spiked an ice-cream headache that made my eyes water.

The arcade seemed to go on for miles. Every time I reached the end of a row of machines, there'd be another one, and as I went farther in, things started to get strange. The kids manning the joysticks were replaced by gnomes, blond gnomes with pebble glasses and leather trench coats. The machines changed too, *Virtua Fighter 3* and *Dance Dance Revolution* giving way to games with more of a Seven Deadly Sins theme. And the images on the screens ... Let's just say, the Concerned Parents Association wouldn't have approved.

Finally I came to a door marked EMPLOYEE INTERVIEWS. I took another sip of Coke, knocked, and went in.

Dixon's office had a single overhead light fixture, like a search lamp mounted in the ceiling—the bulb was like a thousand watts or something, and if it had been angled at the door instead of aimed straight down, I'd have gone blind on the spot. A long folding table had been set up in the cone of the lamplight. The left side of the table was piled with paper, mostly old-fashioned computer fanfold printout. The right side was reserved for a sleek laptop, its screen flickering with a cascade of green figures.

Dixon stood with his back to the door, flipping through a sheaf of printout and pretending he hadn't heard me come in. I took this for a standard interrogation tactic: he wanted me to speak first, to establish that he was the one in charge. Instead I drank more Coke, slurping it. The belch at the end seemed to get his attention.

"It's 8:09," he said. "I told you to be here at eight."

"Yeah, well, you didn't tell me about the walk in from the street. How long is this building, anyway?"

He turned around. Some sort of device had been attached to his glasses: a tiny arm extended from the top of the right lens, dangling a clear plastic rectangle a half-inch in front of it. The rectangle flickered, green, in tandem with the flickering of the laptop on the table. It was completely geeky, but it was also kind of hypnotic.

"Do you know why you're here?" Dixon asked.

Another interrogation tactic: get me to guess what I'd done, and maybe I'd volunteer something he didn't know about. I shrugged and played dumb. "True thought it might have something to do with my background check. So what, did you find some unpaid parking tickets?"

"*Der schlechte Affe hasst seinen eigenen Geruch.*"

"Excuse me?"

"It's a saying we have in Malfeasance. Not as pithy as '*Omnes mundum facimus,*' but it serves us."

"Well don't keep me in suspense. What does it mean?"

"It's an observation about human nature," Dixon said. "One difficulty we have in running these background checks is that our information-gathering apparatus is so effective, we end up drowning in data. Of course we have technology to help sort through it, but even machines have their limits, and a brute-force search of an entire life—particularly one that hasn't been all that well-lived—eats an enormous number of computing cycles. So we try to find clues to help us narrow the search space ... Loosely translated, *Der schlechte Affe hasst seinen eigenen Geruch* means that people are most deeply offended by moral failings that mirror their own. The minister who preaches a tearful sermon against fornication: he's the one you'll find sneaking out of a brothel at midnight. The district attorney who crusades against illegal gambling: look for him at the track, betting his life savings on Bluenose in the fifth."

"If you're trying to say that people are hypocrites, that's not exactly a newsflash. And what's it got to do with me?"

"Who told you to search John Tyler's office?"

"No one."

"You just intuited somehow that there was something to find?"

"No, I was just being nosy. I'm like that."

"How many other offices did you search?"

"Well ... none."

"What about the nurses you've been having breakfast with? Did you go through any of their purses?"

"No."

"What about their lockers?"

"No, but—"

"So you're not *that* nosy. Why single out Dr. Tyler?"

"I thought he was cute, OK?"

"Oh. So you were stalking him?"

"No! I was just checking him out ... I mean, I don't know, maybe I did get a vibe off him."

"A vibe."

"Yeah, like you said, an intuition. That there was something not right there."

"But then what about the nurses?"

"What about them?"

"Two of them have been stealing painkillers—shorting their patients' dosages—and giving them to their boyfriends to sell. Strange you didn't get a vibe about that. Maybe if they were taking the drugs for *personal use*, your intuition would have picked up on it ..."

"Look, where are you going with this? You think I zeroed in on Tyler because I'm *like* him?"

"Are you?"

"Hey, if you're worried I've got my own collection of magazine clippings, you're welcome to search my apartment."

"We already did."

"OK ... So you know your schlecky-affa-whatever theory doesn't hold water."

"It's often a related transgression, rather than the exact same one," Dixon said. "Just to be thorough, I ran a check of your reading history to see if there were any signs of inappropriate sexual interest." He held up the batch of printout he'd been looking at when I came in. "That search was more fruitful. Tell me, do you recall stealing a book from the San Francisco Public Library when you were twelve years old?"

It was such a left-field question I almost laughed, but the funny thing was, I knew exactly what he was talking about. When he said, "Do you recall," it was like my brain got zapped with some kind of flashback ray.

And what was he talking about? What was the book?

Anaïs Nin's *Delta of Venus*. Moon's mother had a copy, and Moon and I used to read it to each other during sleepovers. Eventually I decided I wanted a copy of my own, and hooking it from the library was easier than shoplifting it.

"How do you know about that?"

"Library Binding," Dixon said.

I thought he was talking about the anti-theft strip: "But I didn't take it out the front door."

"No, you tossed it out of the second-floor girls' bathroom window. That branch of the library lost a lot of books that way."

"OK, I'll cop to stealing it. But what's so inappropriate? I mean, *Delta of Venus* is smut, but it's literary smut."

"It's a curious sort of literature, though, isn't it?" Dixon said. "For example, the third story in the book— the one entitled 'The Boarding School'—concerns a young student at a monastery who is ogled by priests and sexually violated by his classmates ... This is what you consider *wholesome* erotic entertainment?"

"I don't remember *that* story."

"Don't you? I'd have thought it was a favorite. According to my records, you read it nineteen times while the book was in your possession."

"According to your *records*?"

"Library Binding." He offered me the printout. "There are some other items here I'd love to get your comments on."

I started going through it. It was crazy: a catalog of every piece of porn and erotica I'd ever laid eyes on. Not just titles, either—there were notes about specific scenes, even specific paragraphs I'd paid special attention to. And you know, it was bullshit, what he was implying, but with all of it thrown together on one big list like that, I could see how someone with an overly suspicious mind might get the wrong idea.

What else was on the list?

Well, De Sade, of course. Assorted Victorian gentlemen—in college, I must have gone through the entire Grove Press library, I mean, who the hell didn't? Henry Miller. William Burroughs. Anne Rice.

At first I was kind of mortified, you know? But as I got further into it—it was a *long* list—I started to hit stuff that was harder to be embarrassed about, books and stories that weren't technically smut at all, even if they did have sex in them. Towards the end the list-maker really seemed to be reaching—there were even a couple of Shakespeare plays, I think. And then on the last page, I found the weirdest entry of all …

"The Bible?"

"November 13th, 1977," Dixon said. "One of the few times you were actually in church. Eyes Only caught you lingering over a passage in Genesis—the one where Lot offers his virgin daughters to the mob in Sodom and Gomorrah."

"Uh-huh … And because I *lingered* over this Bible verse, you think I might want to sacrifice a real virgin to an evil mob?"

"If you'd lingered over it *nineteen times*, I'd certainly have cause to wonder. Just the once, we can probably write off to prurient interest … Although I do find it curious you were laughing as you read it."

"Right." I shoved the printout back into his hands. "I get it."

"You get it?"

"Yeah. You can tell True to get bent."

"Ah … You think Mr. True told me to give you a hard time about this."

"I questioned his call on Tyler, didn't I? But this isn't even *close* to being the same thing …"

"You are laboring under at least two misimpressions right now," Dixon said. "The first is that I care whether you're comfortable with Mr. True's policy decisions. Trust me when I tell you, putting low-level operatives' minds at ease isn't one of my concerns in this life."

"What's the other misimpression?"

"That I disagree with you about Dr. Tyler. If it were up to me, the organization would deal much more aggressively with him—and *all others like him*. Unfortunately, like you, I have to defer to Cost-Benefits. And even if the decision was mine to make, my dream solution wouldn't be feasible."

"Why not? Because everyone has sick fantasies?"

"No. That's just something people who have sick fantasies tell themselves, so they can feel normal. But there *are* enough of you to make a clean sweep logistically impractical ..." He waited a beat before adding: "People who *act* on their sick fantasies, though—that's a more manageable number."

And just like that, I finally got it, what this was really all about: he knew about the pet boys.

"I know about the pet boys," Dixon said.

The pet boys?

Yeah, OK, how do I explain this ... You remember how, when I was talking about my twenties, I said there were times when I had a little *too* much fun? This was like one of those times.

It was a couple summers after I got kicked out of Berkeley. Weekdays I was working this roach-infested burger joint in the Tenderloin. On Friday and Saturday nights I had a different gig, at a liquor store across from the Golden Gate Panhandle. There were a lot of street kids in the Panhandle, and every night I'd get a bunch of them coming into the store, trying to buy booze.

Now the legal drinking age was twenty-one, which would be ridiculous in any jurisdiction, but what made it especially silly in California's case is that we also had the death penalty, and you know what the minimum age for that was? Eighteen. So think about that, you're old enough to get a lethal injection, but you've got to wait three more years before you can buy a beer. Does that sound logical?

It sounds like a novel justification for violating state liquor laws. I assume you sold alcohol to these street kids?

Well, not *all* of them. I used my discretion. If the kid carried himself like an adult, and didn't come off like someone who was going to get blitzed and go leaping in front of a trolley—and if his phony I.D. wasn't *too* bad—then yeah, I'd give him the benefit of the doubt.

And when you say "give," was that a free gift, or did it come at a premium?

You're asking whether I took bribes?

That's what I'm asking.

I might have had a tip jar ... Hey, I was poor. And besides, it was part of the maturity test: if you don't understand you've got to pay in order to play, maybe you're *not* grown up enough to drink yet ... You know, if you're going to look at me like that, I may as well stop right now, because I'm not even at the bad part yet.

I'm sorry. Please continue.

Yeah, OK, so one night this kid came in, six foot, husky, but baby-faced, and right away I pegged him as underage: old enough for the needle, maybe, but not for the bottle. I watched him while he circled the store, to make sure he didn't steal anything, and also because, you know, it wasn't exactly a chore to look at him. Eventually he picked out a liter of Stoli and brought it to the counter.

"I.D.?" I said, and waited for his pitch. A lot of them had a spiel they'd go through, you know, "I was sick the day this photo was taken, that's why it doesn't look like me." But this kid didn't say a word, just handed me a driver's license with the name Miles Davis on it. I checked the picture, and it's this black guy with a trumpet.

Miles Davis. The jazz musician.

Yeah. So I looked at the kid, and there was maybe a *hint* of a smile on his lips, but other than that he was completely straight-faced. And I'm like, "Miles Davis, huh?" And he just looked back at me, cool as can be, like, yep, that's me. So then I'm like, "You're looking awfully pale tonight, Miles." And he said: "I have a skin condition."

Well, that was good enough as far as I was concerned. If you can come up with a line like that and deliver it deadpan, you deserve a drink. So I went to give the tip jar a shake, but he was already there, slipping in a dollar. "You're the man, Miles," I said, and rang him up.

Fast forward a couple of hours: after I locked up the store for the night, I went into the Panhandle to score some dope, and found Miles sitting at the base of a statue, smoking a joint. I went over to him: "Can I get a hit off that?" He gave me a toke and made room for me to sit.

"So Miles," I said, taking a pull off the Stoli bottle, "do you live around here?"

"Actually," he said, all Mr. Casual, "I'm looking for a place. What about you?"

"I'm thinking of becoming a landlady." Which came out lamer than I intended, but it was OK—we were already rubbing shoulders, so it's not like I needed a *great* line.

I took him home with me. In the morning I woke up alone in the futon, which wasn't a huge surprise, but then I smelled smoke, and I was like, shit, did he set the place on fire on his way out?

Before I could jump out of bed, though, Miles came in, carrying this cutting board like a serving tray, loaded with goodies: an omelet, cinnamon toast, coffee, juice, even a little sprig of grapes. I'm like, "What's this?" and he said, "Full service." He got me all propped up on a nest of pillows like the Queen of Sheba, and put the cutting board in my lap.

I was blown away. No one had *ever* made me breakfast in bed before, and frankly, at that point, the food could have tasted like crap and I wouldn't have cared. But when I took a bite of the omelet it was actually really good.

So I ate, and meanwhile Miles went over to my dresser and opened up the box where I kept my drug stash. I watched him roll himself a joint, sunshine streaming through the window while he did it, and all at once it struck me, full light of day, he was even more baby-faced than I'd thought. So I put my fork down, and I said, "How old are you really, Miles? Nineteen?" He didn't say anything, didn't even look at me, just went on rolling that joint, but he smiled in a way that told me the answer was no. And I'm like, "Eighteen?" Still no. So I'm like, oh boy ... "Seventeen?" Still no. "*Six*teen?" Finally, his smile changed a little. "Oh great," I said. "The cops are going to love this." And Miles reached back into the drug box and pulled out this big bag of pills I had in there, and said, "I can tell you're really worried about the cops."

So now that you knew he was only sixteen, what did you do?

What do you think I did? I kept him.

Kept him?

Duh, breakfast in bed, of course I kept him. Gave him a key and told him he could stay as long as he liked. We worked out a deal: he kept the place clean, cooked for me when I was home, and, you know ...

And how long did this arrangement last?

A few weeks. Until one morning he took off for real, along with my stereo and half my dope. I should've been pissed about that, but I couldn't get too worked up; he'd earned it, and anyway I'd have probably done the same thing in his shoes.

And after he left, there were others?

Yeah, but I don't want you to think I was a total slut about it. I did wait a while, to see if he'd come back. But eventually, yeah. It became like a regular thing for me, all that summer and fall. Picking up strays.

Were they all underage?

They were all old enough. As far as specific ages, after Miles, I didn't even ask.

But you referred to them as pet boys.

It wasn't me who started that, it was Phil. He showed up one morning uninvited, and before I could get rid of him, my latest houseguest came walking through the kitchen without a shirt on. So Phil's like: "The cat wasn't enough? You're keeping pet *boys* now?"

He didn't approve.

Yeah, well, no surprise there. Phil always was kind of a prude ... And look, I'm not defending it, OK? I know it was wrong, but you've got to understand, it was a different time. It wasn't like today, where whenever you turn on the news some high-school teacher is being dragged off in handcuffs. San Francisco, 1990, picking up teenage boys in the park wasn't this huge perversion, it was just ... decadent.

But of course it's one thing to be comfortable with that in your own mind, and a whole other thing to sell it to a cop or a judge, let alone some four-eyed freak who spends his days cataloging sin. So when Dixon said, "I know about the pet boys," my first thought was, *Jane, you've got some explaining to do.*

Little did I know. I still hadn't really grasped the whole Eyes Only thing, how pervasive it was. I figured Dixon must have heard *stories* about the pet boys, like maybe his people had tracked down one of the neighbors from my old apartment building. I wasn't expecting *video*.

But then somebody hit a dimmer switch on the overhead light, and suddenly this little back room became an amphitheater. You know that Sony Jumbotron screen they've got in Times Square, the one that's like forty feet wide? Imagine that popping up on a wall in this space that you thought was maybe fifteen by twenty.

The wall lit up and started filling with this photo array of pet boys. All of them, even the one-night stands that I didn't really consider part of the official count. The pictures were practically life-size, at least it *seemed* that way, and each one had a caption: MILES DAVIS MONROE, AGE 16—the 16 was flashing in red—JORDAN GRAHAM, AGE 17, VICTOR TODD, AGE 17, NICHOLAS MARTINESCU, AGE 16, et cetera, et cetera.

How many "et ceteras"?

Let's just stipulate that it was a big frigging wall and leave it at that, OK? It took a long time to fill up, and meanwhile I was sucking down Coke, and my wristband, which was obviously some sort of lie detector, was tingling like mad, and I just knew that whatever I said next was going to be judged really severely. So I thought, and I thought, and I was still thinking when the last picture appeared, and finally I opened my mouth and said the exact wrong thing:

"How much trouble am I in?"

"Well, let's see," said Dixon. The overhead light came up again, and he was holding a big red book with the words CALIFORNIA PENAL CODE on the cover. "Unlawful sexual intercourse with a minor, age sixteen or seventeen, a misdemeanor, three months to a year per count, 189 counts ... Providing alcohol to a minor, age sixteen or seventeen, for immoral purposes, a misdemeanor, three months to a year per count, 131 counts ... Providing illegal narcotics to a minor, age sixteen or seventeen, for immoral purposes, a felony ..."

I started to do the math in my head, but then I was like, wait, he knows how many times I did it? And so I took another look at the picture array and saw that all the shots were framed the same way, with the pet boy sitting at the foot of my futon and the image angled like the person holding the camera was standing on the futon's headboard, which you think I might have noticed at the time. Then the flashback ray hit me again, and I remembered that very first night with Miles, me handing him a fresh joint and then looking up at the wall above the headboard and winking, conspiratorially, at—

"My Marlene Dietrich poster."

"Eyes Only," Dixon said.

I was screwed. I was so screwed. I'd had that Marlene Dietrich poster since freshman year at Berkeley, it had hung on the wall over every bed I'd ever owned, and if Marlene was a narc for Panopticon—

"I'm screwed." The Coke can was empty now; my head felt three sizes too big, and totally detached from my body. I said to Dixon: "So when are the cops coming?"

"Why would the police be coming?"

"Because ... I'm a criminal."

"Yes, you are," Dixon said. "And if I were an agent of law enforcement, I'd be all too happy to see you locked away in a cell. But I work for the organization, and the organization doesn't fight crime, it fights evil."

"So you're saying ... this wasn't evil?"

"It was reckless. And appallingly selfish. You were certainly old enough to know better. But you appear to have acted without malice, and inasmuch as it's possible to judge such things objectively, most of these young men were unharmed by their association with you."

I didn't miss the qualifier: "Most of them?"

"Why don't *you* tell me who I'm thinking of?"

I didn't have to guess. I turned back to the photo array, to the picture in the bottom right-hand corner, my very last pet boy: Owen Farley.

"Age nineteen," Dixon observed. "A little old for you, wasn't he?"

"No," I said. "He was the youngest one of all, in the way that mattered. He was like ..."—and I hesitated, realizing I was about to bury myself, but there was no choice really, so I went on—"... he was like the boy in the Anaïs Nin story. Innocent. Or no, not innocent. Delicate. *Fragile*."

"Now we're getting somewhere. Tell me what happened."

"You already know what happened."

"I want to hear how you tell it."

Well, I *really* didn't want to do that, but Dixon just kept staring me down, and then the tingling in the wristband started to get painful, so finally I gave in and told the story:

By the middle of fall, the pet-boy thing had started to get old. I guess the novelty wore off. The thing about teenage boys, you know, they're actually not all that interesting as company. I mean even Miles, with all that he had going on upstairs, he wasn't much to talk to.

So I started to get bored. And there were other things going on, too. My boss at the liquor store finally got wise to the fact that I'd been risking his license with my tip-jar scheme; he not only fired me, he kept my last paycheck and said he'd turn me in if I made any trouble about it. So because of that I got behind on my rent, and then also, I was doing a few too many drugs, which hurt my finances even more and made it hard to get out of bed in the morning, which started causing problems at my other job ...

So all of this was sort of snowballing, right? And then one day out of the blue I got a call from Carlotta Diaz saying she'd just bought a house in Bodega Bay, and would I like to come visit her? And I was like, that's great, I'll get out of the city for a while, get straight, get my head together, and make a fresh start. So I told Carlotta yes, and we set a date.

And not long before I was due to leave, I was coming back from working a last shift at the burger joint, and that's when I saw him.

He was a street preacher. I never found out where he came from, but it must have been some little church town out in the boonies where they raise kids under glass. What brought him to S.F. I don't know, but he couldn't have been off the bus more than five minutes.

He was standing on the sidewalk in the heart of the Tenderloin, testifying about Jesus to a pack of transvestite hookers. The hookers were having a grand old time cracking on him, but he was impervious to catcalls—not thick-skinned, you understand, just clueless. He called the hookers "ladies," and from the way he said it you could tell he wasn't being sarcastic or politically correct. He didn't get the whole cross-dressing thing; he thought these really were women.

So I stopped to watch this travesty, right? And seeing how green this kid was, how totally out of his depth, the thought came to me: *If I wanted to, I could take him home and really blow his mind.*

Now you can believe this or not, but this was a departure for me. I mean, with the other pet boys it had all been about fun, and free housekeeping. This was the first time I ever consciously considered messing with some kid's head, *leaving marks* ... And some part of me knew that was a *bad* idea, that I'd be crossing a line I didn't want to cross. Normally, I wouldn't have. But I was leaving for Carlotta's in less than a week, and that changed the calculus a little. It's like, if you're a sane person, ordinarily you'd never touch heroin. But if it's the night before you're going to give up *all* drugs, and somebody offers you a line to snort ...

So I was actually contemplating this, seducing this little preacher boy. And *still* I probably wouldn't have gone through with it, except that as I was standing there, the kid suddenly noticed me, and said: "Ma'am, can I share some good news with you?" And it must have been pretty obvious what was going through my head just then, because one of the hookers called out: "Honey, I think she's going to give *you* some good news!"

And me, I just smiled, and stepped over the line: "I'd be happy to hear your good news, but you're going to have to come with me."

"Come with you, ma'am?" he said. "Where?"

"To my apartment. I need to get off my feet. Are you hungry?"

As easy as that. He fell in beside me and we started for home.

Now here's another weird thing: I was telling Dixon

about this, right? And the whole time, he's goggling at me from behind those glasses of his, but even so, and even knowing what ultimately happened, I started to get into it. I mean, I remembered what it was like that day, bopping down the street, the kid next to me jabbering about the love of Christ, and me feeling like the lioness leading the lamb back to her den ...

So I got to the part where we were in my apartment, and I literally, God help me, offered the kid milk and cookies, and ducked into the bedroom to "change into something more comfortable." And then the Jumbotron came alive again, and suddenly I was looking at a video of what actually happened in my kitchen that day.

It was a two-shot, a close-up and a wide-angle. For the close-up, they must have had Eyes Only on one of the Keebler elves on the cookie box, and the wide-angle, I guess that was from the Quaker Oats canister over the sink. The video picked up right at the point where I came out of the bedroom, wearing this semi-see-through kimono. And like I said before, I know I'm not God's gift, but if you're doing a Mrs. Robinson routine, you don't need to be a knockout, just, you know, presentable. But on-screen, I looked really bad, *scary* bad ... All those drugs I'd been doing, I guess they'd taken more of a toll than I'd realized. There were these dark bags under my eyes, and my skin was blotchy, and my hair was a freak show, and, you know, I do *not* have a mustache problem, but I swear I could see a shadow on my upper lip. I was a hag, basically.

And the kid, he was sitting there with a mouth full of cookies, terrified, and not in a good way ...

Is there a good way to be terrified?

Well, you know, there's *virgin* panic, that feeling you get when it's your first time, and you weren't expecting it, but all of a sudden here it is ... But this wasn't like that. It's like I said to Dixon, this kid wasn't an innocent. The fear on his face, you could see it in the close-up, it wasn't like, *Oh my God, I'm about to get laid*, or even, *Oh my God, what's going on here?* It was, *Oh my God*, not again …

Like he'd been seduced before?

Like he was *damaged*. Like it was too late for *me* to mess with his head, because somebody else had already *been* there, and all I was doing was plugging into this old nightmare. Only I couldn't see that, because I was a fucking stoned-out hag.

You can imagine, watching the replay on this was complete torture. Seeing just how oblivious I'd been to the way this kid was feeling. And the *things* coming out of my mouth … Thank God, after I finally took him by the hand and started leading him into the bedroom, the screen went dark.

But it wasn't over. "What happened next?" Dixon said.

"Just kill me now," I begged him.

"If you'd prefer, we could watch it …"

In case you're wondering, there *are* worse fates than death.

So I got the kid into the bedroom and I started undressing him, and even at the time, I knew there was something wrong. He was too passive—not *nervous* passive, more like catatonic. And then after I got his pants off, got him onto the futon, suddenly he wasn't passive, suddenly *I* was the one who was scared, because this kid, he might have been younger than me, but he was bigger than me too, and all at once he was on top of me, with his face like an inch from mine and this *fever* in his eyes, and now he was the one running it, right, and it wasn't *fun*, it was starting to hurt …

And then … Ah, man, this is bad …

What?

He called me "sister."

Sister as in a nun, or …?

What, like one is less fucked up than the other? I

don't know, but at that point I just flipped out. I started hitting him—maybe I asked him to stop first, but probably I just started whaling on him. I hit him, punched him, four or five times, in the face, and finally he rolled off me, and I sat up, and he was just lying there on his back, shaking and crying.

And I was like, I can't deal with this, I can*not* deal with this, so I went and locked myself in the bathroom and waited for him to leave. And a little while later I heard this thump and I thought, front door, thank God, even though the sound wasn't right for that. So I gave it another ten minutes and came out, holding this toilet plunger like a club.

I did a sweep of the apartment. Kitchen: empty. Good. Living room: empty. Good. Bedroom: empty? The *futon* was empty, but the bedclothes were heaped in a pile on the floor on the far side, and then I saw this foot sticking out. "Oh, shit."

Some instinct made me look over at the dresser. My drug-stash box was open. Marijuana was scattered all over the dresser top, and the pill bag had been turned inside out. "Oh, *shit*."

I ran to him and dug him out from under the sheets and blankets. He was facedown, unconscious, and he'd thrown up at least once, but thank God he hadn't choked on it—he was breathing, he still had a pulse. As I slapped his face to try to revive him, I ran a mental inventory of what had been in that pill bag: uppers and downers mostly—hopefully they'd counteract each other—but also some mescaline tabs I'd been saving for my last day in town. Not the healthiest mix.

The kid's cheeks were raw from the slapping but he wasn't waking up. His breathing was getting sketchy, and I realized I was going to have to call an ambulance. I dithered, trying to come up with an alternative.

How long?

Three, four minutes, tops—I swear—but this kid, he

wasn't growing any new brain cells in the meantime, you know what I'm saying? At least I didn't try to put him under the shower—I knew from experience that doesn't work—but still ...

Anyway, I finally called 911. The dispatcher came on: "What's your emergency?" And I'm like, "Accidental drug overdose ..." She went through the standard Q&A—"What kind of drugs?" "Is he conscious?" "Have you checked his airway?"—and then she asked me where I was located. This was back before they had caller I.D., right? So I was about to tell her, but then I took another look at my dresser, at all that dope scattered around.

And the dispatcher said, "Miss? Are you there?" And I said, "Yeah, I'm here," and gave her the address of the building across the street. And she's like, "Is that an apartment building?" and I said, "Yeah, I think so," and she said, "You *think* so?" and I said, "I mean it is—just hurry up and get here, OK?" And she said, sounding skeptical now, "What's the apartment number?" and I told her, "Don't worry about it. Tell the paramedics I'll meet them on the sidewalk." I hung up before she could argue.

The hospital was six blocks away, so I had like zero time. The one small blessing was that the kid had put his clothes back on before he took the pills, so I thought, *At least it won't be obvious what we were up to.* I forgot that *I* wasn't dressed ... I wrapped him in a blanket and used it to drag him—no way could I carry him—and on the way out of the bedroom I bumped into the dresser. A bunch of stuff fell off, including a Valium that he'd missed. I popped that right away, thinking I was definitely going to need it.

I dragged him out the door and down three flights of stairs. I must've banged up his legs and his tailbone pretty bad, but there was nothing I could do about that—I was busy making sure he didn't hit his head, and at every landing I had to stop and check that he hadn't swallowed his tongue. Then one landing from the bottom I heard this click, an apartment door opened up, and this old Ukrainian lady who was always giving me dirty looks came out to see what the racket was about. And I, I was beyond reason at this point, I just smiled at her and said something like: "Allergy attack ... Doctor's on his way ... Nothing to worry about!" She made this little, like, *warding* gesture with her hands, and shut the door again.

So I got the kid down to the lobby—my back was *killing* me by now—and of course the ambulance was already outside, and the paramedics were talking to the super of the building across the street. I dragged the kid out onto the stoop and started shouting, "Hey, over here!" and as everybody turned to look, I felt this breeze, and that's when I realized, I was still wearing nothing but my kimono, and it was flapping open in front, and I'm like, *Oh great.*

The paramedics came running. They got the kid unwrapped, started checking him over, and we did another Q&A: "What did he take? What did he take?" One of the paramedics, he was all about saving the kid, and I liked that, that he barely even looked at me. The other one though, he was older, beard stubble, he *did* look at me, and he was pissed. He said: "Why did you give the dispatcher the wrong address? Are you too high to remember where you live, or are you just scared?" And I'm like, "I don't live here," and he's like, "Yeah, *right.*"

Then the other paramedic—he'd been listening to the kid's heart with a stethoscope—said, "We've got to go, *now.*" So they put the kid on a stretcher, and I knew I should just shut up, be invisible, but as they were bundling him into the back of the ambulance, I said, "Is he going to be OK?" And the angry paramedic looked at me again, and said, "You want to come to the hospital with us? Or do you want to *hide*?" And I pinched the front of my kimono closed, and said, "I've got to get some clothes on …" And he's like: "Yeah, *right*."

They got into the ambulance, and as they were driving away, I saw the angry paramedic on the radio, talking to somebody, and I was like, if the Ukrainian lady hasn't called the police *already* …

I ran back upstairs and got dressed. I took a plastic bag and swept as much of the marijuana as I could into it, and hid it in the back of a closet along with my drug-stash box. Then I got out—I thought I heard a siren outside, so I left by the fire escape—and stayed out.

I called Carlotta and asked if it was OK if I came a few days early. She said sure, so I got a car, some boxes, and a little extra Valium, and after midnight I went back to my apartment to pack. I just took the essentials—I had to leave the furniture behind, but that was OK, most of it wasn't paid for anyway.

As I was packing, Phil showed up.

In the middle of the night?

Yeah, I told you, he had a knack for knowing when I needed him. "Phil," I said, "I think I really fucked up here." And he was like, "Yeah, I tried to warn you …" And then he just sat there, looking sad, which got me packing even faster. By sunup I was done, and by early that morning I was in Bodega Bay. End of story.

You never called the hospital to find out what happened to the boy?

It's not malfeasance if you behave like a decent human being. The way I thought about it was like this: aside from the Officer Friendly types, cops are generally lazy, and tracking me to Carlotta's would be difficult enough that they probably wouldn't go to the trouble unless the kid died. So it followed that if I *didn't* hear from the cops, he must be OK … And I never did hear from them. Even after I came back to S.F.—you know, I had other scrapes with the police after that, but the thing with the street preacher never came up. So I told myself I'd dodged a bullet, and swore I'd learned my lesson.

And had you?

Hey, after that day? It was a year and a half before I had sex with *anyone* again, and when I did, the guy was like thirty-five—a *mature* thirty-five.

So like I said, I counted myself lucky, and moved on. I tried to forget it had ever happened, you know? But Panopticon never forgets. They miss stuff, or misfile it, but if they know about it at all, they never really forget … And when the truth finally comes back around, all those excuses you thought were so clever end up sounding like the bullshit that they are.

So I finished my story and stood there staring at the video wall—it was all just Owen Farley's picture, now— while I waited for Dixon to pass final judgment. But Dixon was waiting too, looking my way but focused on a point a half inch in front of his right eye. The little computer screen flickered like mad, and my wrist was tingling so much my hand had gone numb.

And so finally I just blurted it out: "Did I kill him?"

"Kill him?" Dixon said. "That's an interesting choice of words."

"It's the right choice. You said it yourself, I was reckless. I knew better. So if he's dead, it's on me. If he's in a coma somewhere, or locked up in a psycho ward, that's on me too. I accept responsibility, OK? No excuses … Whatever you're going to do to me, just do it."

Seconds ticked by, and I felt another tingling, at the back of my head. I thought: that's where he's going to shoot me, the other Bad Monkeys operative who's sneaking up behind me even now, waiting for Dixon to give the nod. I tried to brace myself.

And then a cell phone rang, breaking the spell. Dixon pursed his lips in annoyance and slipped the phone from his pocket. "Yes?" he said. "Oh, it's you … I didn't realize you were monitoring the session … Yes, I'm looking at the results now. I'd have to call them inconclusive, but I was going to ... Really ... Really ... Is there some factor here that I'm not aware of? ... *Really* ... Well, it would have been helpful to know that before ... Yes, I understand ... Of course it's your call, but for the record, I still don't think it's wise to ... Yes ... Yes ... As you wish ..."

He snapped the phone closed, and then, turning, pressed a single key on the laptop. The computer screen went dark. The video wall went dark, too.

"You're free to go," Dixon said.

"What? But what about ... You never answered my question."

"Owen Farley is alive. No thanks to you."

"Is he OK, though? What happened to him? Is he—"

"Don't push your luck," Dixon said sharply.

"OK ... But when you say I'm free to go, does that mean ... Am I in the clear on this? Am I still in Bad Monkeys?"

"For now," Dixon said. "Unless ..."

"Unless?"

"Unless you have something else you'd like to confess."

"No." I hooked a finger under the wristband and popped it loose, then started massaging the feeling back into my hand. "No, that's OK. I'm done confessing for now."

"Then get out. And Jane?"

"Yeah?"

"I'll be *seeing* you ..."

white room (v)

"INTERESTING," THE DOCTOR SAYS.

"What is?"

"In addition to my duties here, I sometimes conduct interviews at a facility called Red Springs, out in the desert. It's—"

"A jail for sex predators," she says, her cheeks coloring. "I know. I saw a sign for it on my way into Vegas."

"*Violent* sex predators," he says, but the correction does nothing to soothe her indignation. "I've spoken to over a hundred of them now, and they break down into two main categories: sociopaths, and a second group I like to think of as *malefactors*."

Still flushed, she says: "Sociopaths are the ones who don't feel guilty."

"Very good. Most people think that sociopaths are the ones who can't tell right from wrong, but of course that's not true. They know the difference—enough to understand they have to hide what they do—they just don't care about it."

"Bad monkeys."

"Oh, the malefactors are bad monkeys, too—and in some ways, they're harder to take. Sociopaths are like Martians: their moral indifference is very strange, but at least their behavior is consistent with it. Malefactors, on the other hand, possess a normal sense of conscience. They experience guilt, and are capable of remorse. But they don't let any of that stop them.

"Which brings me to my point," the doctor says. "Another way of distinguishing sociopaths from malefactors is through the types of lies they tell. Sociopaths lie to other people. Malefactors do that too, but first they lie to themselves. In order to justify their actions, they often construct very elaborate fantasy scenarios ..."

Her ire finally dissipates. She snorts. "So this is your new theory? I dreamed up the organization to help cope with my repressed guilt about the pet boys?"

"You think it's a silly idea?"

"That Dixon was some kind of enabler? Yeah, I do think it's silly. If you'd met him, you'd know why."

"He did clear you."

"No, he didn't." She starts to get angry again. "Did you not get the point about the phone call? Dixon didn't clear me. Dixon wanted to burn me. At the very least he wanted me kicked out of Bad Monkeys, and if he could have sent me someplace like Red Springs, that would have made his day."

"But that isn't what happened."

"Because Cost-Benefits overruled him."

"So you were cleared. By very smart, well-informed people."

"But why would I do it that way? If I were just imagining the whole thing to ease my guilt, why would I put myself through the wringer? Why not just have Dixon say, 'Hey, so you crossed a line, it's no big deal.'"

"Because you don't believe that," the doctor says. "You think it is a big deal. And before you could accept absolution, you wanted—needed—to be taken to task for what you'd done."

"You've got it all figured out, huh?"

"Not all. By your own account, your involvement with the organization goes back long before your involvement with the pet boys. And while you may have been carrying a significant amount of guilt over what happened to Owen Farley, I doubt that incident alone was enough to give rise to such an elaborate coping mechanism. It's too little, too late. So that leaves me with the same question Dixon had: Is there something else you'd like to confess?"

"*No,*" she says firmly, and then again: "No." She leans back in her chair and looks away; her lips move as if to shape the word "no" a third time.

But what actually comes out—after a long pause, and in tones so low as to be barely audible—is: "Not yet."

Scary Clowns, Shibboleths, and the Desert of Ozymandias

AFTER MY RUN-IN WITH DIXON, I didn't get another Bad Monkeys assignment for almost three months. I knew from what Annie had told me during training that that kind of downtime wasn't necessarily unusual, but under the circumstances I couldn't help worrying about it.

Did you think you'd been fired after all?

No, I knew it wasn't that—I could still get Catering on the phone anytime I wanted, they just didn't have anything for me. Then when I asked to speak to True, they kept telling me he was unavailable, and so from that I got the idea that maybe he was upset.

About what? The pet boys?

More likely this other thing I'd done. Back at that rooftop buffet meeting, right before he left, True had warned me not to take Dr. Tyler's case into my own hands: "I know you'll be tempted, especially once your Malfeasance interview is out of the way, but don't do it. Julius Deeds was strike one; Annie Charles was strike two; I trust I don't need to tell you what happens after strike three."

Of course this meant I had to quit my job at the nursing home. Maybe I'm the biggest hypocrite in the universe, but I just didn't trust myself to rub shoulders with

that sicko every night and *not* do something. So I quit,
but then during my last shift I broke into Tyler's office
again and found that Catholic school-uniform catalogue
he kept hidden in his filing cabinet, and left it on his
desk. It wasn't anything that'd get him into trouble if
someone else saw it, but I knew that he'd know that
somebody was on to him.

And what did you hope to accomplish by doing that?

Christ, talk about a Bob True question. I don't *know*
what I hoped to accomplish; I just *did* it, OK? But because of Eyes Only, Panopticon knew I'd done it, and
I'm sure they told True, and if it wasn't bad enough to
count as strike three, still, I'd disobeyed a direct order.
So I figured the lack of assignments might be True's way
of punishing me: unofficial suspension.

Meanwhile, Dixon kept dropping hints that he was
still on my case. I got another floor-sweeping gig at this
office building on the waterfront. It was a lot quieter
than the nursing home, just me and a security guard,
which should have been great: no boss, whole place
practically to myself, plus the vending machine on the
top floor had this glitch where if you hit the buttons
just right, you'd get two sodas for the price of one. But
I started getting creeped out. The company that owned
the building imported bobblehead dolls from Taiwan,
and those freaking things were everywhere, not just
watching me but *nodding* at me. It got so I couldn't go
more than half an hour without running down to the
security station to calm my nerves.

One night I went in there and the guard had his TV
on. *The Graduate* was playing. Not just any part of *The
Graduate*, either—the first thing I saw coming in the
room was Anne Bancroft putting her stockings on for
Dustin Hoffman. So I'm like, "Can I change this?", and
the guard shrugged and said sure, so I flipped channels, into the middle of another bedroom scene: Bud
Cort lying next to Ruth Gordon in *Harold and Maude*.

So I flipped channels *again*, and it was a commercial, and I was like, OK, but then the announcer's voice said, "Coming up next on A&E, *The Mary Kay Letourneau Story* ..."

And you thought this was Dixon's way of taunting you? By manipulating the TV schedule?

If it had just been the once, I might have put it down to coincidence. But after that, whenever I got near a television ... I mean, I know they like to repeat stuff on cable, but how many times can they cycle through the same handful of shows?

And it wasn't just TV. I started noticing little digs in the radio playlist, too. I'd be in the shower, singing along with KFOG, and all at once I'd be like, oh, "The Kids Are All Right," are they? And if it wasn't the song itself, it was the band ... The Pet Shop Boys. Remember the Pet Shop Boys? They dropped off the charts, what, a decade ago? But suddenly they were in heavy rotation again.

Michael Jackson too, I suppose.

Don't even get me started on Michael Jackson. If I never hear "Billie Jean" again in this life ...

So what did you do about this ... harassment?

At first I tried to ignore it; when that didn't work, I went back to popping Valium. That helped for a while, but then Dixon started to play nasty. One day in the grocery checkout I realized I'd forgotten to get butter, and when I ran back to the dairy case, someone had turned all the milk cartons so that the missing-kid photos were face-out. They were all boys, and all looking at me with these disappointed expressions.

That was just too much. I mean, *Harold and Maude*, OK, that was funny in a demented sort of way, but this, to me, this was no joke.

So next I got this idea that I should leave town again. It didn't really make sense, because Dixon's jurisdiction wasn't limited the way the SFPD's is—Malfeasance is everywhere. But it was all I could think to do at that point.

What made you choose Las Vegas as a destination?

It wasn't my choice. Where I *wanted* to go was the Pacific Northwest, Seattle or maybe Portland. I figured it'd be a nice change of climate, plus that part of the country is Mecca for serial killers, so I knew I'd have lots of work once True let me out of the doghouse. But it turned out True had other plans for me.

I went to this travel agency that specialized in helping people plan moves, and asked for some info on Washington and Oregon. The woman behind the desk looked at me like I was nuts. "The economy up there is terrible right now. Have you thought about Nevada?"

"Nevada?"

"Las Vegas is booming. It's one of the only cities in the country that hasn't been hurt by the recession. They're building thousands of new homes a month."

"Sorry, I'm not interested."

"No, really, you should think about it. Just wait here, Jane, let me get you some literature ..." She went into a back room, and I got the hell out of there. I hadn't told her my name.

Back at my apartment, I gulped down three Valium and turned on the TV. I'd programmed it to skip over stations that showed movies or sex-offender trials, which didn't leave a whole lot. Can you guess what the theme on the Travel Channel was that night?

Las Vegas?

Three shows in a row. You'd almost think the L.V. chamber of commerce was paying the network to advertise. And then when I clicked over to ESPN, they were covering a poker tournament at Binion's Casino.

I switched off the TV and picked up the phone.

"Jane Charlotte."

"Yeah, I'm calling for Bob True again. Tell him I got the message."

"Look behind you."

I turned around to see True coming out of my kitchen. "What's in Las Vegas?" I asked him.

"An operation we believe you'd be perfect for."

"You don't have anything perfect someplace nicer?" True just arched an eyebrow, as if to say, *You want me to cut you off for* another *three months?* "Yeah, OK," I said. "So what is it?"

"The details will be given to you by your handler after you arrive."

"You're not supervising me on this one?"

"I'll be along later, but during the initial phase of the operation, you'll be working with a colleague of mine named Robert Wise."

"Is everyone in Cost-Benefits named Bob?"

"Wise isn't with Cost-Benefits," True said. "He's a Scary Clown."

"You're teaming me with a Clown? What kind of op is this?"

"It's not the nature of the operation so much as its location. The Scary Clowns consider Las Vegas to be their fiefdom, and they are extremely territorial. It's not really possible for us to run an operation there without including them. But don't worry, Wise is a good man. He's … much less random than some of the others."

"Great. So when do I leave?"

"We need you ready to go by Thursday. Catering will handle the travel arrangements."

"OK. I'm going to need some money, though. The bobblehead people aren't going to give me a paid vacation, and I'm already way behind on my rent."

"Yes, I know. I was just coming to that." He handed me a Jungle Cash ticket that had already been scratched off.

"Um, True," I said, looking at the prize amount. "This is too little."

"It's enough for a long-term storage locker. A small one. You don't have that many possessions."

"You want me to give up the apartment?"

"Weren't you planning to do that anyway?"

"Well yeah, but ... How long is this Vegas operation supposed to last? I mean, does it make sense for me to burn all my bridges here?"

True held up the crumpled eviction notice that he'd fished out of my kitchen garbage can. "I'd say this bridge is already blazing, wouldn't you?"

I put my stuff in storage. I stopped by the bobble-head company, intending to give my notice, and instead managed to talk this guy in payroll into giving me two weeks' pay in advance. Then I called Black Helicopters, the subdivision of Catering in charge of transport. Even though I should have known better, I was honestly expecting them to fly me to Vegas. Hah.

"At five p.m. this evening," the voice on the phone said, "go stand in the parking lot outside the Safeway supermarket in Pacific Heights. Someone will park within sight of you and leave their keys in the ignition."

"What kind of car will it be?"

"At five p.m. this evening, go stand in the parking lot outside the Safeway supermarket in Pacific—"

"Yeah, yeah, I got that. But how will I know it's the right car?"

"The license plate will have an even number."

It was almost six by the time a black SUV pulled into the Safeway lot, driven by a mother with two kids; the kids were screaming at each other, which gave their mom a perfect pretext to forget her car keys. The SUV's license number ended in an 8, and it was a Nevada plate, which I thought pretty much clinched it—but just in case, I waited until Mom had dragged the kids into the store before making my move.

I found a Mobil credit card in the glove compartment

and used it to top off the tank. Then I blew town. As I drove south, I thought about the Scary Clowns.

The Clowns are the remnant of another secret society that got taken over by the organization way back in the day. They specialize in psychological ops: mind-fucking for the greater good. Like everybody else, they're supposed to answer to Cost-Benefits, but because of their special history they're actually semiautonomous, and their insistence on playing by their own rules creates a lot of headaches for the bureaucracy.

What sort of headaches?

Well, one of the things that distinguishes the Clowns is that they're a lot less publicity-shy than the other divisions. They consider urban legends a form of tradecraft. It's how they got their nickname.

I don't recall an urban legend about scary clowns.

It was a variation on the old Men in Black gag. Used to be, when the organization got wind of a predator operating in a small town or a suburb, they'd send in a bunch of guys in freaky clown makeup to drive around and menace the locals. The idea was to raise awareness, get people to lock their doors and stop trusting strangers, until Bad Monkeys could eliminate the threat. It was a pretty effective gimmick, but they had to stop doing it after this one clown actor named Gacy got a little too into his role.

John Wayne Gacy was an organization operative?

Not one of the better ones, but yeah. He'd worked in Panopticon before switching to psy-ops, so he knew how to spoof Eyes Only surveillance; that's how he managed to rack up so many bodies without getting caught. And then when the cops nailed him, before the organization could? You can bet heads rolled in Malfeasance over *that* screwup.

Anyway, after that, they quit using the Scary Clown gimmick—mostly—but the name stuck.

So this was the group I was going to be working with. You can see why I felt kind of ambivalent about it. The job wasn't likely to be boring, but if I drew the wrong psycho for a partner, I might find myself wishing I was back with the bobbleheads.

I stopped in Bakersfield for a late dinner. Not long after I got back on the highway, the gas gauge, which had been telling me I still had almost a third of a tank left, suddenly dipped into the red zone. Fortunately there was a Mobil sign at the next exit.

The Mobil station was in a one-stoplight mountain town that had rolled up its sidewalks hours earlier. Coming down the main drag, I got a weird vibe. The street was deserted, but the kind of deserted you see in a horror movie, right before the zombies start coming out in droves. I'd been planning on pumping my own gas, but when I got to the station I pulled up to the full-service island instead.

The gas-station attendant wore a hooded sweatshirt that hid his face in shadow. "Chilly night," he said, when I cracked the window. "Would you like to come inside for some coffee?"

"No thanks. Just fill it up with unleaded."

I kept an eye on him while he pumped the gas. As he was putting the gas cap back on, he did this funny ten-second freeze with his head cocked, like he'd just heard a branch breaking out in the dark somewhere.

Then he was back at my window: "You sure you don't want that coffee?"

"Positive."

"It's *really* good." He tilted his head, and his right arm started twitching. "*Trust* me, you'll be *very glad* you tried it."

"Sorry, I'm a Mormon. Caffeine even touches these lips, I go straight to hell." I made my own twitching motion with the credit card, and reluctantly he took it from me. He went into his office and stood just inside the door, tapping his feet. Then he came back out again.

My NC gun was stuffed in a brown paper bag next to my seat. I reached for it as the attendant came around to my window for the third time.

"This card's no good," he told me.

"Oh yeah?" I said, slipping the gun off safe. "I hear it works a lot better if you actually run it through the machine."

"It's *no good*." His whole body was jerking violently to one side now.

"OK, give it back to me then. I'll pay cash."

"It's against the rules for me to give it back. I'm going to need you to *come inside* with me."

"Yeah, right."

"Miss—"

"You want to keep the card, go ahead and keep it. But I'm not going anywhere with you."

"Miss, *please* ..."

I came this close to shooting him. But as he leaned in to plead with me, I finally got a glimpse of his face, and saw that he was scared silly. And then—probably because I was already in a horror-movie frame of mind—it occurred to me that I'd heard this story before somewhere.

"Tell me something," I said. "Are you acting weird because there's a guy with an ax crouched behind my back seat?"

The gas-station attendant blinked. "You *know* him?"

"Well, we haven't been formally introduced, but I'm pretty sure his name is Bob."

"Oh," the attendant said. "OK. I'll just go run your card, then ..."

He went back into the office; I looked in my rearview mirror. "Robert Wise, I presume?"

"If I weren't," Wise said, "you'd be dead. Or wishing

you were." He got up, and despite the tough talk and the double-bitter in his hands, my first impression was that he wasn't all that scary. He didn't look like an ax murderer; he looked like an army ranger who'd gotten lost on his way to chop some firewood.

"How long have you been back there?" I asked him. "Since Bakersfield?"

"Does it matter?"

"I just want to know how cranky you are. If you've been sitting on the floor all the way from S.F., your butt must be pretty sore by now."

"You're funny," said Wise. "True mentioned you were funny." Then he said, "Wait here," and got out.

I watched him walk towards the gas-station office, ax swinging at his side. As Wise came in the door, the attendant looked up from the credit-card machine and started to raise his hands. Then the office lights went out.

Two minutes passed. Wise reappeared, minus his ax. He trotted back to the SUV and got into the front passenger seat. "Here," he said, handing me the credit card.

"Uh ... What did you just do?"

"Don't worry about it."

"What did you do, Wise?"

"I'll tell you later. Right now, we need to get away from here." He glanced at his wristwatch. "Sometime in the next forty-two seconds would be good."

The wristwatch glance stopped me from arguing. I put the SUV in gear and drove, counting "one one thousand, two one thousand," under my breath. When I got to "forty-two one thousand," bright light flared in the rearview.

I took a hand off the wheel and reached for my NC gun. The paper bag was empty.

"That's all right, Jane," Wise said. "I'll hang on to the weapon for now. You just concentrate on driving. And don't worry about that guy back there—he had it coming, I promise."

"What the *hell*—"

"Just drive."

I drove. Wise didn't speak again until we were in Nevada. A few miles past the state line, he had me leave the highway for an unpaved road that snaked north into the desert.

"We're not going to Vegas tonight?"

"No. My place."

The road ended at a fenced compound whose gate opened automatically for us. Wise directed me inside, to a long, low, warehouse-style building with a sign that read LAWFUL GOOD PRESS. As soon as I'd parked, he took the keys.

"It's OK," I told him. "I'm not going anywhere. I'm too tired."

"Yeah, well, this way I don't have to worry about you driving off in your sleep."

"What if I walk off in my sleep?"

"There are coyotes," said Wise. "So don't."

I followed him into the warehouse, to a musty room where a cot had already been set up for me. "Bathroom's straight back if you need it," he said. "Other than that, if you get an urge to snoop around—"

"I know. Coyotes."

I woke up in the morning to a vision of swastikas. To the left of my cot was a bookcase labeled ARYAN LITERATURE, filled with display copies of books with titles like *A Hoax Called Auschwitz* and *The Illustrated Protocols of the Elders of Zion*. I got up, rubbing sleep from my eyes, and checked out the other bookcases lining the room, each with its own subject: White Supremacy; Black Supremacy; Religion; Firearms and Silencers; Knife-Fighting and Martial Arts; Bomb-Making; Biological Warfare; Torture Techniques; Confidence Games; Phony I.D.

and Identity Theft; Computer Hacking; Money-Laundering and Tax Evasion; Stalking; Revenge.

I'd wandered over to Bomb-Making and was leafing through *The Patriot's Cookbook: A Step-by-Step Guide to Brewing Explosives and Chemical Weapons at Home* when Wise came into the room. He was showered and shaved, and in a much mellower mood than the night before. "Found something you like?"

"Lawful Good Press," I said. "Is that a joke?"

"I don't know. Are you laughing?"

I held up *The Patriot's Cookbook.* "Is *this* a joke?"

"It's no substitute for a college chemistry degree, if that's what you're asking."

"The recipes don't work?"

Wise made a seesawing motion with his hand. "The quality of the information varies. The smoke- and stink-bomb recipes are pretty solid; the ones for TNT and plastique, not so much."

"What about this one?" I pointed to a line in the table of contents that read, "Sarin Gas."

"Look at the equipment list."

I did. "What's a Gallinago flask?"

"A very specialized piece of hardware—so specialized, it doesn't actually exist. But if you ask for it at a chemical-supply house, or try to search for it on the Internet, bells go off in Panopticon."

"Are the books bugged, too?"

"Some of them. Eyes Only on selected volumes, plus Library Bindings on some of the hate litera-ture. And of course we keep a mailing list." He took a remote control from his pocket and pointed it at the picture of the Reichstag that hung above the Aryan Lit. bookcase; the picture slid aside, revealing a computerized map of the U.S. covered in blinking points of light. "Green dots are customers we believe to be harmless—people who think it's cute to have *How to Find Your Ex-Wife* as bathroom reading copy.

Red dots are customers who want to do damage. Yellow dots, we're not sure yet."

"Lot of red dots around Vegas right now," I observed.

"Yeah, we noticed that too. But here, take a look at this ..." He pressed another button on the remote, and all the dots vanished except for one in southern California. A picture and a name appeared at the bottom of the screen. "Recognize him?"

"The gas-station attendant."

"He had some unfortunate ideas about anthrax and the U.S. Postal Service."

"If he was a bad monkey, shouldn't I have taken care of him?"

"Well, if you'd bothered to check the back of your vehicle for stowaways, we would have had time to discuss that. As it was, it just seemed simpler to handle him myself. Plus I really was feeling pretty cranky. You hungry?"

Besides the printing press and bindery, the building had a full industrial kitchen. I sat at a stainless-steel counter making small talk while Wise cooked me breakfast.

"So how'd you end up a Clown?" I asked him. "I mean, axwork aside, you seem like a normal guy."

"Don't let the haircut fool you," Wise said. "I was originally in intel, but when I came out here to start up the Press, the head of the Scary Clowns made me an offer."

"Panopticon to Clown seems like a popular career path. Did you know—"

"Gacy?" Wise shook his head. "Before my time."

"What about a guy named Dixon? You ever cross paths with him?"

"You could say so. I was his Probate officer."

"You *trained* Dixon? ... So does that mean you were in Malfeasance?"

"No, regular Panopticon. Dixon was too at first, but he was bucking for a Malfie post from day one."

"Did you like him?"

"He was a good student. A little overzealous, maybe. Why, what's he to you?"

"He's running my background check."

Wise laughed. "I bet that's fun."

"Thrilling. Listen, maybe you can explain something to me: when Dixon called me in for an interview, I had to wear this wristband ..." I described it to him.

"Sounds like a shibboleth device," Wise said.

"What's a shibboleth?"

"It's from the Book of Judges in the Old Testament. The men of Gilead went to war against the men of Ephraim, and the Ephraimites got slaughtered. When the survivors tried to pass themselves off as members of another tribe, their accents gave them away: Ephraimites couldn't pronounce the 'sh' sound, so when they said the word 'Shibboleth,' it came out 'Sibboleth.'"

"And a shibboleth device ...?"

"Same basic idea. It's a tool for sorting good monkeys from bad monkeys."

"By the way they talk?"

"By the way they feel. The device tests for inappropriate emotional responses. Like, someone tells you your mother died, and you're happy instead of sad. Or someone makes you talk about this shameful thing you did, only you're not ashamed." He laughed again. "You look worried. Don't be. I don't know what went on between you and Dixon, but if he had any serious doubts about you, you wouldn't be here. This operation's too important."

"What is the operation, anyway?"

He handed me a silver medical bracelet like the kind epileptics wear. On one side was a cluster of Egyptian hieroglyphs over the legend OZYMANDIAS LLC. On the other side was an inscription:

in case of death
keep body cool & call
1-800-EXTROPY
for further instructions

$50,000 cash reward

"You know what cryogenics is?" Wise asked.

"Sure. It's where they put you on ice until doctors can invent a cure for whatever killed you. I didn't know there was a rewards program, though."

"That's the deluxe version. The goal is to get the cadaver into cryostasis as quickly as possible, to minimize postmortem decay."

"Let me guess: this is one of those clever-sounding ideas that turns out not to be."

"There *is* a contradiction," said Wise, "between wanting to live forever, and offering a cash bounty for the discovery of your corpse." He passed me a stack of what looked like baseball cards. But the pictures were of both men and women, and the stats on the back weren't sports-related. "These are all the customers of the Ozymandias Corporation who've died within the past six months."

I counted thirteen cards. "How big is their client list?"

"Not that big. Going by the average of previous six-month periods, there should be two cards in that stack at most."

"So someone's killing them off for the bounty money … But wouldn't that be kind of hard to get away with? I mean, you'd think the company would get suspicious when the same person kept claiming all the rewards."

"The bodies were all discovered by different people," Wise said, "and there's no obvious connection between any of the discoverers. But we believe a connection exists."

"So it's an organized racket? Murder for profit?"

"Profit, and one other motive."

"What?"

"Evil. We believe the killers' ultimate goal—after making as much money as possible—is to attract the attention of the police."

"Aren't the police already paying attention?"

"Not yet. But their involvement is inevitable if the deaths continue at this rate—and the first thing they'll do when they launch their investigation is order an autopsy of all the bodies."

I thought about it. "Autopsies mean thawing them out ..."

"Thawing them out, and cutting them up."

"So not only are they dead before their time, they lose their shot at resurrection."

"You find that amusing?"

"Well no, I think it's horrible, but ... come on. The whole cryogenics thing is bullshit anyway, right?"

"Yeah, like organ transplants. Or cloning."

"OK," I said, not wanting to argue the point, "OK, back up, I still don't understand why the police aren't already investigating this. If thirteen people were *murdered*—"

"You didn't look closely enough at the stats."

I shuffled through the cards again. "Cause of death: heart attack ... Cause of death: heart attack ... Cause of death: stroke ... Cause of death: heart attack ..." I looked up. "Are you guys missing an NC gun?"

"Along with its owner." He laid one more card on the counter.

"Jacob Carlton."

"Former Good Samaritan, transferred to Bad Monkeys in 1999. He disappeared last June during an operation in Reno. Originally the thinking was he'd been taken out by the guy he was hunting, but now it looks like there's another explanation."

"So how do we find him?"

"We believe Carlton has taken a job inside the Ozymandias Corporation. Panopticon's been trying to bug
their headquarters for weeks, but the surveillance equipment keeps malfunctioning. You and I are going to go in
there today, posing as clients."

The Ozymandias facility was another forty miles out
in the desert. "If they're in such a hurry to freeze people,"
I asked, as we drove across the wasteland, "wouldn't it
make more sense to build the place in town?"

"Zoning regulations," Wise said vaguely.

"They have those in Vegas?"

The first sign we were getting close was a shimmer
of color on the horizon. I thought it was a heat mirage,
but within another mile the shimmer had resolved itself
into a green circle with a white building at its center.

A big cargo helicopter came screaming overhead as
we passed through the gardens of Ozymandias to the
visitor parking lot. The helicopter touched down just
east of the building, and a team of guys in moon suits
came running to unload a silver body bag and hustle it
inside.

"OK, so what's our cover?"

"We're married," said Wise. He handed me a ring.
"Mr. and Mrs. Doe."

"Jane Doe? Yeah, that's not suspicious."

"Don't worry about it. When we get inside, I'll be
doing the talking. You just nod your head and keep your
eyes peeled for Carlton." He opened the glove compartment and brought out my NC gun. "One more thing,
we'd like to get him alive if we can."

"No problem." I set the gun's dial to NS, narcoleptic
seizure.

Coming in the building we got hit with a blast of arc-
tic air, like the company wanted to let us know right
away it could deliver. We went to the reception desk,
where a woman in four layers of wool printed us badges
and told us a Dr. Ogilvy would be right with us.

Ogilvy reminded me of Ganesh. There wasn't much of a physical resemblance—except that he was small, and looked like he'd be easy to beat up—but he had a nervousness about him, and also a sadness, like this wasn't the career he'd planned on having. Once he'd introduced himself and got his game face on, though, he was pretty peppy. "Well, Mr. and Mrs. Doe, thank you so much for coming out here today! Let's go back to my office and talk about what Ozymandias can do for you!"

Ogilvy's office had a big bay window that looked out on an acre of fruit trees and flower bushes. The greenbelt was shot through with rainbows from an automated sprinkler system, and if I'd had a tab of acid I could have stared at it all day. But Ogilvy didn't offer us any drugs, just comfy chairs and tea. Then he got down to business: "I understand you're interested in purchasing one of our life-extension plans."

I must have looked like I was going to make a crack, because Wise laid a hand on my arm before answering, "Yes."

"And will this be for both of you, or ...?"

"Neither," Wise said.

"Neither." Ogilvy's eyebrows went up and down a few times. "Is it a gift, then? We do have gift packages, it's actually fairly common, or well, not *common*, but ... For the friend who has everything, or a valued employee about to retire ..."

"It's for our son."

"Oh! Oh, I see. Your son ...?"

"Philip."

"I see. And how old is Philip?"

"He's ten."

"And is he ... ill?"

"He was in an accident. He was playing outside, and his sister was supposed to be watching him, but ... Well, you know how kids are. She got distracted."

"Oh, how terrible."

"It's not her fault, really. She should never have been given that responsibility. If anyone's to blame, it's my wife and I."

"Oh no," said Dr. Ogilvy. "No, don't think that way! These things, you know, they just happen sometimes."

"Anyway, Phil's in the hospital now, in intensive care, and we're praying that he'll pull through, but if he doesn't ... We want to be ready."

"Of course. Of course."

"So what we'd like," Wise concluded, "is to have a look around your facility, here, and maybe meet some of your people ..."

"Of course! I'd be happy to give you a tour right now! Let's—" The phone rang, and Dr. Ogilvy started. "Oh dear! I'm sorry ..." Peering closer at the blinking light that accompanied the ringing: "Hmm, line three, I'm sorry, you know I really should take this ... Would you mind if—"

"It's fine," I said, getting up. "We'll wait for you outside."

I practically dragged Wise from the room. As soon as we were out the door, I lit into him: "What the hell was that about?"

"What was what about?"

"Our son *Phil*? Who had an *accident*? While his *sister* was watching him?"

Wise was blank-faced. "I have no idea what's eating you. Everything I said in there was part of a script. I'm just following it."

"What script?"

"The one Cost-Benefits gave me for this op. You think I make this stuff up as I go along?"

"Who in Cost-Benefits—"

"All right then!" said Dr. Ogilvy. "Are we ready for the tour?"

We headed down the hall towards our first stop, with me still staring daggers at Wise. Meanwhile Ogilvy, either because he'd picked up on the tension or because it was part of his standard sales pitch, launched into a rambling explanation of the company name: "It's from the poem by Percy Shelley."

"Ozymandias, King of Kings," said Wise. "'Look on my works, ye mighty, and despair.'"

"Yes! That's the one. And of course, 'my works,' that's meant to be ironic, since as the poem goes on to say, there's actually nothing left of those works, other than the inscription that brags about them. Which, given what we do here, may seem like a strange allusion to be making. But you see, there's actually a double irony, because it turns out Shelley picked on the wrong king. At the time he was writing, 1817, I believe, Egyptology hadn't gotten off the ground yet, so one pharaoh was as obscure as any other. Today, though, thanks to science, things are very different. Ozymandias—aka Ramses the Great—is not only one of the most famous rulers in history, but we know, contrary to what Shelley wrote, that a lot of his works *did* survive."

"So what's the point?" I interrupted, not wanting to fall asleep before I had a chance to finish grilling Wise. "Don't speak too soon?"

"Exactly!" said Dr. Ogilvy. "*Exactly.* Don't speak too soon! And we believe a similar caution applies to what we're doing here. Our industry, Mrs. Doe, perhaps I don't have to tell you this, but it has its share of skeptics. Some people, I won't call them ignorant, but some ... *uninformed* people, think cryogenics is, well—"

"A load of crap?"

"—a fantasy. An optimist's pipe dream ... But the same thing has been said about a lot of scientific advances."

"Like organ transplants," I said. "Or cloning."

"Yes! Yes! You *do* understand. What one generation mocks, the next takes for granted. And I promise you, Mrs. Doe—we'll pray for your son, of course we will, and we'll hope for the best—but even if the worst happens, he won't be lost forever. I guarantee, we *will* bring Phil back ... And here we are!"

We'd come to a security door marked CRYOSTASIS A. Ogilvy swiped a keycard through a reader on the wall and the door slid open, hitting us with another blast of cold air.

I stepped inside, expecting a morgue-type setup, bodies filed away in lockers along the wall. Instead, Ozymandias' clients were arranged on freestanding racks, encased in tall metal cylinders like giant thermoses—what Dr. Ogilvy called "cryopods." There were six pods to a rack. They hung upright, but could swivel to a horizontal position for loading and unloading. At the far end of the room, a team of moon-suit guys—probably the same ones we'd seen on the helicopter pad—had just cranked a pod into the loading position; white vapor boiled out of it as they removed the end cap.

One series of racks held smaller containers, each about a third the size of a normal cryopod. I said: "Please tell me those aren't babies."

"Oh no," said Dr. Ogilvy. "Children are kept in Cryostasis B. This is an adults-only chamber. Those are heads. The, uh, budget option," he explained, wincing a little. "Not that there's anything wrong with that, you understand—once we have the means to reanimate a dead body, growing an entirely new one shouldn't be much harder. Personally, though, I'd rather not present a revival team with any *unnecessary* challenges."

Cryostasis B was almost identical to Cryostasis A, except that the racks were spaced farther apart to make room for padded benches. "For visitors," Dr. Ogilvy explained. "Friends and loved ones of our adult clients are welcome to visit at any time as well, but for reasons I'm sure you can appreciate, visits here in the nursery are much more common. Incidentally, purchase of a Platinum Lazarus or higher-premium plan entitles you

to unlimited shuttle service to and from McCarran
Airport ..."

Figuring it might blow our cover if I slugged him, I
stepped away while Ogilvy continued his pitch. I went
over to the nearest rack and pretended to examine one
of the pods.

A clanging noise caught my attention. I leaned sideways and looked around the rack to where a maintenance
hatch had just opened in the floor. Another moon-suit
guy climbed up out of it. As he turned to drop the hatch
cover back in place, I saw his face.

Jacob Carlton.

"Mrs. Doe?" Dr. Ogilvy said. "I was just telling your
husband something that I think you—"

"Be with you in a minute!" I drew my NC gun and
stepped quickly around the rack, but Carlton had vanished.

"Jane?" said Wise. "What is it?"

A loud *boom!* from beneath the floor shook the pods
in their racks. The lights flickered, and the steady hum
of air-conditioning and refrigeration units gave way to
a sick stutter.

"It's you-know-who!" I called to Wise. "I think he
just sabotaged the electricity!"

"What?" said Dr. Ogilvy. "Oh no, sabotage is impossible here, we have *excellent* security! And the power system has *two* backup generators."

On cue, a second explosion rocked the building. An
alarm sounded.

"Oh dear," said Dr. Ogilvy. "Perhaps we'd better—
urk!"

"Wise?" Gun at the ready, I stepped back around the
rack and saw the doctor lying facedown on the floor.
Wise, who'd dived for cover behind a batch of frozen
heads, mouthed the words *Over there* and pointed.

I made my way from rack to rack towards Carlton's
hiding place. I was nearly there when a third explo-

sion knocked out the last of the power. In the seconds
of pitch-blackness that followed, I heard running footsteps.

Battery-operated safety lights came on. I ducked
past the last rack in time to see an emergency-exit door
swinging closed. I shouted to Wise, "I'm going after
him," but when I reached the door I paused to look
back. The room was already noticeably warmer, and
wisps of vapor were curling off the cryopods.

I went through the door. A twisting corridor led me
back out to the main hallway, where I found two more
bodies on the ground, another doctor and a security
guard. The guard had gone down swinging, a nightstick
still clutched tightly in his fist. Right next to him on the
floor, nearly invisible in the amber glow of the safety
lights, was an orange pistol.

I tucked Carlton's NC gun in my waistband and followed the signs to the nearest exit. Carlton was stuck
there, his final escape from the building blocked by a
set of automatic doors that were no longer automatic.
You're supposed to be able to slide those things open
manually, but it helps to have both hands, and Carlton's
right arm hung limp, a casualty of the guard's nightstick. Now he'd pulled out a club of his own—a monkey
wrench—and was using it to bash out the door glass.
I snuck up behind him and waited until he'd removed
enough of the glass to give me a clear field of fire. Then
I put him to sleep.

A hot desert wind blew in through the shattered
door. Looking out, I realized that the power failure had
killed the garden's sprinkler system, so the plants were
doomed, too. But it wasn't the fruit trees I was worried
about.

"We blew it, didn't we?" I said, as Wise came up behind me. "They're all going to thaw out."

"I thought you didn't believe in the resurrection."
Wise crouched down, pulled the hood off Carlton's

moon suit, and laid a pair of fingers on Carlton's jugular. "God damn it! I told you we wanted him alive!"

"He is alive. He's just sleeping."

"Yeah, sleeping like those corpsicles back there."

"No ... I had it on stun, see?" I turned the gun to show him, but the dial was on the MI setting. "Oh shit ..."

"Oh shit what?"

"This must be his gun. I picked it up back there, and ... Christ, I must have confused it with mine."

"Good job."

"Look, I'm sorry. It was an accident."

"Yeah, you're prone to those, aren't you?" He stood up. "All right, let's get out of here."

"What about him?"

"Leave him. He's useless to us now."

"And what about ...?" I gestured in the direction of the cryostasis rooms.

"Nothing we can do."

"The organization doesn't have some kind of crack repair team that could get the power back online? What about the Good Samaritans, isn't this right up their alley?"

"Nothing we can do," Wise repeated. "Now come on." He stepped through the door into the dying garden. "We can't stay here."

white room (vi)

"ARE YOU READY TO TALK ABOUT what happened to Phil?" the doctor asks.

Yet another evidence folder lies open on the table, turned so she can read the top page of the police report inside. But she refuses to look at it. She hunches back in her chair, keeping her eyes downcast, fixed on the cuffed hands in her lap.

"Jane," the doctor prompts her.

"It's a free country," she finally says. "You talk about whatever you like."

"All right ... Let's start with what *didn't* happen. Your brother wasn't swept up in some comical marijuana raid. And despite what you seemed to be suggesting in our last session—"

"I didn't *suggest* anything."

"—he wasn't in an accident. Your mother thought *you* had done something to him—that's what she told the 911 operator when she first reported him missing, and it's why she attacked you in the police station. But she was wrong, too. According to witnesses, your brother left the community garden in the company of a man whose description matched that of a recently paroled felon, a convicted child molester and suspected child murderer named John Doyle.

"A child molester," the doctor says. "But I doubt the police would use that expression in front of a fourteen-year-old girl, particularly one who was wracked with guilt. They'd probably just refer to him as a bad man … or a bad monkey."

She still won't look up, but her lips curl in a bitter smile. "Theory number 257," she says. "Jane's psychotic break begins with euphemism."

"Well you tell me, Jane: is it just a coincidence that all your missions for the organization somehow involve threats to children or young men?"

She doesn't answer.

"Something else I found interesting …" He lays a hand on the folder. "The reporting officer: Buster Keaton Friendly. That really was his name … But you've been lying about yours, haven't you? Or at least, not telling the whole truth. Charlotte is your middle name. Your *full* name is Jane Charlotte—"

"Don't," she says, at last raising her eyes to meet his. "Just don't. That's *not* my name. She made that very clear."

"She?"

"My mother. Last thing she told me before she sent me packing, I wasn't ever to use that name again. Which was ridiculous, since it wasn't her name either, it was my goddamned father's, and she hated him almost as much as she hated me … But that didn't matter, she said. What mattered was it was Phil's name, so it couldn't be mine. She said she'd kill me if she ever caught me using it: 'I'll choke the life out of you,' quote unquote. So no, I wasn't lying."

"OK. But the story you first told me about your brother and the marijuana patch. You do acknowledge now that that was false."

Sighing: "Yeah, I acknowledge it."

"And the other encounters with your brother over

the years—his visits with you in Siesta Corta, and your relationship once you'd returned to San Francisco—"

"That stuff was all true."

"Jane ..."

"I mean, OK, he wasn't really there, but the conversations we had, the advice he gave me ... Look, I *knew* Phil. I might not have liked the little shit, but I knew him, he was my brother, and I know what kind of person he'd have grown up to be, if ... So those conversations I told you about, they were genuine. They were *accurate*."

"But he wasn't really there."

"Yeah, all right, no."

"Because he's dead."

"No!" She bristles. "That's *not* true."

"Jane ..."

"Even the police could never say that. They never found a body. They never found *anything*, and Doyle—"

"Jane, the man was implicated in the killing of two other children. I'm sure you want to believe your brother survived, but—"

"No! I mean, yes, I wanted to believe that, and for years belief was all I had, but now, now I *know*. Phil's alive."

"How do you know that?"

"For Christ's sake," she says, "what do you think this whole story I've been telling you is about?"

"You found your brother?"

"Yes."

"In Las Vegas."

"Yes ... Only I didn't find him, exactly, I mean I haven't *seen* him, but I know he's here. And I know what really happened to him."

"And what did happen to him?"

"Well, Doyle took him. That part's true. And it's probably also true that Doyle *wanted* to kill Phil, the same way he killed those other kids. But he wasn't allowed to."

"Who stopped him?"

"The other bad monkeys, of course."

"The *other* bad monkeys."

"The ones who put him up to it," she says. "The anti-organization. The Troop."

Bad Monkeys, Inc.

TRUE WAS WAITING FOR US AT A roadside diner just outside the Vegas city limits. A waitress with a name tag that read HI THERE! I'M JANE! took us to his booth, then hovered while Wise decided between the blueberry and the chocolate-chip pancakes. I spun my wheels, impatient to ask the question that had been gnawing at me for the past three days; but when the waitress finally left us alone, True beat me to the punch.

"It's time we had a talk about your brother," he said.

"Fine. Let's talk. Let's start with the fact that you know about him. You've known all along, haven't you?"

"Of course."

"And you never thought to mention it? Like when you were recruiting me, maybe? 'By the way, one of the reasons we think you'll be really good at hunting down scumbags is because one of them took your brother.'"

"That *is* one of the reasons we thought you'd be good at it, as a matter of fact."

"Then why not say anything?"

"If I'd told you we knew about your brother's kidnapping, you'd have wanted to hear what else we knew. Then I would have had to lie, which I don't like to do, or put you off, which would have made us all unhappy.

You're a difficult enough person to deal with when your wishes are being granted."

"Why would you have to lie to me?"

"To preserve operational security."

"You mean this operation? It's got something to do with Phil?"

"Yes."

"Then Phil is ... He's alive? He's OK?"

"He's alive."

I must have blanked out for a minute, because suddenly Jane the waitress was back with our breakfasts. When she started talking to Wise about syrup flavors, I gave her the eyes of death and said: "Fuck off. Now." She did, and I turned back to True: "Tell me everything."

True prodded one of the eggs on his plate with a fork, dimpling the yolk. "*Omnes mundum facimus,*" he said. "We all make the world ... And we, the organization, try to make it better. Have you asked yourself yet whether there might be *another* organization, devoted to the opposite goal?"

"What, a bunch of people trying to make the world worse? No. It wouldn't make sense."

The yolk broke and started bleeding over True's plate. "Why not?"

"What would they get out of it? I mean, OK, it can be fun to cause trouble, and there are people who get off on destruction in a big way, but you can't build an organization around that. When bad people work as a team, it's for something like money, or power."

"You're saying that evil is a means to an end, never an end in itself. But what if evil was more than just a label for antisocial behavior? What if evil was a real force working in the world, capable of drawing people to its service?"

"I already told you, I don't believe in God." Then, anxious to get to the point, I said: "But what do I know, right? You're saying this anti-organization exists?"

"It exists," True said. "We believe it has *always* existed, in one form or another. In its most recent incarnation, it styles itself the Troop."

"The Troop? Like a monkey troop?" I started to laugh, but then I remembered: "Arlo Dexter's notebook."

"Yes. Until we recovered the briefcase, we couldn't be sure it wasn't a coincidence, but it's clear now the Troop recruited Dexter."

"OK ... But what does this have to do with my brother?"

"Not everyone who joins the Troop does so willingly," True said. "The foot soldiers and support staff are volunteers, but in every case where we've positively identified a Troop leader, that person has turned out to have been abducted as a child."

"Hold on ..."

"The Bible says that if you train up a child in the way he should go, when he is old, he will not depart from it. It may be that the Troop shares that philosophy, and crafts its leadership from an early age in order to ensure loyalty. But we think the real reason they steal children and turn them into monsters is because it is such an awful thing to do."

"You're telling me my brother's a bad monkey? That's bullshit! Phil was a good kid."

"Of course he was. Corrupting a *bad* child wouldn't be nearly as evil an accomplishment ... Your brother *is* a high-level Troop member, working for their equivalent of Cost-Benefits."

"Well first of all, I don't believe you," I said. "And second of all, I haven't forgotten my job description. If you think I'm going to kill my own brother ..."

"We don't want you to kill him. We want you to help us find him."

"Right, so somebody *else* can kill him? Sorry, I pass."

"Your brother has grown up to be a very dangerous

individual, Jane. The Ozymandias operation—the murder of the clients, the sabotage of the facility—that was his handiwork."

"No it wasn't! That was *your* guy, Carlton."

"Jacob Carlton was seduced by the Troop," True said, "and perhaps we do share some responsibility for allowing that to happen. But he took his final orders from your brother."

"Right. But you don't want to *kill* Phil for that, you just—"

"We want him stopped. Your brother is one of the Troop's most effective strategists. Depriving them of his services would be a major achievement. But we—I—would like to accomplish something more. I'd like to try to save him."

"Save him ... You mean like deprogram him?"

True nodded. "I have to tell you up front that the odds of success are slim. What we know of Troop indoctrination methods suggests that they are very thorough and very difficult to break. Your brother may prefer death to redemption. But because he didn't choose the path he is on, redemption is still a possibility. I'd like to give him the chance."

"What if he doesn't go for it, though? Let's say I bring him in alive, and he tells you to stick your redemption. What then? You let him walk?"

"No. If he's truly beyond saving, we obviously couldn't let him go. But we don't have to execute him, either. We can keep him contained, indefinitely."

"You mean lock him up somewhere? I thought you didn't—"

"It's not our usual policy with irredeemables. It ties up resources and creates a security issue. But we can do it, if circumstances warrant. So what do you say, Jane? Will you help us try to save Phil?"

Of course I was going to say yes. I just needed a minute to let my brain catch up, to process everything I'd

been told. But I guess True read my hesitation as un-
certainty.

"There is another factor you may want to consider,"
he said. "We chose you for this operation because we
believe you are uniquely suited to draw your brother
out into the open."

"You think I'll make good bait, you mean."

"Yes. And there's already evidence that your brother
is moving to take that bait."

"What evidence?"

"The Ozymandias operation. I understand you were
upset about the script."

"That business about Wise and me having a son
named Phil? Yeah, I was upset."

"Yes, well, we didn't write that. The two of you *were*
meant to pose as man and wife, but the script we com-
posed in Cost-Benefits said nothing about a dying son
or a disobedient daughter."

"So someone rewrote the script before Wise got it …
And you think that someone was Phil?"

"More likely a deep-cover agent working on his be-
half."

"And what's his point? What's he trying to tell me?"

"Obviously he's aware you're working for us. This
could be his way of letting you know that he knows.
Perhaps he hopes to recruit you. Or …"

"Or?"

"You understand, the indoctrination process your
brother was subjected to would have been extremely
unpleasant. So while he may be a committed Troop
member now, that doesn't mean he's grateful for being
delivered into the Troop's hands in the first place."

"You're saying Phil's *mad* at me?"

"If he is, can you blame him?"

"I … No. No. But if he wants revenge, why wait until
now?"

"Perhaps he felt the life you were living before you

joined the organization was revenge enough. The point is this: we can't force you to accept this mission. But saying no to your brother, whatever he has planned, may not be so easy."

"Well, that works out just great for you, doesn't it?"

"Don't misunderstand. We're not going to abandon you to the Troop if you turn us down. But your best and safest course is to work with us on this ... There's also the matter of atonement. I don't know how much you care about that, but—"

"Atonement? I let Bad Monkeys Incorporated steal my brother, True. How do I atone for that?"

"By stealing him back. Will you do it?"

Like I even had a choice. "Where do we start?"

"With the man who took him. John Doyle."

"*He's* still alive?"

"Not for lack of trying on our part," True said. "In the weeks before he kidnapped your brother, Doyle was the target of a Bad Monkeys operation. He survived one execution attempt, and then, after abducting Phil, he disappeared completely. That was our first clue that he was more than just a lone predator. In the decades since, he's popped up periodically—usually on some mission for the Troop—only to vanish again before we could get to him. Then, a few days ago, Doyle checked into the Venetian Hotel on the Vegas Strip ..." True set a wrinkled newspaper, the *Las Vegas Tipster*, on the table. Under the headline CASINO GUEST AIDS IN MANHUNT was a face I'd last seen in a police mug shot twenty-three years ago. Doyle's hair was white now, and he'd lost some teeth, but there was no question it was him.

My palms were suddenly sweating. "When did you spot him?"

"Almost immediately," True said. "It is Sin City, after all: our surveillance coverage of the Strip is more comprehensive than the casinos' own. Also, he registered under his real name."

"Sounds like I'm not the only one being used as bait. You have his room number?"

"He's staying in one of the penthouse suites."

"OK, then. Let's go see him ..."

Wise, who'd been quietly eating his pancakes this whole time, put down his fork and cleared his throat. "Not so fast," he said. "Before you go to the Venetian, we need to make a stop at Harrah's."

"What for?" asked True, looking annoyed.

"Love wants to meet her."

"Who's Love?" I said.

"I thought we agreed we weren't going to have this sort of interference," said True.

"I don't know what *you* agreed to," said Wise, "but my orders come from the man himself. Love isn't happy with the way the Ozymandias op played out. Before we take this any further, he wants to be sure of her."

"And he couldn't have met with her yesterday, or the day before?"

"He's got a full schedule. This is when he had time."

"Who's Love?" I repeated.

"The Trickster-in-Chief," said True. "The leader of the Scary Clowns." To Wise: "Very well. We'll go see him."

"Not 'we.' Love wants to talk to her in private. You're welcome to wait in the casino, but she goes up to the Mudgett Suite alone."

At that point, True got more pissed off than I'd ever seen him. He bitched at Wise about how totally unacceptable this was. Wise listened impassively, like he knew True had to complain for the sake of form, even though it wasn't going to change anything.

A new waitress came to collect our plates. Once we'd settled the bill, Wise was in a hurry to get going, but when we got outside, I broke away from him and followed True to his car.

"What's this Mudgett Suite?" I asked him. "And what did Wise mean about Love wanting to be sure of me? Am I going to have to do another one of those shibboleth tests?"

"I don't know," True said, still steaming. "As you may have gathered, I wasn't consulted about this."

"Well OK then, let's just blow him off. Go straight to the Venetian."

"No. That won't work."

"Jane!" Wise called. "Come on!"

"True …"

"No." He shook his head firmly. "Go with him. I'll meet you afterwards."

I could see there was no point in arguing, so reluctantly I let him go. As I headed back to the SUV, I heard True get into his car, start the motor, and drive off. The sound of the engine was just beginning to fade with distance when the world changed color again.

I was far enough from the blast this time that I didn't fall down, just stumbled. When I caught my balance and looked back, I saw True's car rolling to a stop in the middle of the road, with all its windows gone and no one in the driver's seat.

I ran for the SUV. Wise had the door open and was reaching for something. He came out holding a fire ax. Then he dropped it and collapsed.

"Wise?" I crouched down to check on him, then looked up, sensing another presence. But the parking lot was empty.

And then it wasn't. Maybe five yards off to my left, the air seemed to shimmer, and this person just … *materialized*. It was Jane, the waitress. She'd swapped her work uniform for a pair of black jeans and a T-shirt silkscreened with a mandrill face, and she was holding an orange pistol.

I jumped up, raising my own gun to fire, but the air shimmered again, and suddenly she wasn't five yards away, she was right in my face. She slapped my gun aside. She punched me, two quick jabs that dropped me helpless to my knees. A hand cupped my chin, and a plastic pistol muzzle pressed against my forehead.

"Welcome to Las Vegas, Jane," she said. "Little brother sends his regards."

She pulled the trigger.

The world went away for a while. When it came back, I was lying in a morgue with my skull blown open. That was my first guess, anyway: I was stretched out on my back on a hard, cold surface; I was paralyzed, blind, and had a headache a hundred times worse than anything I'd ever experienced.

A couple centuries went by while I waited for someone to either cut my chest open or dump me into a coffin. Then the pain lowered a notch, and I could see again—not *well*, but enough to know that I still had eyes. The feeling came back in my arms, and I ran my hands over the thing I was lying on. It wasn't a metal slab. It was lumpy, and covered in some kind of stiff hide: a leather couch. I raised a hand to my scalp. It hurt, but it was still there.

Now that I knew my brains weren't going to fall out, I started to wiggle my head around experimentally. That's when I saw the clown. He was about nine feet tall. He wore a cone-shaped hat cocked to one side, and a frilly silk suit with a ruffed collar and cuffs. His face was painted white; there was a black teardrop under his left eye and a wicked red grin around his mouth. He stood just at the end of the couch, above and behind me, poised like he was about to bend down and take a bite out of my face.

The sight of him got me up. There was a blur of motion and pain, and then I was at the couch's far end, screaming at the top of my lungs. The screams drove needles into my brain, but the clown didn't react, just stood there leering at me, and around the time my voice gave out I realized he was a mannequin, set up on a wooden pedestal.

I panned my head around slowly, wary of more surprises. The room was lit by old-fashioned gas lamps, their flames set just high enough to throw shadows. The lamps weren't the only antique touch: the wallpaper, rugs, and most of the furniture looked like they could have come straight out of a Victorian-period shop. The only exception was a television, set up discreetly in a corner under a faded poster advertising something called the World's Columbian Exposition.

There were no windows. The only exit I could see was a set of double doors. I wanted to run to them, but to do that I'd have to go past the clown mannequin.

The TV came on, showing a blue screen. It cast more light than all the gas lamps combined, and by its glow I saw a figure sitting in the shadowy hollow of a wing chair. Something told me this *wasn't* a mannequin.

"*Phil?*" I whispered.

The figure leaned forward. Pebble-glass lenses flashed in the blue light. "Guess again."

"Dixon ... You work for the Troop?"

The lenses tilted as he cocked his head. "What an interesting question. I was just going to ask you the same thing."

"You mean you're a prisoner too?"

"A prisoner?"

"Yeah. Isn't this ... Where are we?"

"The Mudgett Suite."

"Scary Clown headquarters? In Harrah's?"

"This week."

"So the Troop didn't capture me? What happened, then? Why does my head hurt like this?"

"You were shot with an NC gun."

"Yeah, I know, but narcolepsy's not supposed to be painful."

"It isn't. You were poisoned by your own endocrine system. The effects are superficially similar to a drug overdose."

"What about Wise?"

"Dead at the scene. He was hit with an aortic dissection and bled out internally."

"NC guns don't have a setting for that."

"Organization NC guns don't," Dixon said. "And organization operatives don't typically plant Mandrill bombs in cars, or feed strychnine-laced apple pie to shadow security teams. Which brings us back to the question of your allegiance."

"You think *I* did it?"

"You're the only survivor of a small massacre. Color me suspicious."

"So I shot myself? With what?"

"When we found you, you were holding a Troop-issue NC gun. Your finger was still on the trigger."

"No. No way. That wasn't mine."

"Of course it wasn't ... Tell me, is there something wrong with your own weapon, that you keep ending up with other people's?"

"She must have planted it on me after she shot me ..."

"She?"

"Jane. The bad Jane, I mean."

"The bad Jane ... Let me guess, she only comes out when you're angry."

"She was a waitress, you asshole. In the diner ... She served us breakfast, but then she disappeared before the check came. She must have left ahead of us and planted the bomb in True's car. Then she came at me and Wise with the gun ... Please tell me Eyes Only caught some of this."

"The Eyes Only devices inside the diner all malfunctioned shortly before you arrived," Dixon said. "But we did manage to get some footage from outside."

A view of the parking lot appeared on the TV screen. It was a high-angle shot, probably from a billboard, centered on the SUV. Wise was standing at the driver's side, yelling my name ... There was an orange-and-yellow flash, followed by a burst of static, and then Wise reached for his ax. I ran into the frame. Now the way I remembered it, I was only drawing my gun at this point, but in the video, I already had it out, aimed straight ahead of me. Wise convulsed and fell down.

"Just wait," I said. "This isn't what it looks like ..."

On the screen, I crouched beside Wise's body, checked for a pulse, and then looked up.

"OK. Just watch, here she comes ..."

But the video cut out at that point and the blue screen returned, overlaid with the words TRANSMISSION IN-TERRUPTED.

"Oh, *come on*!" I shouted. "What the fuck, does it only work when it makes me *look bad*?"

A high giggle filled the room. "She has a point, Dixon. Eyes Only coverage has been very spotty lately."

The clown mannequin had come to life and was stepping down off its pedestal. Even with both feet on the floor, it was still very tall.

"That's not unusual, where the Troop is involved," Dixon said.

"No, I suppose not," said the clown, and then nodded to me. "Welcome to my demesnes, Jane Charlotte. My name is Robert Love."

"I didn't do this," I said. "I'm being set up. My brother—"

"I know all about your brother. He's been a thorn in my side for some time now."

"Yeah, Phil can be like that. And he's mad at me. And"—I pointed a finger at Dixon—"*he* doesn't like me either. Whatever he's told you—"

"I'm aware Mr. Dixon isn't fond of you. You're not fond of me either, are you, Dixon?" He raised a finger to the teardrop under his eye, and pouted. "No love for Love ... But then it's not an inquisitor's job to be affectionate, is it?"

"Look," I said, "if I were going to stage an attack, why would I do it this way? I mean, shoot myself with a gun that I couldn't get rid of? What sense does that make?"

"It does seem rather stupid," Love allowed. "But then, evil is so very tricky, sometimes ... Perhaps you are telling the truth, and you've been framed. Or perhaps we're meant to believe that you've been framed so that we'll trust you, and not recognize that you really are working for the Troop." He stroked his chin theatrically. "What a puzzle ... Are you a good Jane, or a bad Jane?"

"What do you want me to do? How do I prove myself?"

"That's the question, isn't it? Your brother is very talented at manipulating perception. It's one of the reasons the Troop prizes him so highly. If he's decided to ruin your reputation, such as it is, there may not be anything you can do." He sighed and shook his head. "Evil ... Tricky, tricky evil ... Do you know, I was almost evil once ..."

"That's swell," I said. "But getting back to me—"

"It was when I was younger. I grew up in the desert, not far from here. Abusively strict father, passive mother ... Well, I won't bore you with the details. I had issues, as they say. And when I finally got away to Berkeley, I went wild."

"You were at Berkeley?"

"Why, do I strike you more as Yale material?"

"What"—I couldn't believe I was asking this—"what was your major?"

"Art. Drama. A few others. Really though, I think it's fair to say my main pursuit in those years was finding novel ways to tax my liver. And pranks. I was quite the merry prankster, at Berkeley ... Then in the middle of my senior year—my *third* senior year—my parents died in a car crash. They left me a great deal of money and a seven-hundred-acre ranch. The acreage was mostly scrub, but the house was nice. So I came home. I had some vague notions about using the land to do performance art, or maybe some installation pieces—build my own Stonehenge on the back forty, stage Druidic rituals—but before that could go anywhere, I got sidetracked by an idea for a new prank.

"My best friend in college liked to tell stories about how he'd been abducted by aliens. You'd think intelligent people would laugh that off, but he was very convincing, and in several cases he not only got his listeners to believe that *he'd* been abducted, he made them wonder whether *they* had, as well.

"One night at the ranch I asked myself whether you couldn't take it a step further: Build an enclosed stage set, designed to look like the interior of an alien spacecraft. Go out and find people—stranded motorists, or just barflies who'd had too much to drink—knock them out somehow, bring them back and put them in it. And do things to them.

"Of course it was a wicked idea. Evil, if you took it far enough. I tried to think of ways to make it *not* be wicked ... What if, I thought, you only did it to *bad* people? Murderers, thieves, people who deserved a good scare. But inevitably, my fantasies turned towards other kinds of people as well ... A pretty girl, say, whose car blew a tire on a back road, and who saw a strange light in the sky. And when she woke up in the spaceship, she wouldn't be alone. There'd be a man with her, a fellow abductee, college age, as scared as she was, and together they'd explore the ship, and see what happened ..."

"These issues you had," I said. "Were they sexual, by any chance?"

"Some of them." Love grinned. "I hear you have a few of those yourself ... Anyway, I decided that while of course I couldn't go through with this prank, there was no harm in at least building the spaceship. I called it my ant farm, because the point was to put living things in it and watch what they'd do, and because, let's be honest, this was very much a boy's toy.

"So I built the spaceship, and then, since I still wasn't ready to admit that I *was* going to use it, I built some other ant farms: A nuclear fallout shelter. A death-row prison wing. Most elaborate of all, a Victorian-era hotel floor with no exits.

"All of this took time, and for most of it I was completely alone. When you're removed from human society for that long, especially if you're intoxicated, ordinary moral inhibitions begin to lose their grip. It's not that you deny the concept of evil, it's that you begin to find it acceptable, even attractive. You start to wallow in it: you ignore the consequences and concentrate on the fun parts.

"But it turned out I wasn't as alone as I thought. My one remaining contact with the outside world was the town of Coleman, where I'd go to pick up supplies. When I bought things, I paid cash, and I put the change in jars on a high shelf in the workshop where I designed my ant farms. In one of the jars, there was a dollar bill that was ... special. The pyramid on the back, it saw what I was about. The organization became aware of me. And it might have ended there, with me dying quietly of a heart attack or stroke, except that the young Cost-Benefits operative assigned to my case, Bob True, had some rather ... *enlightened* ideas about the difference between thought and deed. Also, the Panopticon agent who first sussed me out—Bob Wise—well, he wasn't as hesitant as True when it came to dealing death, but he did think my ant farms might be useful as an intel-gathering tool.

"So they didn't kill me. They decided to study me. They built an ant farm around my ant farms. The town of Coleman: they bought it. That wasn't as hard as you might think. It was … What was the name of that town where you spent your teenage years? Little Nap?"

"Siesta Corta," I said.

"Right," said Love. "Compared to Coleman, Siesta Corta was a metropolis. Coleman was just a saloon with a gas pump and a mail drop. The organization bought it and brought in their own people. The night I finally came looking for an ant to put in my ant farm, they were waiting for me.

"The setup was perfect—too perfect. They'd doubled all the saloon staff I might recognize, and there was a pretty girl sitting at the bar, slightly drunk, looking *exactly* like the pretty girl I'd fantasized about … She smiled at me and encouraged me to sit with her, and in that moment, I knew two things: First, that I'd walked into a trap. And second, that since what I'd been planning to do was clearly evil, the people who'd set the trap must be good. So good could be tricky, too. That was a revelation to me."

"Uh-huh," I said. "So you just saw the light then?"

"It wasn't exactly Saul on the road to Damascus," said Love. "But it was a significant epiphany. So I looked at this pretty, helpless girl who wasn't helpless at all, and said to her, 'I surrender.'"

"And they *recruited* you?"

"Well. It wasn't *quite* that simple. The road from there to here was a long and twisted one, and along the way I gave True more than a few opportunities to regret his leniency towards me. But in the end, yes, here I am, running the circus.

"And the reason I'm telling you all this," Love continued, "is that I want you to know I *understand* evil. I've been there; I've felt its draw, and almost succumbed.

"I understand it, but I don't condone it. I know that

I was lucky. The organization would have been right to put me down. And if I'd gone ahead and done to that pretty girl what I was thinking of doing ... A quick death would have been a mercy to me.

"So maybe you are a good Jane. We'll proceed on that assumption for now. And if you *are* a good Jane, then all will be well: if the Troop wants to play tricky, we'll show them what tricky really is.

"But if you're a bad Jane? If you're lying to us now, if even a drop of True or Wise's blood is on your hands? ... You'll weep before we're through. True was enlightened; Wise was patient. I'm neither. Are we clear?"

"Yeah," I said. "I think I have the ground rules straight."

"Good." He brightened, and held out his hand—like I was really going to touch him after hearing that story. "Let's go in the next room. We'll talk strategy ... and see what we can't do about that brother of yours."

white room (vii)

IN THE WHITE ROOM, ONE LAST PROP has been laid on the table.

"Where did you get this?" she says.

"From Officer Friendly."

"You *found* him?"

"It wasn't difficult," says the doctor. "He's retired now, but he draws a pension, so his address is on file. I thought he would be worth contacting. Most of the policemen I know, over the course of their careers, have a handful of cases that continue to haunt them long after they are officially closed. With Officer Friendly, I had an inkling that your case might be one of those."

Wary, now: "What did he tell you?"

"You know that even after she learned about John Doyle, your mother still blamed you for your brother's abduction. And she wasn't just accusing you of being irresponsible: she believed you'd abandoned your brother in the garden deliberately, as you'd abandoned him many times before, *hoping* that something would happen to him."

"My mother was out of her mind."

"She made some outrageous claims. The social worker thought she was paranoid, and Officer Friendly

wanted to agree, but his patrolman's intuition told him
not to dismiss her so quickly. So when he volunteered to
drive you to your aunt and uncle's house, he wasn't just
being kind—he wanted to spend more time with you."

"That son of a bitch ... He actually thought I *wanted*
Phil to get kidnapped?"

"He wasn't sure. It bothered him that he wasn't sure.
Unfortunately, the car ride didn't settle the matter. He
said you *seemed* like a normal, if very troubled, girl—
one who'd done a careless thing and was now putting
up a tough front to keep remorse from eating her alive.
Ordinarily, he said, he'd have been worried about you
hurting yourself, especially if your brother was found
dead. But he couldn't shake the feeling that you were
hiding something, and that made him wonder if your
remorse was just an act.

"So he went back to your mother. She repeated her
claims: That you were an *evil* child. That you hated your
brother. That you'd intentionally put him in jeopardy as
a way of getting rid of him."

"If I was so evil," she says, "why did she make me
watch Phil? I mean, does that make sense, that you have
your monster daughter babysit the brother she's trying
to kill?"

"Officer Friendly asked her about that. She said she
didn't have a choice—as a single mother working to
support two children, she couldn't afford a real babysit-
ter ..."

"Oh, *that's* good. Why didn't she just get a pit bull to
watch Phil? I hear they're *great* with kids."

"She also said she'd been in denial about your true
nature. She said of course you were no angel, she'd always known that, but it was only now she saw what a
devil you were."

"And Officer Friendly bought that?"

"No," the doctor says. "He thought it was nonsense.

He was about to concede that the social worker had been right after all. Then your mother said one more thing.

"She said she should have known that this was going to happen—she'd had a clear warning, and she'd never forgive herself for ignoring it. Officer Friendly asked what she was talking about, and she said that the day before your brother was abducted you'd all been at the post office together. Your mother left the two of you in the lobby while she went to stand in line, and when she came back, your brother was crying. It was obvious something had frightened him badly, but he wouldn't say what, and neither would you. Then that night, he woke up screaming. She asked him again what was wrong, and he told her that the man who collected children for the gypsies was coming to get him. 'Jane showed me his face,' he said.

"It sounded like more paranoia, but when Officer Friendly went to the post office to have a look around, he found this tacked up on a bulletin board in the lobby. 'Jane showed me his face ...'"

She's silent a long time before asking: "Did he tell my mother about this?"

"No," says the doctor. "It's possible she'd already seen it, but he saw no reason to upset her further if she hadn't. It's not as if it were evidence—at least, not the kind he could act on. But you can see why he kept this, even after the hunt for Doyle was abandoned. And you can understand why, when I called him a few days ago, he knew right away which Jane I was referring to ... So what about it, Jane? How does this figure into the story you've been telling me? Or does it?"

"Of course it does."

"Really? Because I was under the impression the story's almost over. Shouldn't this have come at the be-ginning?"

"Sure, if I was an *honest* person ... I wanted to forget it all, you know? What happened to Phil, or even that I had a brother. Well, I couldn't do that. I got good at lying about it, but that's not the same as forgetting. But this ..." She nods at the piece of paper on the table. "This I almost did manage to forget. I thought I was the only one who knew—other than Phil, I mean. But it turns out it's not just Panopticon on the lookout for bad behavior."

"You're losing me again, Jane."

"Just listen," she says. "I'm getting to it."

The Good Jane and the Bad Jane

WHEN LOVE FINALLY LET ME GO, I went down to the street and stood there taking deep breaths until I was sure, absolutely sure, that I was really outside, on the actual Vegas Strip, and not in some ant-farm extension of the Mudgett Suite. What ultimately convinced me wasn't the air quality so much as the sheer number of tourists bumping past me on the sidewalk: even the organization, I figured, couldn't afford to hire that many extras.

It was late afternoon. *Which* afternoon was harder to say, but that didn't matter: I had a job to do. Panopticon had confirmed that John Doyle was in his suite at the Venetian. It was time to pay him a visit. I joined the flow of pedestrians headed north, past the Casino Royale to the fake Doge's Palace.

The tourist crowd inside the Venetian was salted with Clowns, white-faced Italian mimes and harlequins. None of them made eye contact with me, but I knew they were watching—when I started to follow the hall of shops towards the Grand Canal, a passing mime caught me by the elbow, spun me around, and pushed me back in the direction of the escalator bank. I rode down to the lower level and found the hotel lobby, where a red-headed bellhop, his long hair combed in a Bozo flip, was waiting to slip me a keycard.

It wasn't until I'd boarded the elevator that I really let myself think about who I was going to meet. I took out my NC gun and checked, twice, that the dial was on the narcolepsy setting. "Do *not* pick up any other weapons," I reminded myself.

The elevator arrived on the penthouse floor. I located Doyle's suite and used the keycard to open the door, stepping through into an entry hall that was larger than most hotel rooms. The walls and ceiling were mirrored and the floor was polished marble, so whichever way I looked I saw infinite Janes holding infinite NC guns that they didn't dare fire.

I followed the hall to its end, to an enormous sitting room with still more reflective surfaces: another mirror wall; a line of floor-to-ceiling windows overlooking the Strip; assorted glass- and marble-topped tables and cabinets. Here, though, my gaze was drawn to the body on the floor, the blood fanning out from it in all directions already beginning to dry to a dull finish.

John Doyle's throat had been slit, and his face, palms, and chest all bore slashing cuts. His legs were curled under him, like he'd been on his knees and flopped over backwards. The thought that he'd died begging for mercy didn't exactly break my heart, but this was obviously a problem as far as interrogating him was concerned.

As I dug in my pocket for my comm unit, I sensed movement in the room. I looked up and saw what seemed like an optical illusion reflected in the mirror wall: there I was, standing over Doyle's corpse, while above and slightly behind me a second Jane extended upside-down from the ceiling. I turned and raised my head; sure enough, there was the bad Jane, standing on the ceiling with her hair and jacket dangling *up*, like gravity was reversed just for her. "Hello again," she said, and while I was still trying to make sense of this, she reached down, grabbed my head with both hands, and gave it a sharp twist.

I woke up paralyzed in a chair, facing the mirror wall. Doyle's body was at my feet, and my NC gun was on a table to my right, within easy reach, if only I could reach. The bad Jane was behind me, standing on the floor now like a normal person, only not normal: as I watched her in the mirror, she kept shimmering, disappearing, and reappearing, just as she had in the diner parking lot.

"How's the neck?" she said, solidifying long enough to lay a cool hand against my jugular. "I hope I didn't overdo it. Phil would be pissed if I did any permanent damage."

I couldn't reach, but I could talk: "What the fuck are you?"

"What, you don't recognize your evil twin? Or do you mean this?" She winked, and winked out. Her voice came from thin air: "It's the drugs, Jane."

"You drugged me?"

"Not you, genius. Me." She was back, crouched behind me with her chin propped on my shoulder. "Altered-state theory, Jane. Remember?"

I remembered.

Altered-state theory, that was a Berkeley thing. She must have gone there too. Small world.

What is altered-state theory?

This stupid acidhead idea about the relationship between consciousness and reality. There was this crazy guy, right, leftover flower child, who used to hang out on campus. He had great dope, and he was willing to share, but it was like the Salvation Army, where before you get the free soup you have to listen to a sermon. So this guy would go on about this theory he had, that any time you altered your perception of reality, there was a corresponding alteration in the way reality perceived you, or something like that ...

Getting stoned changes the laws of physics?

In a nutshell. Which, you don't have to tell me, is the kind of insane logic that makes people jump off of buildings thinking they can fly. But this guy, he'd spent a lot of time refining his hypotheses, and if you pointed out that gravity doesn't seem to care how you look at it, he'd say that it wasn't a one-to-one correspondence, consciousness was obviously more flexible than truth, and so you'd need a big change in perception to produce even a small change in reality. In other words, ordinary drugs weren't strong enough, usually, to let you do magic. But he claimed to have heard rumors about this other, much more potent class of drugs, called X-drugs. With X-drugs, he said, you really *could* fly, bend time and space, or even go back and undo history.

So the bad Jane—

—was telling me the Troop had access to X-drugs Which I would have laughed off, if she hadn't been so busy demonstrating her powers.

Did it occur to you that it really was you who'd been drugged, and that this "demonstration of powers" was simply a trick?

Of course it occurred to me, but the thing is, I didn't *feel* drugged, I felt sober. Trust me, I know the difference.

I'm sure you do. But by your own account, at this point you were recovering from an overdose.

A *simulated* overdose. I wasn't—

Simulated, but still ... And you'd just been knocked unconscious a second time.

I know all that, but it doesn't change the fact that I wasn't the one who was tripping, *she* was.

Of course, I still tried to deny it: "You're full of shit! X-drugs don't exist!"

She laughed, faded out, and phased back in again.

"Do you really want to waste time pretending you don't believe me?" she said. "Or can we get down to business before J.D. here starts to stink?"

"What business? What does Phil want from me?"

"We'll come to that. But first, check out the painting."

A portrait of a Renaissance nobleman hung on the wall behind me. The bad Jane angled my head like a camera, aiming it at the portrait's reflection in the mirror, and zoomed in my perspective until I could make out individual brush strokes. Closer still and I began to see, very faint around the portrait's eyes, the outline of a pair of lenses.

"Panopticon."

"Yes," the bad Jane whispered. "They're watching. They *think* they're seeing. They know we can jam their signal, but what they don't know—Shh! Don't tell!—is that we can also substitute a *false* signal. Would you like to know what we're feeding them now?"

My point of view zoomed out again, until I could see the whole mirror wall. It flickered, and suddenly in the reflection John Doyle was alive again, down on his knees in front of me. I had my NC gun leveled at his chest and was forcing him to keep still as I took swipes at him with a knife.

"Ouch!" the bad Jane said, as my reflection made a particularly nasty cut across Doyle's scalp. "You know, I don't know what Love's orders to you were, Jane, but I'm pretty sure he didn't tell you to do *this* ..."

Unable to take the pain anymore, Doyle tried to pull away. Instead of shooting him, my reflection bent forward and slashed his throat. As blood geysered from the wound, I felt real wetness splash me in the chair.

"Oops!" said the bad Jane. "You really want to stand *behind* the person when you do that ..." She clucked her tongue as the vision in the mirror faded. "So what do you suppose Dixon is thinking right now?" As if in answer, the elevator dinged off in the distance. "Uh-oh. This can't be good ..." I heard the suite's outer door burst open. Footsteps echoed in the hall of mirrors. "All right, Jane, you're on. Think fast."

She slapped the back of my neck, and I could feel my arms and legs again. I dove for my gun, but by the time I got turned around in the chair she'd disappeared, and I found myself drawing down on a pair of harlequins. They were armed with horns: rifle-length, brass-belled instruments with rubber squeeze-bulbs.

"Put down the weapon, Jane," the lead harlequin said. Then he clapped a hand to his head and dropped dead of an aneurysm.

"I didn't do that!" I shouted at the remaining harlequin. Weirdly enough, he believed me. Instead of blasting me with his horn, he pivoted towards the mirror wall.

Then he was dead, too.

The bad Jane's gun hand extended from a ring of ripples in the mirror glass. "There are more of them on the way," I heard her say, as the hand withdrew. "You'd better get out of here."

I tried to find my comm unit, but she'd taken it. "If you can hear me," I told the nobleman's portrait, "I didn't do this!" The nobleman stared back skeptically.

I left the suite and ran to the elevator. When the doors opened on the lobby a minute later, the corpse of Bozo the bellhop fell into the car. I stepped over the body and saw two more harlequins coming for me. I ran the other way.

A flight of stairs brought me up beside the Grand Canal. A gondola floated by, the tourists inside it all staring. Although I'd tucked my NC gun back in my jacket, my hands and face were still covered with John Doyle's blood spatter. "It's just ketchup!" I called to them. Hurrying along, I rounded a bend in the canal and came face-to-face with a mime, who immediately drew a hatchet from his belt.

"Wait!" I said. "I surrender!"

The hatchet clipped a lock of my hair as it flew past my head.

"I *surrender*, God damn it!"

The air behind the mime shimmered. The bad Jane reached around with her knife, and the front of the mime's white blouse turned red.

"You see?" the bad Jane said, as the mime crumpled. "Not a drop on me!"

Wink. Gone again.

And I ran on, past more staring tourists, through a door marked NO ADMITTANCE, down another hall and some more stairs, coming out finally on an underground loading dock.

A sports car idled at the dock's edge. "Get in," the bad Jane said.

I felt the weight of my NC gun pressing against my ribs. My hand twitched.

"Try it and I'll leave you here," she said. "You *don't* want that."

Behind me, a door banged open.

"Last chance …"

I got in the car. An ax blade kissed the back bumper as we pulled away.

"Better buckle up," the bad Jane advised, steering us up a ramp and out onto the Strip. As I clicked my safety belt into place, I heard a squeal of tires and looked back; a subcompact stuffed with Scary Clowns was coming up fast behind us.

The bad Jane saw them too. "All right," she said. "Let's play." She shifted into a higher gear and began zigzagging through the traffic. The subcompact, nimbler than it looked, kept right on our tail. Hatchets started thunking off the sports car's trunk.

My hand was twitching again. I asked myself: *if* I could get my gun out from under my seatbelt, and *if* I managed to shoot the bad Jane before she shot me or stabbed me in the neck, and *if* I brought the car to a stop without crashing it, would the Clowns let me live long enough to explain what had really happened?

"I wouldn't put money on it," the bad Jane said. The rear windshield exploded, and a hatchet buried itself in the back of her headrest. I screamed; she laughed.

Up ahead, two identical trailer trucks rode side-by-side with an open lane between them. The trucks' back panels were unmarked, but as we got closer, I saw that their mud flaps were decorated with mandrill faces.

"Pattycake, pattycake," the bad Jane said, and flashed her high beams. The trucks began drifting towards each other. The bad Jane floored the accelerator and zipped through the narrowing gap; when the Clown car tried to follow, the trucks swerved aside, causing their trailers to swing together like clapping hands. The subcompact was caught and crushed.

That took care of the pursuit, but not the threat of looming death: the sports car was doing like a hundred and ten, and the light at the approaching intersection had just turned yellow. "What do you think?" the bad Jane asked me. "Can we make it?" Laughing hysterically, she took her hands off the steering wheel. The light turned red. I covered my eyes.

When the car jerked sharply to the right I was sure we'd been hit. The seatbelt cut into my waist and chest; the shift in g-forces combined with a sudden loss of friction was the cue that we'd left the ground and were tumbling through space. I braced myself for a final impact that never came.

Slowly the car leveled out. There was a light jolt as the tires reestablished contact with the road, and our speed began to drop back into a saner range. The blare of horns had already faded, leaving only the purr of the motor and the steady rush of air through the broken back window.

When I pried my hands from my face, we were out

in the desert under a starry sky. The lights of Vegas and the last rays of sunset were just a glow on the horizon behind us. The bad Jane wore the satisfied smile of someone who's just had amazing sex.

"Evil," she said, in answer to my stare, "is just *so* much cooler than even you know."

The road we were on led to a ramshackle house that stood alone in the middle of the wasteland. The bad Jane parked the car and got out. By the time I staggered from the passenger side, she was at the front door with her back to me, which would have been a perfect opportunity if my NC gun hadn't disappeared. "Sorry," she said, without bothering to turn around. "I'm a little too tapped out to play hide-and-seek right now, but if you give me a chance to recharge, I'll be happy to go again."

The house was just a shell; beyond the front door, metal steps led down into an underground complex. The first room we came to was a cross between a bomb shelter and a den: the walls were reinforced concrete, but there was a gas fireplace and a fully stocked bar.

"I've got sandwiches in the refrigerator if you're hungry," the bad Jane said. "And mineral water and juice to drink—I'd offer you something stronger, but I'm guessing your head's in a weird enough space as it is." When I didn't answer, she shrugged and said, "Suit yourself. *I* definitely need a little something ..."

While she rummaged in the fridge, I went over to the shelves that flanked the fireplace, drawn by a familiar row of yellow book spines: Nancy Drew mysteries. Tucked into a gap in the line of books was an autographed photo of Pamela Sue Martin.

"There you are," the bad Jane said, holding up a glass vial filled with clear liquid. She fitted it into an auto-injector and shot the full dose into her arm. "Ah-h-h ..." Her outline got fuzzy, then snapped back into sharp focus. "That's better." She ejected the empty vial into a trash bin. "You wouldn't *believe* how expensive this stuff is ... And before you get any ideas, you should know that it's DNA-specific. If you're not me, all it'll do is give you a really bad trip, the kind you don't come back from."

"So when are you going to tell me why I'm here?" I said. "What does Phil want from me?"

"What does *Phil* want?" She rolled her eyes. "This isn't about Phil, Jane. It's about you, playing for the wrong team."

"You want me to join the Troop."

"No, that's backwards. *You* want to join *us*. And we're going to grant your wish."

"My wish? My *wish* is to get my brother back, and for you to go to—"

"Are you auditioning, Jane?" She grinned. "Trying to show me what a great bullshit artist you are? Trust me, I know you've got *that* down cold. And hey, it's a useful skill, we can definitely put it to work for the Troop, but right here and now? I need you to start coming clean with yourself." She pointed to a door at the end of the bar. "In there."

"In there what?"

"The thing you've been denying for the past twenty-three years. Your true nature. Go on in and check it out."

I looked at the door. I didn't move.

"*Go on*," she said, and the door opened on its own, and then I was moving—not *walking*, you understand, just moving. I passed through into this darkened space, and the door slammed shut behind me, so it was like total blackout, and that was bad, not for the dark itself but because I knew it wouldn't last. She gave me a few seconds to think about what was coming, and then she said, "Now *look*," and the lights came on, and there he was, staring at me from every angle. John Doyle.

His wanted poster, you mean. The one from the post-office lobby.

Yeah. Officer Friendly may have kept one copy, but the Troop had a million of them. Every inch of wall space in this room was plastered with them. The ceiling, too, and I didn't even need to look down—I could feel the paper crackling under my feet.

"He really was a creepy guy, wasn't he?" said the bad Jane. "Some child molesters, you know, they're actually very sweet when they want to be, but J.D. wasn't one of those. He was more the come-with-me-now-kid-or-else type."

"Did Phil ... He told you what I did?"

"At the post office? Yeah, that's still kind of a sore spot with him, but he told me. Showed me the tape, too."

"The—"

"The surveillance tape. Probably you guessed this already, but the organization doesn't have a monopoly on Eyes Only technology. We've got our own version. Have had for years."

"The wanted poster ...?" I said. She nodded. "And that's ... how you find victims?"

"Recruits," she said. "Yeah, that's one of the ways. You think about it, it's not a bad profiling strategy: show someone the face of evil, see how they respond. Your brother's reaction was classic. That look of vulnerability on his face, like he was just begging someone to come in and start rewiring his brain—I can see why the powers that be snapped him up. What I don't understand is why they didn't recruit you at the same time."

"Me?"

"Jane ..." Suddenly she was right behind me, with her hands on my shoulders. "Don't be coy, now. You know what I'm talking about."

"No."

"You were standing behind Phil, just like this, whispering in his ear, saying ... Let's see, what were your exact words again? Oh yeah: 'That's the guy, Phil, the one who kidnaps little kids for the gypsies. I told him all about you: where you live, where you play, where you *sleep* ...'"

I shut my eyes.

"'... and when he comes for you, Phil, you'd better not scream or try to run away. That'll just make him mad, and then he'll *hurt* you. And don't go crying to Mom about this, either. She can't protect you. He'll hurt her too, maybe even kill her, and he'll still take you away afterwards.'"

"I was just messing with his head!" I said. "I was teasing him! I didn't know—"

"*Teasing* him?" She touched the side of my face and I flinched. "I think you're teasing *me*, Jane. I mean, I saw the tape. Phil was practically pissing himself from fear, and you: you were into it. Teasing! You were *being evil*. You *liked* it. You were *good at it*. Good enough to make a casual observer think that maybe you'd had some *practice* ..."

"Fuck you! I wasn't—it was just that one day."

"Yeah, right. That's a hell of a coincidence, Jane. The *one time* you give in to a sadistic impulse, put on a performance that couldn't have been better if you'd been *trying out* for the Troop, and we just happened to be there to record it ... You know what I think? You had ten years with Phil before we took him, and I bet if we picked any day out of those ten years and put J.D.'s poster in a room with the two of you, we'd have caught something just as telling. Jane being evil? Hah. How about Jane being Jane?" She touched my face again, and whispered: "Bad monkey."

This time instead of pulling away I turned on her, but my fists punched empty air. I heard the sound of her laugh off to my left and lunged for it, still swinging.

"Open your eyes, Jane," she said. "I know you don't want to see, but you're never going to catch me blind."

I opened my eyes. She was right in front of me, and this time I actually managed to get my hands around her throat before she melted away.

"Stop *doing* that!" I complained, as she rematerialized, just out of reach.

"All right," she said. "You want a fair shot, I'll give you one. Here, I'll even give you a handicap ..." She brought out the knife she'd used to kill John Doyle, and tossed it to me. "Now come on," she said, showing me her empty hands. "No tricks this time, I promise."

"OK," I said. "Just one other thing ..." And I lunged at her, leading with the point of the knife blade. She sidestepped, caught my wrist, and threw me face-first into the nearest wall.

"So where did it all go wrong?" she asked, pinning me effortlessly. "After such a promising start ... Were you actually *sorry* when Doyle took Phil away? Or was it that business with Whitmer? I mean, no offense, that was pretty impressive for a fourteen-year-old, but still. You think taking out a serial killer makes you some kind of *saint*?"

She released me and stepped back, and I whirled around, slashing with the knife.

"Or was it the organization?" she said, dancing clear of the blade. "Talking to Catering on the phone, I can see how that might have an effect on a young girl, even a bad seed. Weird though, how they waited so long before actually recruiting you ... Why do you suppose that is?"

I cut at her again, and this time she ducked beneath my arm, hooked a boot behind one of my ankles, and jerked my feet out from under me.

"Was that just a bureaucratic oversight, you think? Or did they maybe have a reason for not rushing to take you on?"

"I had a life," I gasped. "They hoped ... They wanted me to do something with it."

"Oh, *that* line." She laughed. "So why *didn't* you do anything with it?"

When I'd landed on my ass, I'd dropped the knife. I tried to pick it up, but she got there first and toed it out of my reach.

"They *did* recruit me," I said. "Maybe it took twenty years, but—"

"Yeah, and how's that been working out? Word from our spies is, not great. Your mission failure rate is kind of an embarrassment. And why is *that*?"

I made another try for the knife. She kicked me in the face.

"What's the problem, Jane? Are you just a titanic fuckup? Or could it be that your heart's not really in it?"

As she hauled back to kick me again I sprang up and locked my hands around her throat. I felt her try to pull away and thought: *Got you now, you bitch!* But then her own arms came up, breaking my grip, and she spun me around and slammed me into the wall again, eye-to-eye with John Doyle.

"Yeah," she said. "I really think that's it, your heart's just not in it. And I think you'll feel a whole lot better once you admit it … Say it, Jane."

"Fuck you!"

"Say it …" She pressed up against me, belly to back, like a full-body hug from behind, and then—the intimacy of it was hideous—our clothes, our *skin*, just dissolved, and we started to merge …

"*Say it,*" she commanded, her voice inside and outside now.

(I'm evil.)

"What's that? I didn't catch that, Jane. Say it again. Say it *loud*."

"I'm—" I said, and then fought it, pushing back until the pressure in my skull was just too great to resist: "I'm evil!"

"Now we're getting somewhere."

She pulled back, *withdrew*, and I collapsed to the floor.

"First time's always the hardest ..." She squatted beside me, hands balanced casually on her knees. "So listen up, Jane, I'm going to tell you what your options are. Option one, you can deny what you just admitted. Go back to Vegas, try and square things with Love—or just run like hell, which amounts to the same thing, except he'll be even less likely to believe you when he catches you. Option two, you can think it over some more. No one knows about this room but me—not even Phil—so you'll be safe here, long as you like. But the lights stay on.

"And then there's option three. You can stop hiding from yourself. Embrace what you really are, what you've always been. Join the Troop, and start making the kind of difference in the world you were *meant* to make. Now"—she leaned forward, lowered her voice—"*I* know what option you're going to pick, because I know which one you *want* to pick. But I also understand you don't want it to look too easy, don't want to seem like you're caving just because I kicked your ass. So we're going to pretend you're going for option two. You stay in here, 'think it over' as long as you need to, to save face—only not too long, OK, because we've got stuff to do. I'll be waiting for you outside when you're ready ..."

When I dragged myself back into the den twenty minutes later, a black case was sitting on the bar. It was smaller than the case the Troop had given to Arlo Dexter, but the style was identical.

"You know one of the great things about evil?" the bad Jane said. "You can't fake it. I mean, think about it, there isn't a good deed you can name that an evil person couldn't do, and still be evil afterwards. But it doesn't work the other way around. You pass *our* shibboleth test, and there's no question that you're one of us."

I popped the latches on the case, lifted the lid. "You expect me to use this?"

"'Expect.' When you say it like that, it makes it sound like there's room for doubt. I have faith in you, Jane."

"Who do you want me to kill?"

"Just some people. Nobody important. It's part of an op you'll be doing for us. For Phil, actually. He's throwing a party next week, and he wants a Clown for the entertainment."

"You mean Love? You want me to kill Robert Love?"

"No, I'm going to kill him. You're just going to bring him in so Phil can talk to him first. And this"—she patted the case—"this is going to help you get him."

I shook my head. "Even if I was willing to do that—"

"God, Jane, don't start backsliding. You want to go another round in the poster room?"

"Even *if* I was willing to do it, there's no way I could get back into the Mudgett Suite now."

"Oh, you could probably get back into it. It's getting out that's hard. But that's OK, you're not going after him in the Suite, you're going to hit him at the tables ... He gambles," she explained. "Baccarat, if you can believe it. I mean, of all the boring games ... But that's his thing, and tonight's his usual night out. Of course he may have changed his plans after your little defection today, but I doubt it. We'll know for sure in about an hour."

"I want to talk to Phil."

"You will. After you grab Love, I'm going to take you straight to him."

"No, I want to talk to him now."

"Sorry."

"I *need* to talk to him, OK?"

"I get that you're anxious," she said. "If it helps any, you should know that Phil is going out on a limb, bringing you in like this. I mean, corrupting organization members is part of his job, but there are special rules where family is involved. If the über-bosses knew he was going after his big sister personally, they'd be pissed."

"Why? The Troop has a problem with nepotism?"

"It's more a question of objectivity. Those old sibling bonds, you know, they can screw up your emotions. So this is technically a breach of protocol. But Phil figures if we bring in Love, the über-bosses will owe him some slack—he's already gotten big points for taking out True and Wise. And with this"—she patted the case again—"there shouldn't be any questions about your loyalties, either ... So just be patient, Jane. Once you're officially on board, there'll be plenty of time for you and Phil to reconnect."

"Once I'm on board," I said. "And what's my job going to be? Phil's assistant? His number two?"

"More like his number three." She grinned. "Now come on, let's get you cleaned up. You've still got J.D.'s blood all over you."

Two hours later I was back in the sports car's passenger seat, wearing a fresh set of clothes. Coming up on the west side of the Strip was the black pyramid of the Luxor, its glass tip shooting a beam of light half a mile into the sky.

My evil twin was giving me some last-minute instructions. "Put these on," she said, handing me an amazingly ugly pair of cat's-eye glasses. "There's a built-in comm unit, and it also transmits video, so I'll be able to keep tabs on you." Noticing my expression, she added: "I know it's a fashion felony, but that's part of the point. It'll help disguise you if you bump into any Clowns on the way to Love's table."

"What about Eyes Only?" I said. "Doesn't Panopticon have face-recognition software that can pick me out, even disguised?"

"Yeah, and that software is *so* reliable ... Don't worry, we've got it covered. The lenses are specially treated so you can see Eyes Only sensors. Go ahead, try it."

I put on the glasses and looked out. Above us, a billboard showed a line of half-naked showgirls, and my attention was drawn instantly to the girl with the biggest
boobs. Her eyes were glowing.

"Of course," the bad Jane continued, "spotting them
is only half the battle. This car's shielded against Eyes
Only surveillance, but outside, you'll need this." She
passed me an expensive-looking wristwatch. "State-of-
the-art jamming device. It'll shut down every Eye within
line of sight."

I read the brand name on the watch face: "Mandrill."

"Yeah." She shrugged apologetically. "I don't want to
be untrusting, but I figure there's still an outside chance
that you and Love are running some kind of elaborate
counterscheme here. So along with the jammer, there's
a destruct mechanism that lets me vaporize you by remote control if I get a bad vibe." Her right arm came
up, and I was staring into the muzzle of my own NC
gun. "Put it on."

I slipped the watchband around my wrist. The clasp
emitted a faint beep as I snapped it closed, and I didn't
need to be told that trying to undo it without permis-
sion would be fatal.

"Good girl," the bad Jane said. She put my NC gun
on safety and dropped it in my lap. "Here we go ..."

Two bright-eyed statues of the Egyptian god Horus
guarded the entrance to the Luxor casino. As I stepped
from the car, the light in their pupils dimmed and went
out. The next test was waiting just inside the casino
doors: a pair of real security guards. When one of them
looked straight at me I thought I was busted, but the
guy just yawned and turned away.

"You see?" the bad Jane said, a voice in my ear. *"It's
like you're invisible ... Walk straight ahead, now. The high-
stakes room is at the center of the casino floor."*

I passed between rows of blackjack tables, a wave of

darkness preceding me as my Troop watch turned every king, queen, and one-eyed jack blind. Next came bank after bank of slot machines. Here the effect was more subtle: even with their Eyes Only devices jammed, the slots had lights to spare.

The entrance to the high-stakes room was a sliding door of frosted glass. The door was triggered by a motion sensor, but my watch seemed to have jammed it, too.

"Problem," I said.

"Don't worry. I'm patched into the electrical system. Before I open the door I need you to pay attention. Love's dressed in a tuxedo. He's sitting at a table with two women; they're his bodyguards. There's also a dealer at the table, a pit boss off to the right, and a couple other dealers cooling their heels at the back of the room. Any of them might be bodyguards, too."

"So I need to shoot six people in, what, three seconds?"

"Two seconds if you can manage it. And don't *hit Love— even if he were light enough to carry, you aren't that invisible. Can you handle this?"*

"Let's find out," I said. "Open the door."

The door slid aside. I stepped forward, raised my gun, and pulled the trigger six times.

"Well," said Robert Love, glancing over the half dozen unconscious bodies sprawled around him, "I see my warning didn't take."

"Shut up." Without his clown outfit, he wasn't nearly as frightening.

"Search him," the bad Jane said.

I set the bomb case on the floor and gestured at Love with my NC gun. "Stand up and lean forward. Put your hands flat on the table." Love did as he was told. I moved around behind him. Feeling under his jacket, I found a hand ax tucked into his cummerbund. I pulled it out and set it aside. I checked his pockets. "He's clean," I announced.

"Good. Now explain to him what the situation is."

"There are some people waiting to meet you in the VIP parking garage," I told Love. "So we're going to walk out of here now. You'll stay in front of me, go where I say, not make any sudden moves, not make trouble."

"Interesting plan," said Love. "But as I can only assume you're taking me to be tortured and murdered, what's my motivation, exactly, for not making trouble?"

I kept the gun on him as I transferred the case from the floor to the table. I showed him what was inside it. "You know what this is, right?"

"I recognize the brand name. I can't say I've seen that particular model before."

"It's got a damper switch on the back," I explained. "If the switch is on, the blast is limited to an area roughly the size of this room. But if the switch is off, everyone within two hundred yards gets turned to ashes."

"I see. And in the latter case, will you be one of the dead?" He tilted his chin to indicate my glasses. "I'm guessing your controller won't be happy if you fail to bring me out of here."

"He's got that part right," the bad Jane said.

I leaned in close and pressed my gun to Love's temple. "If I fail this mission," I told him, "it means I've blown my only chance to see my brother again. And if that's true, I don't care what happens to me. Are we clear?"

"Yes," said Love. Then he smiled. "So shall I keep my hands up while we're walking, or will that be too conspicuous?"

"Don't worry about being conspicuous." I pulled back but kept the gun pointed at him. "Take your clothes off."

"What?"

"Strip. Everything, even your socks and shoes." I lifted the bomb out of the case, then pulled up the case's lining to reveal a button-down shirt, khakis, and a pair of loafers. "These should fit you. The stuff you're wearing now goes in a pile on the floor. Put your little ax in the pile, too."

"… and as far as the organization knows, I died in the explosion." He nodded. "Tricky. Very tricky."

"Dixon will figure it out eventually. But by the time he does, it'll be too late to do anything."

"So you get to see your brother again, *and* stick it to Dixon on your way out. I can see now why you turned."

"*Less conversation, more action,*" the bad Jane said. "*We don't have forever here.*"

"Let's go," I said, waving the gun. Love changed his clothes. When we were ready, I set the timer on the bomb.

Neither one of us looked like a high-stakes gambler now, but my invisible status held, and nobody paid us any mind as we left the room. We crossed the casino floor without incident, the bad Jane directing us towards a private elevator whose doors opened as we approached. I pushed Love inside.

In the parking garage the bad Jane, maybe worried about a last-minute change of heart on my part, was standing back at a safe distance from the elevator. She'd called in backup: eight guys dressed as parking valets, all packing Troop-issue NC guns. The bad Jane's own gun was still holstered, but she held the detonator for my wristwatch ready in her hand.

I'd taken off the glasses but my vision was crystal-clear. Even from fifty feet away, I could make out the little hairs on the back of the bad Jane's thumb as it hovered over the detonator button. I could see, and count, the beads of sweat on the foreheads of her backup team, and the grains of dust on the van they'd brought to carry Love away in. I saw the eddies of hot air rising from the engine of the bad Jane's sports car where it sat parked beside the van. And I saw the bad Jane's jaw muscles tighten, as she realized her concerns about a double-cross were justified.

"Where is he?" she said.

"Where's who?"

Her thumb tensed. "Don't fuck with me, Jane. Where's Love?"

"Oh, *him* ... He got off between floors. He claimed it was a security issue, said he knows too much to let himself be captured. Personally, I think he's just a wimp about being tortured by psychopaths." I waited a beat, then added: "Oh yeah. He said to tell you the Scary Clowns have sealed off all the exits from this building. None of you are getting out of here alive."

Her backup guys started exchanging glances, but the bad Jane herself was unmoved by the threat. "None of us?" she said. "Not even me?"

"Especially not you. I'm going to kill you myself, right after you tell me where Phil is."

"Sure you are ... Good-bye, Jane."

As Love and I had walked through the casino, we'd passed by a Vegas version of an old-fashioned carnival wheel. Now I imagined that time was like that, a big wheel of fortune, and I reached out, mentally, and stopped it in its spin. Next I focused on my arm, telling myself that the bones in my wrist and hand were elastic. When I felt them start to stretch, I brought my arm up sharply. The Mandrill watch slid off with its clasp still fastened, and went flying across the garage like a guided missile, zeroing in on a cluster of four parking valets.

I let go of the wheel of time. The bad Jane's thumb came down, and half of her backup detail disappeared in a yellow-orange flash.

"What the *fuck*?" the bad Jane said. Some instinct had enabled her to protect herself by redirecting the energy of the blast around her; her hair was mussed, but otherwise she was untouched. Her surviving minions weren't as lucky: dazzled by the explosion, they were staggering in blind circles.

I held up the auto-injector I'd found in Love's pocket when I'd searched him. "Love took a sample of my blood before he let me out of the Mudgett Suite," I explained. "He wouldn't say why, but when you told me that X-drugs were DNA-specific, I started to get an idea."

"The Scary Clowns have X-drugs?"

"Yeah. And speaking as a connoisseur of controlled substances? I'm pretty sure their shit's *better* than yours, Jane."

"Let's find out," she said. "Let's play."

She dropped the detonator; I dropped the auto-injector; we both went for our guns. We both tried to stop time again, too, and in the slow-motion world that resulted, the shots we fired were actually visible. The bad Jane's NC gun spat thick jagged bolts the color of arterial blood; my own gun sprayed wispy white lines of narcolepsy. None of the shots connected, and after dodging back and forth for a moment, we both rolled for cover.

Crouched behind the polished bulk of a silver Mercedes, I listened to the stumbling of the parking valets until I had a clear picture of where they all were. Then I thumbed the dial on my NC gun to MI and popped up firing. I'd killed three of them and was about to shoot the fourth when I heard the beep of a Mandrill bomb being activated, and the soft swoosh as the bad Jane lobbed it overhand in my direction. I put a hand on the roof of the Mercedes and flipped myself up into the air. My foot connected with the incoming bomb and kicked it back the way it had come, with a slight course correction; it smacked into the chest of the last valet and detonated.

The blast, much more powerful than the previous one, broke the windows on most of the cars in the garage; as I dropped back to the ground I had to cover my head against a shower of safety glass. By the time the rain stopped the bad Jane had gotten back in her sports car and was revving the engine for a getaway. As she reversed out of her parking slot, I jumped up again, using the hood of the Mercedes as a springboard to launch myself through the air. I landed on the roof of the sports car even as the bad Jane was shifting into forward gear; when she hit the gas, I reached down through the broken front window and gave the steering wheel a hard yank. I rolled clear as the car swerved into a concrete pylon.

The crash killed the sports car's engine. The bad Jane fought free of the deflating air bag and crawled out over the crumpled hood. Back on my feet, I tried to draw a bead on her, but then another Mandrill bomb came skittering across the garage floor, its countdown timer reading 0:01.

I closed my eyes and teleported behind another concrete pylon. The bomb detonated, shattering more glass. An alarm began to wail—and beneath that, I heard the bad Jane's footsteps receding, and the sound of a stairwell door.

The stairs led back up to the casino level. By the time I got there, the bad Jane was out of sight. As I stood searching for some sign of which way she'd gone, a security guard approached me. I recognized him as the same guard who'd eyeballed me when I'd first entered the building, and I hesitated, not sure whether he was a Troop member, a Scary Clown, or a civilian.

A second security guard tackled me from behind. He locked an arm over my windpipe and tried to shove me up against the wall, but he was no bad Jane: I melted out from under his chokehold, reappeared behind him, and gave him a double shot of narcolepsy to the back of the head. Then I turned to deal with the first guard, but he'd already been knocked senseless by a burst of sound from a brass-belled Clown horn.

"Hello again, Jane," Robert Love said. "Enjoying the rush?"

"Yes, actually ... But you could have told me in advance."

"What, and spoil the surprise? That wouldn't be very tricky." He giggled, but then his grin turned to a grimace. "Ouch!"

"Love?"

I was worried he'd been shot, but he didn't fall down. He stretched out his arm, opening and closing his fist. "Must've pulled a muscle climbing out of the elevator ... No matter. Listen: I've got Clowns on X-drugs guarding all the primary exits, but that will only delay her. You need to hunt her down before she finds another way out."

"Right ..." I stared at the casino floor, focusing on the individual fibers that made up the carpet. Out of the thousands of random impressions left by passing gamblers, a fresh set of footprints appeared, as visible to me as tracks in grass. "Got her."

I sprinted away at superhuman speed. The bad Jane's trail led out under the pyramid atrium, where another pair of security guards tried to get in my way. I'd just finished taking them down when I heard a horn blast off in the distance. I ran towards it, and the bad Jane came darting right in front of me, her hair more than just mussed, now—she looked like she'd been through a tumble dryer. She saw me and tried to snap off a shot, but the barrel of her NC gun had cracked, rendering it as harmless as the toy it appeared to be. A look of real fear came into her eyes then, and she took off in a blur.

I stayed right on her heels. I could sense that she was almost out of power, in need of another dose, but between the Mandrill bomb explosions and the horn blast, any X-drug vials she was carrying would have shattered by now. All I had to do was keep pressing her until she was completely tapped out.

I chased her into a corner of the atrium, where she broke through another stairwell door. The stairs went up, the flights staggered to follow the incline of the pyramid. The geometry of it made me dizzy, so I forced myself not to look up the central well and just concentrated on running. By the time I passed the fifth landing, it was more like flying.

We flew up and up, all the way to the top—I nearly caught her at the three-quarter mark, but she put on a final burst of speed and pulled away again. Then I was at the top landing, in front of a door that radiated heat. The door was unmarked, but if you were going to make a sign for it, the symbol off the organization coin would have been a good choice.

I nudged the door open and stepped into the eye of the pyramid. It was like stepping into the sun: the Luxor's searchlight was the size of a swimming pool, and though it pumped most of its energy into the sky, enough reflected back off the inside of the glass cap to turn the room into a bake oven.

My pupils shrank to pinpoints as I climbed onto the catwalk that encircled the searchlight. The air above the light was one big heat-shimmer, but I thought I glimpsed a human outline on the far side of the catwalk.

"You might as well show yourself," I said. "I know you're here, and you don't have enough juice left to get past me."

She solidified. "Careful with the gun." She gestured at the glass walls. "If you miss ..."

"I'm not going to shoot you. I need you awake so I can beat the truth out of you."

"The truth." She smiled. "You sure you want the truth, Jane? Because the truth is, even if you get me to tell you where Phil's hiding, you won't save him. He belongs to the Troop now. You might catch him, but you won't turn him. He'll curse you for even trying."

"Why don't you let me worry about that?"

"I know you *are* worried about it. That's why there's a part of you that really would like to shoot me, to shut me up before I can talk. Go on, check it out."

I glanced down at the gun in my hand.

The dial was turned to the MI setting.

"Yeah," the bad Jane said. "If you kill me, Phil gets away, and then you can go on pretending there's hope. But there is no more hope, Jane. You had your chance to protect Phil twenty-three years ago. Now he's got power, and position, and a purpose—more than *you* ever had—and he's never going to give that up willingly. He might have shared a little of it with you, but that chance is gone too. So all that's left is death. You can hunt him down and execute him, like the bad monkey he is. Is that the truth you're looking for, Jane? You want to be responsible for finishing Phil off?"

As she talked, she moved along the catwalk towards me. She started to get a little too close for comfort; I took a step back and my heel caught, throwing me off-balance. It was all the opening she needed. She came forward in a blur, chopping her hand against my wrist to make me drop the gun. Then her hands were around my neck.

"Don't fight it," she said. I tried to melt away, but she held on to me firmly, using the last of her power. "Don't fight it, Jane … You know this is the best way." She bent me backwards over the catwalk railing. I felt the heat of the light scorching me. "Just let go. Just let go. No more guilt for you, no more screwups, and Phil gets to go on …"

With the last of *my* strength, I reached up, placed a palm flat against her chest. I pushed, *merged*, my hand passing through her jacket, her skin, her breastbone. I grabbed her by the heart, and squeezed.

She gasped and let go of me. She tried to step away, but I lifted her off the ground.

"Now," I said. "You're going to tell me where my brother is ..."

Her arms and legs started flailing like mad, but her slaps and kicks were nothing to me. I pivoted around, lifting her over the railing to dangle her above the searchlight. I concentrated; the light blazed up, not just *like* the sun now, until I could see all the way through her, all the way to her soul. Steam, then smoke, curled off of her.

"Tell me where he is," I said. I gave her heart one more squeeze.

She threw her head back, screamed it out; the words echoed off the glass tent as the light continued to blaze.

"Thank you," I said. "And good-bye, Jane."

I opened my hand. Her body, limp now, slipped free. Descending, she flashed into fire, the light consuming her more thoroughly than a Mandrill bomb. Not even ashes were left.

Tapped out, dripping with sweat, I slumped against the catwalk railing.

A dark shape moved at the edge of my vision. There was a flash of pebble glasses.

"Well," Dixon said. "That was rather medieval."

"I didn't like her," I told him. "I don't like you much, either. But that doesn't matter now ... I know where Phil is."

"Yes, I heard. I hope she wasn't lying."

"She wasn't. But we're going to have to move fast. By now Phil will know that this operation has gone wrong. When the bad Jane doesn't report in, he'll run."

"Not to worry." Dixon flipped open his cell phone. "I have a Bad Monkeys strike team standing by."

"I don't want any help. Just get me to him, I'll go in alone."

"You aren't going in at all. Even if I trusted you, you can barely stand."

"Even if you *trusted* me? What ... Wait. What do you mean, 'strike team'?"

"What do you think I mean?"

"No. We're supposed to bring Phil in alive. Love promised me he'd honor True's deal."

"Love is on his way to the hospital," Dixon said. "He had a heart attack—a real one. That puts me in operational command."

"It doesn't change the deal! You can't—"

"You know that bomb you left on the baccarat table? The technician we sent in to defuse it said that the 'damper switch' was just a dummy. If it had gone off, it would have killed everyone in the casino."

"It wasn't Phil who put me up to that. It was *her*."

"It was his plan. This is the sort of thing your brother does for the Troop. This is what he *is*, now ... And I am not going to go in soft and risk letting him escape, just to assuage your guilt about being a bad sister."

"You prick," I said. "You're just doing this to spite me!"

"I'm doing it because it's the right thing to do." He raised the cell phone to his ear.

I scooped my NC gun off the catwalk.

"Don't be a fool," Dixon said.

"Don't think I won't ..." The dial was still on the MI setting. I tried to switch it back to narcolepsy, but it must have been damaged in the fall. It wouldn't budge.

A cold smirk formed on Dixon's lips as he watched me struggle with the dial. "How very convenient," he said. "To stop me, you'll have to kill me ... And as there are no witnesses, you'll be free to blame the bad Jane ..."

"Shut up!" I banged the dial against the catwalk railing. It still wouldn't turn. "Put down that goddamned cell phone!"

"No."

"I'm not going to let you kill my brother, Dixon."

"And what about all the other people *he'll* kill, if he gets away? I suppose you'll blame their deaths on the bad Jane, too."

"Dixon—"

"Go ahead," he said, staring me down. "Pull the trigger. Prove me right."

"No."

"No?"

"No ..." Relaxing my grip, I let the gun drop. It bounced off the catwalk and vanished into the light.

Behind the pebble glasses, I caught the tiniest flicker of relief. "That's better," Dixon said. "Now—"

Before he could finish his sentence, I dipped my hand in my pocket and came out holding the bad Jane's knife.

"I'm not going to let you kill my brother," I repeated. "But you're wrong about the rest of it. I take full responsibility. For everything. For Phil."

Then I flicked open the blade and stepped towards him.

white room (viii)

"SO YOU KILLED DIXON TO PROTECT your brother."

"No, I killed Dixon because I *didn't* protect my brother ... and because I finally realized I couldn't save him."

The doctor shakes his head. "I don't understand. If you thought Phil couldn't be saved—"

"I didn't say that. I said *I* couldn't save him. The bad Jane was right about that much: I'd missed my one chance, and all I could do now was get him killed ... But Phil could still save himself." She looks the doctor in the eye. "I don't care what the Troop did to him, what they made him do, I have to believe there's some part of him that's not irredeemable. He was a good kid, you know? He deserved better than me for a sister ... But I was what he got, and if I wasn't strong enough to bring him home, I could at least buy him some more time to find his own way back.

"So that's my story." She shrugs and sinks back in the chair. "What do you think?"

"I'm not sure what you want me to say, Jane."

"That bad, huh?"

"I could point out some more holes in the narrative, if you like," the doctor says. "I could tell you that there

have been no reports of bodies found at the Venetian:
no butchered guests up in the penthouse, no mimes
with their throats slit beside the Grand Canal. I could
tell you that the security guards at the Luxor are quite
certain there was only one Jane, not two, running amok
in the casino that night, and none of them witnessed
any laws of physics being broken—just a lot of punching
and kicking. I could tell you that, but then you'll tell me
that Catering covered up what really happened, and if
that explanation still leaves a few loose ends, well, it's a
Nod problem."

"Good to see you finally catching on," she says. "So
what about Dixon? What did they make him out to be?
Another security guard? A hotel employee who got in
my way?"

"He was a social worker," the doctor tells her.

"Dixon, a social worker?" She laughs. "That's rich!
Let me guess: he worked with street people, right? *De-ranged* street people?"

"Homeless addicts."

"Sure, of course. And that night—don't tell me—that
night, he just happened to be passing through the Luxor
and heard one of his new clients had gone berserk. So
he decided to help track me down and ended up getting
stabbed for his troubles."

"The police don't know how Dixon came to be in that
room with you. But that scenario sounds plausible."

"Yeah, except for one thing: I'm not deranged. I
mean, my *story's* crazy, I know that, but I'm lucid."

"You're lucid now," the doctor says. "But that
night?"

"Yeah, well ... Those X-drugs really were something.
Too bad I won't be getting any more."

"Jane—"

"I talked to Phil again, you know," she says. "I mean,
not *really* ... But after I killed Dixon, when I was sitting
at the top of the stairs waiting to see if the cops or the

Clowns would come for me first, I pretended Phil was there with me. I told him I was sorry. I'd never done that, you know, in all the conversations we'd had, but this was like the last time, so I apologized for being such a lousy sister, for leaving him that day ... I told him that no matter what bad things he'd done for the Troop, it wasn't his fault, it was all on me. I said I hoped he'd find a way to get free of them—that he could, I *knew* he could, if he really wanted to."

"And what did Phil say?"

"He didn't say anything. He just listened." She looks the doctor in the eye again. "I hope he listened."

Before the doctor can respond, his pager goes off.

"Time to go?" She sounds disappointed.

"I have to step out for a moment," the doctor says. "But I would like to talk some more. If you don't mind waiting ...?"

"No, I don't mind." She shows him her bracelets again. "It's not like I've got anywhere to be."

He stands up and reaches for the tape recorder, then hesitates. "Did she say anything else?"

"Who?"

"The bad Jane. Before you dropped her—did she say anything else about Phil, or the Troop?"

"No. I mean, it's not like she was super-articulate with my fist in her chest. It was all she could do to scream out a few words ... Why?"

"Just curious," the doctor says. He presses the STOP button on the recorder. "I'll be back shortly ..."

He goes to the door and tries to open it, but it's been locked from the outside. "Guard?" he calls. "I'm ready to come out now ... Guard?" He raises a fist, knocks. "Guard!"

Behind him, there is a thunk of handcuffs hitting the table. He looks over his shoulder. She is leaning forward, aiming a bright orange pistol at him. "What on earth ...?" he says. "Where did you ...?" Then he sees

it: the black tile in the floor has been flipped up to reveal
a compartment underneath.

"Phil," she says.

He blinks. "Is this some kind of joke? Did … Did Dr.
Chiang put you up to this?"

"It's no joke, Phil. I wish it was."

He stares at her for a moment, glances at the tape
recorder, and then he is hammering on the door.
"Guard!… GUARD!"

"There's no one out there to help you, Phil. This isn't
the county jail. You're in an ant farm in the desert."

He stops pounding. He turns around slowly, a new
expression on his face.

"Yeah," she says. "Sorry. I lied to you about Dixon:
I probably *would* have killed him, but he was smart
enough not to give me a reason. By the time he showed
himself on the catwalk, the strike team was already on
its way, and he sent them in with strict orders to take
you alive—not because he's a nice guy, you understand,
but because even he didn't dare break the deal Love
made with me … Love said the Clowns had a way to
trick your memory, make you think you'd come to me
on your own, to pump me for intel, which would give
me a chance to try to reach you. Dixon said it would
never work, that you had no conscience left for me to
reach, but I told Love I was sure I could pull it off …"
She sighs. "But I was wrong about that, wasn't I, Phil?"

She picks up the tape recorder and slams it down
hard. The case splinters, revealing the flat disc of the
Mandrill bomb inside. There's a nervous pause as they
both wait for the timer to finish counting down, but
when it reaches zero, there's no explosion, just a short
buzz. A word appears in the digital readout:

SHIBBOLETH

Then the lead H flickers and goes out:

S IBBOLETH

"Jane," he says. "I can explain ..."

"Yeah, I'll bet you can," she says. "But there's not much to explain, is there? It was a simple test. You didn't have to confess, or break down crying, or anything dramatic like that. All you had to do was walk out of this room without trying to kill me."

"Jane ... Jane, please."

"I'm sorry, little brother. I tried. I gave you every chance I could. But this is my half of the deal ..."

"*Jane!*"

"Bad monkey," she says.

She pulls the trigger.

The NC gun makes no sound.

He convulses. One hand grabs the knob of the door behind him; the other flies up to his chest. A strangling noise issues from his throat; his face reddens and his eyes bulge. *Her* eyes widen, as she leans farther forward, taking it all in. His knees start to buckle.

And then, right at the point where he should fall dead of a heart attack, he catches himself. He stops gasping for breath. His legs straighten and his arms return to his sides.

She pulls the trigger again. Once again the NC gun is silent, but it's a different kind of silence—the kind that signifies impotence. This time he doesn't react to the shot. He stands tall, his face returning to its normal color. She switches the gun's dial from MI to CI, aims straight at his head, and tries once more.

Nothing. He doesn't even blink.

She is not pleased with this outcome.

"Phil," she says.

"Jane," he replies.

"You're not the ant in this ant farm, are you?"

"No."

"I am."

"Yes."

"Well, fuck," she says, and tosses the useless gun on the table.

There's a knock at the door. Phil steps aside, and Dixon enters the room. She greets him with a sour look.

"How long have you known?" she asks.

"That you are a deep-cover agent, working for the Troop? From the beginning," Dixon says. He gestures to Phil. "We were warned about you."

"Then why recruit me?"

"As an experiment. We'd been aware for some time that the Troop was attempting to infiltrate the organization. We'd enacted countermeasures, but were uncertain how effective they were. Recruiting you offered us an opportunity to test them."

"So the idea was to see how long it would take to catch me if you didn't already know?"

"Yes."

"It was a lot harder than you thought, wasn't it?"

"Yes," Dixon says. "Of course I expected you to be a good actress, well practiced in passing yourself off as a charming misfit rather than the monster that you really are, but your ability to fool shibboleth devices came as a shock. Your emotional control was remarkable, especially in someone who *seemed* so impulsive. For a while I almost despaired of catching you out."

"So what finally tipped it?" She glances at Phil. "Him?"

Dixon nods. "Even the most self-controlled person is subject to temptation. You were able to conceal your enthusiasm for more mundane acts of evil, but I thought your composure might crack if you were presented with a chance to commit a truly extraordinary sin."

"So you sent me to hunt down my own brother."

"To kill him, on the pretense of saving him."

"How'd you know I'd go for it, though? I mean, if he's really Troop, then we're technically on the same side."

"Technically," Dixon says. "But it is true, isn't it, that your brother's abduction by the Troop was no coincidence?"

"Of course it wasn't a coincidence," she says. "He was my ticket in. They wanted a sacrifice to prove that I was serious. But they didn't tell me they were going to *adopt* him."

"I assumed as much. I thought the discovery that your brother was not only alive, but occupying a position of importance in an organization to which you were little more than a peon, would undermine whatever loyalty you had."

"So this whole thing …" She waves a hand at the room. "This … *play* … It was all so you could read my heart the moment I pulled the trigger?"

"Yes," Dixon says. "And the results, I'm happy to report, are conclusive. You're evil."

"Yes I am," she says, unable to resist a smile. "But you know, you didn't have to go to so much trouble. You could have just asked my mother."

"Perhaps I would have, if she were still alive."

"Yeah, it's a shame about that. You know they never found the truck that hit her?" She sees Phil bristle and her smile broadens. "So what happens now? You turn me? Make me a double agent?"

Dixon shakes his head. "You're a bad monkey. Now that that's out in the open, the organization has no further use for you."

"Right." She nods, then shrugs, accepting the inevitable. "Oh well, I had a nice run. Did some good damage along the way."

"Some," Dixon agrees. "But less than you believe … The beginning was real," he explains. "But after the Arlo Dexter mission, Cost-Benefits became concerned that it was too dangerous to leave you running around loose, even under close surveillance. True began pressuring me to kill you and be done with it. Ultimately I convinced him to accept an alternative. We gave you to the Scary Clowns. Everything that has happened to you since you met Robert Wise has been simulated."

"Simulated," she says. "You mean the Ozymandias facility ... The diner ... *Vegas* ...?"

"Dreamscapes and ant farms, all of it."

"No way! That ... They can't *do* that!"

"Love will be pleased his illusions were so effective. It turns out I owe him an apology. When I first saw the script his people had prepared, there were a number of plot twists that I was sure would give the game away. But the Clowns' understanding of human gullibility is greater than mine."

She thinks about it. "X-drugs don't exist?"

"Drugs that allow you to stop time and fly around like a martial-arts superhero? No, they don't exist."

"Well, that's embarrassing ... So if the scene at the diner never happened, that means—"

"True and Wise are both still alive," he says. "Oh, and Love didn't have a heart attack."

"What about John Doyle?"

"Bad Monkeys killed him twenty years ago."

"And the bad Jane?"

"Roberta, actually. Roberta Grace. My protégée. She's already back at Malfeasance, preparing to use what we've learned from you to weed out the Troop's other moles."

"And what about *him*?" she asks. "Is he really my brother?"

"Yes. And he really does work for the Troop. But really, he works for the organization."

"How? He was ten when they took him. Don't tell me you recruited him before that."

"No, and we didn't recruit him afterwards, either. He came to us. The Troop's indoctrination specialists had done their best, but your brother proved to be something they never planned on. Incorruptible."

"Incorruptible!" She snorts. "The little shit just didn't have what it takes to be a bad monkey, that's all!"

"You asked on the day we met, what it is that I want," Dixon says, ignoring her outburst. "The answer is: to demonstrate the futility of evil. You and your brother, each in your own way, have helped me do that. But your part of the demonstration is over now."

He opens his coat to reveal another NC gun. This one does not resemble a toy. It's black, and its dial has only two active settings. Dixon draws it from its holster, then turns to Phil and asks with uncharacteristic deference: "May I?"

"No," Phil says. "She's mine."

"Of course." Dixon hands off the pistol, and brushes his palms together as if wiping away dust. "Good-bye, Jane Charlotte," he says. "We won't meet again in this life—or in the next, I hope." He leaves the room.

"Prick," she says, as the door shuts behind him. Then she looks at Phil and her demeanor softens. "So, little brother. I guess congratulations are in order."

"Are they?"

"Don't be a sore winner, Phil."

"You think this is winning for me, Jane?"

"Bad monkey dies, good monkey lives to fight another day …"

"That's Dixon's victory," he tells her. "Dixon took for granted that you passed the shibboleth tests by hiding your true self. I was hoping that there might be another explanation."

"Oh my God," she says. "You actually thought I might be *good*?"

"Conflicted, let's say."

"Oh my God … You wanted to redeem me." She shakes her head in wonder. "How has the Troop not seen through you yet?"

"The answer to that is simple enough. Evil people are easy to fool."

She laughs. "Guess I can't argue with that. Still, I don't know what the hell you were thinking. After what I did to you ..."

"About that," he says. "I know I probably can't trust your answer on this, but I have to ask: When you gave me to them, was that ... Did you hate me?"

"Was it personal, you mean? Eh, not so much ... *Mom* was personal," she says. "Definitely. But with you, well, it was a little personal maybe—you were my brother, after all—but mostly it was just, what did Dixon call it, 'a truly extraordinary sin'? Yeah. I guess I do have a weakness for those." She looks over at the door, not too hopefully. "So listen, I know you can't let me get away clean, but is there any chance I can talk you into giving me a thirty-second head start?"

"Sorry, Jane."

"Fifteen seconds, then. Come on, Phil, you said you wanted to save me. I could still have a change of heart."

"If you do, you'll have to take it up with God. How do you want it?"

"Yeah, OK ... I'll take the stroke. Less painful than the heart attack, and maybe I get a nice light show on the way out."

He nods, and fixes the dial on the CI setting. He takes a deep breath. Lets it out slowly.

His efforts to steel himself are a fresh source of amusement to her: "Jesus, Phil, I'd have shot you ten times already."

"Sorry," he replies, but still he hesitates. She watches him, drawing strength from his ambivalence. As the gun comes up, she is calm, and her final words are almost kind.

"It's all right, little brother," she says. "I'm ready. Send me to Nod."

Acknowledgments

FIRST, THANKS TO THE USUAL SUS-
pects: my wife, Lisa Gold; my agent, Melanie Jackson;
and my editor, Alison Callahan. Thanks also to Lydia
Weaver, Olga Gardner Galvin, Jeanette Perez, Matthew
Snyder, Harold and Rita Gold, Kathy Cain, Charles
McAleese, Michael Hilliard, and my unpaid P.R. staff
at Queen Anne Books: Patti McCall, Cindy Mitchell,
Tegan Tigani, Lillian Welch, Hilary Vonckx, Torrie
Marshall, Hollis Giammatteo, Mary Helbach, Irene
Piekarski, Anne Wyckoff, and Nichole Mogen.

Louis Collins and the Book Club of Washington
were my test audience for the first draft of *Bad Monkeys'*
opening chapters, and their positive response convinced
me that this was indeed the book I wanted to be working on. Jennifer Smith, Christopher Bodan, and Zoe
Stephenson read the finished manuscript and cleared up
a few lingering questions. Zoe Stephenson also double-
checked my Latin, and John Crowley triple-checked
it. Anna Leube helped me with my German. Josh Spin
answered my off-the-wall medical questions with his
usual aplomb. Philip K. Dick, Trey Parker, Matt Stone,
David Simon, Lawrence Sutin, Neal Stephenson, David
Friedman, Bruce Schneier, Jan Harold Brunvand, Neil

Steinberg, and the Reverend Jack Ruff provided inspiration, insight, and/or clever anecdotes. Thank you all.

In the muse department, thanks to Pamela Sue Martin, Liz Phair, and Evil Willow.

And finally, thanks to the National Endowment for the Arts, whose grant of a Literature Fellowship helped buy me the time I needed to finish this novel. The government may not fight evil, but it does have its moments of grace.

About the Author

MATT RUFF WAS BORN IN NEW YORK City in 1965. His father was a hospital chaplain who descended from a line of peaceful Midwestern dairy farmers; his mother was a missionary's daughter who grew up battling snakes and scorpions in the jungles of Brazil. Between the two of them, he received an interesting moral education.

Ruff published his first novel, the cult classic *Fool on the Hill*, in 1988. His most recent novel, *Set This House in Order*, won the James Tiptree, Jr., Award, a Washington State Book Award, and was nominated for the International IMPAC Dublin Literary Award. He is also the recipient of a 2006 National Endowment for the Arts Literature Fellowship.

Ruff lives in Seattle with his wife, Lisa Gold.

Visit Matt Ruff on the web at www.bymattruff.com.